The Rebels and Other Short Fiction

Irish Studies

James MacKillop, *Series Editor*

Select titles in Irish Studies

Carmilla: A Critical Edition
Joseph Sheridan Le Fanu; Kathleen Costello-Sullivan, ed.

Irish Women Dramatists: 1908–2001
Eileen Kearney and Charlotte Headrick, eds.

J. M. Synge and Travel Writing of the Irish Revival
Giulia Bruna

Kate O'Brien and Spanish Literary Culture
Jane Davison

Laying Out the Bones: Death and Dying in the Modern Irish Novel
Bridget English

The Midnight Court / Cúirt an Mheán Oíche: A Critical Edition
Brian Merriman; David Marcus, trans.; Brian Ó Conchubhair, ed.

The Snake's Pass: A Critical Edition
Bram Stoker; Lisabeth C. Buchelt, ed.

Standish O'Grady's Cuculain: A Critical Edition
Standish O'Grady; Gregory Castle and Patrick Bixby, eds.

The Rebels
and Other Short Fiction

RICHARD POWER

Edited and with an Introduction by
James MacKillop

Syracuse University Press

Syracuse University Press
Syracuse, New York 13244-5290

First Edition 2018

18 19 20 21 22 23 6 5 4 3 2 1

∞ The paper used in this publication meets the minimum requirements of the American National Standard for Information Sciences—Permanence of Paper for Printed Library Materials, ANSI Z39.48-1992.

For a listing of books published and distributed by Syracuse University Press, visit www.SyracuseUniversityPress.syr.edu.

ISBN: 978-0-8156-3568-0 (hardcover)
978-0-8156-3586-4 (paperback)
978-0-8156-5434-6 (e-book)

Library of Congress Cataloging-in-Publication Data

Names: Power, Richard, 1928–1970, author. | MacKillop, James, editor.
Title: The rebels and other short fiction / Richard Power ;
edited and with an introduction by James MacKillop.
Description: First edition. | Syracuse : Syracuse University Press, 2018. |
Series: Irish studies | Includes bibliographical references.
Identifiers: LCCN 2018005402 (print) | LCCN 2018015542 (ebook) |
ISBN 9780815654346 (e-book) | ISBN 9780815635680 (hardcover : alk. paper) |
ISBN 9780815635864 (pbk. : alk. paper)
Classification: LCC PR6066.O98 (ebook) | LCC PR6066.O98 A6 2018 (print) |
DDC 823/.914—dc23
LC record available at https://lccn.loc.gov/2018005402

Manufactured in the United States of America

Contents

Acknowledgments

The generosity of the Power family has made this publication possible, beginning with Richard's widow, who had me as a guest in her home and showed me two trunks of untouched stories. Richard's daughter Frances's contributions have been invaluable, beginning with the text of "Night Thoughts." Richard's late brother, P. Victor Power, was the principal source of biographical information in the introduction. Donna Davis of the Village Scribe and Ronan Doherty of Maynooth conscientiously digitalized the texts. Others who assisted or encouraged in significant ways include Cheryl Abbott, Karen Bakke, Mary DesRoches, Marilyn Lonergan, the late Etaín Ó Síocháin, William Reardon, Bruce Stillians, and Margaret Whitfield.

Thanks to Elly Shaw of *Combar* for gracious permission to republish "Deór na hAithrí," which appeared in volume 9, no. 10 (Deireach Fómhair 1950): 9–11.

Introduction

Winter 1969–70 began well for Richard Power. His second novel, *The Hungry Grass*, had just been published in London and New York to widespread critical acclaim. *Time* magazine, which rarely acknowledged Irish fiction, proclaimed that the author was "brilliantly in control of his story." Given the novel's subtlety and pathos, *The Hungry Grass* also held a surprisingly high place on the Irish best-seller list. This led to an invitation to appear on Gay Byrne's *Late, Late Show*, in effect the national forum. Power, not one for self-promotion, declined. A full-time father and civil servant, he instead followed his usual regimen of stolen late night hours to produce twelve thousand words of his next novel, *The Mohair Boys*.

A frequent hiker with an athletic build, Power nonetheless had some health concerns. He had suffered a heart attack in September 1968. Then, on a snowy night on February 12, 1970, Richard Power, just short of his forty-second birthday, died in his sleep in Bray (located just outside Dublin). He left behind six children, aged three to thirteen. Also cancelled was Power's progress along the camino real to the literary pantheon. Obituary after obituary remarked on how much was expected from him. The Irish-language poet Máirtín Ó Direáin eulogized him. Novelist Benedict Kiely wrote, "All who value the state of Irish letters must mourn his passing."[1]

The three volumes published in his lifetime might imply—wrongly—that his output was meager. They are the two novels—*The*

1. *Hibernia*, February 20, 1970, 20.

Land of Youth (1964) and *The Hungry Grass* (1969)—and the Irish-language fictionalized memoir, *Úll i mBarr an Ghéagáin* (1958), translated as *Apple on the Treetop* (1980). But he wrote more than fifty short stories in both English and Irish, thirteen plays (some under pseudonyms), six film scripts, and an untraced cache of journalism and miscellaneous prose, some of it unsigned or pseudonymous. In total, their weight is more substantial than the three published volumes. A banker's son who never knew affluence or leisure, Richard Power seems rarely to have known an unproductive moment.

Richard Power had little craving for ease or creature comforts. His wife, Ann, said of her husband, "He could sit all day in a hard chair."

Power's writing career began in adolescence and continued until his death. On the testimony of the author's brother and translator, Victor Power, Richard published an essay on *Hamlet* in some ephemeral outlet while still in high school. Although his family was monolingual, Richard embraced the Irish language from an early age and composed a story in Irish that was read on Radio Telefis Éireann (RTÉ). Richard used the Irish form of his name, Risteárd de Paor, with his first certain publication at age twenty-one—an account of an earthquake in Japan, "Gaeilgeóir a tSeapáin," which appeared in *Comhar* in November 1949. He began publishing short stories in English, such as "Saving the Bacon," which was published in *Pioneer* in January 1950.

As a writer reluctant to promote himself, who died just as his star was on the rise, Power was likely to be swept aside and forgotten. He did not, however, die in obscurity. His passing was worthy of six column inches in the *Times* of London on February 13. Robust sales for *The Hungry Grass* meant that many libraries shelved copies, and hardcover copies remained on the used-book market as far-flung readers "discovered" it, even after a paperback edition appeared in 1973. Liam mac Austin dramatized *Úll i mBarr an Ghéagáin* on RTÉ in April, May, and June 1978, and Owen Ashe followed with a radio dramatization of *The Hungry Grass* in December 1978.

Many of Power's contemporaries kept his name alive on the literary scene. Editor and journalist David Marcus published an excerpt from *The Mohair Boys* on the "New Irish Writing" page of the *Irish Press* in February 1971. Alongside was a tribute from fiction writer Val Mulkerns, comparing Power's unfinished work with Kingsley Amis's *Lucky Jim*. Also in 1971, Maurice Harmon, professor at University College Dublin and editor of the *Irish University Review*, announced the publication of a volume titled *Three Recent Irish Novelists* for a Bucknell University series. The monograph was never published, but the book's subjects were Richard Power, Aidan Higgins, and John McGahern. Many of Power's champions had been personal friends, like journalist and novelist Bernard Share; librarian, film critic, and raconteur Alf MacLochlainn; and medievalist Proinsias MacCana. Power had known some of his American advocates as well, such as novelist J. F. Powers, whose *Morte d'Urban* was compared with *The Hungry Grass*. The Irish-born but New York–based poet and man of letters Padraic Colum, although forty-seven years older, was an early Power enthusiast. For a jacket blurb Colum wrote that Power was "the finest writer to come out of post-revolutionary Ireland." Other Americans knew Power only from his work, like *New Yorker* short-story writer Elizabeth Cullinan, but Thomas Flanagan, author of *The Year of the French*, became a close pal. Academic interest in Richard Power began a few years after his death. Larry McCaffrey, cofounder of the American Conference for Irish Studies, recommended the author to students and colleagues, and facilitated a link to the Iowa Writers' Program. Papers on Power began to appear in the mid-1970s on forums like the Modern Language Association. John V. Kelleher of Harvard, the unofficial dean of Irish studies in America, cited Power frequently in lectures. In a 1980 interview he asserted that *The Hungry Grass* was the finest novel by an Irishman in the previous fifteen years.[2]

All the while *The Hungry Grass*'s readership continued to grow. The disappearance of used copies caused London's Pan Books to produce a paperback edition in 1978, followed by Dublin's Poolbeg Publishers in 1988. In 2016 London's Apollo Books issued a new edition, which

2. Interview, Cambridge, Massachusetts, January 8, 1980.

prompted much comment in Dublin and elsewhere. The *TLS* (*Times Literary Supplement*) proclaimed that the new edition "returns to print a neglected work of literary merit." In the *Irish Times*, the influential literary critic Eileen Battersby hailed the reissue and announced that Father Conroy, protagonist of *The Hungry Grass*, "is wonderful company and one of the most memorable creations in Irish literature." A commentator on RTÉ was the most generous: *The Hungry Grass* is "easily one of the finest Irish novels ever written—no tricks—just genius."[3]

Power is an Anglicization of the Hiberno-Norman name *de Paor*, known since the twelfth century, and long associated with what is now Waterford and nearby counties. Portions of west Waterford are still known as "Power country." To the east of Waterford once lay the Ring Gaeltacht on a peninsula in Dungarvan Bay, the only spot on the east coast where spoken Irish remained dominant among native speakers until the beginning of the twenty-first century. Although Richard lived in metropolitan Dublin during his mature years, and raised his own family in Bray, he was always aware of his Waterford roots. Some references incorrectly describe him as being born there. Father James Corbett, the model for Father Tom Conroy in *The Hungry Grass*, lived in Old Parish near Ring, County Waterford, although the location is not made specific in the novel.

Richard's father, Patrick Joseph Power, was born in Kilrossanty in central Waterford. No friend of the Irish language, he preferred to play golf at the County Kildare County Club. He might read as many as a dozen books a year, according to Richard's brother Victor, but spectator sports were a higher priority. He became president of the Irish Rugby Football Union. After entering the banking industry, he moved his family to different parts of the country so that Richard was born in Dublin on February 24, 1928—the same year as William Trevor and Thomas Kinsella. Richard spent his early childhood in Naas, County Kildare, a Dublin exurb. He was sixteen when his father

3. For Battersby's quote, see *Irish Times*, September 17, 2016; for RTÉ commentator's quote, see *Irish Times*, October 13, 2016.

died in 1943, and the family learned that he did not have a life insurance policy. Victor reported on his family's departure from a comfortable lifestyle, and the necessity to take in boarders. His mother's coping mechanism was to read novels continuously. The family somehow retained the means, once they moved to Dublin, to allow Richard to attend the Synge Street Christian Brothers Academy, where he distinguished himself. It was also with the Christian Brothers, not at home or in some remote, turf-drenched cottage, that Power began his impassioned study of the Irish language.

Power's pursuit of a college education was circuitous. Initially he received a scholarship to study engineering at University College Dublin (UCD), but he had to abandon his studies when Victor entered the seminary, and the family's limited resources went to support that effort instead. On leaving UCD, Power secured a position in civil service; two hundred applicants had competed for four openings. The government would be his principal employer, with important interruptions, for the rest of his life. An enlightened supervisor allowed Power to pursue a degree in Commerce and Public Administration at Trinity College, Dublin—Oscar Wilde and Samuel Beckett's alma mater—which was still perceived as a citadel of the Anglo-Irish Ascendancy. Power's attendance required written permission from the famously unflinching Archbishop John Charles McQuaid. The same generous administrator who had recommended Trinity College agreed to allow Power to attend lectures in English and Irish literatures. By 1953 Power achieved two degrees simultaneously—one in Commerce, as the civil service had asked, and a dual external degree in English and Irish.

This fiendishly exacting schedule did not prevent him from entering into student life. He made a lifelong friend of novelist and journalist Bernard Share, poets Richard Murphy and Richard Kell, and critic-translator Douglas Sealy. Together they founded the student literary journal *Icarus*, providing a first platform for Richard Power's initial burst of productivity.

One of the author's strongest stories, "The Threshold," appeared in *Icarus* in January 1951; two years later it would appear in the *Saturday Book* in London. Shortly after came "Alone" (October 1951) and "Republicans" (February 1952). These led to a step up in prestige when "Peasants" appeared in *Bell* (December 1952), Seán O'Faolain's journal, the best venue in Ireland for a young writer to find attention. All of these stories are included in this volume.

The pressure of working in a government office and taking courses when he could did not impede Power's creative output. He began publishing in Irish even before his first stories appeared in *Icarus*. "Deór na hAithrí" appeared in *Comhar* in October 1950, winning his first literary award, the Comh-Caidreamh Prize. The original Irish text is included here, along with Victor Power's translation, "Tears of Prayer." Tellingly, Power employed Irish to deliver the grittiest story in the collection, an urban tale of the humiliations of soul-beating poverty. Five other stories published in Irish followed, with still more in manuscript only. Not one is set in the Gaeltacht. The lengthy "Níl Miss Culshaw sa Bhaile" depicts an interracial relationship in London.

Prose was Richard's preferred medium, but he also published poetry in both *Comhar* and *Icarus*.

At Trinity College Power met a beautiful Anglo-Irish student named Ann Colvill. Deep personal and artistic bonds drew them together; she wrote both criticism and fiction, including "Summer Afternoon" (October 1951), for *Icarus*. She was from an Anglo-Irish family that had been prominent in Dublin political and commercial life for centuries up until 1916. Ann has been renowned for her trenchant wit. They married in November 1955, and together had six children: Patrick, Robert, John, Frances, Sarah, and Richard Jr. Ann survived Richard, and spoke at celebrations for the reissue of *The Hungry Grass* in 2016.

Power's heart may have been with the external degree in English and Irish literatures, but the courses in commerce and public administration sustained his daily bread. Departing from Trinity College, he returned to the civil service.

Power was employed in the Department of Local Governments, the same office in which the novelist Brian O'Nolan had toiled. We know him better as Flann O'Brien and columnist-humorist Myles na Gopaleen. Although his offices were housed in Dublin Castle, Power frequently described the daily routine there as "Dickensian"; dull work, taxes and accounting. Eventually Power moved to a more rewarding position, in which he was in charge of the fire brigades. Finally, he was appointed press officer. He told Bruce Stillians in Iowa that he was "writing speeches for the commissioner of sludge."[4]

The Department of Local Governments, however, would lead to creative enterprise. The department issued short documentary films for educational purposes. A word man rather than a visual artist, Power wrote at least six film scripts, four of which were part of his work at the department. The first, only eight minutes long, *A Tale of Two Bicycles* (c. 1961), directed by Billy Bowles, advocated for bike safety with wit and irony. Others are *Game of Chance* (c. 1967), directed by Jim Mulkerns; *Water Wisdom* (c. 1967), directed by Colm Ó Laoghaire; and *To Save a Life* (n.d.), directed by George Morrison. A fifth film script, never produced, "A Boy in Ireland," is held in the archives of the National Library of Ireland. Although no one would make many claims for these five items, through this work, Power associated with significant creative people such as George Morrison, one of Ireland's best known documentarists, remembered for the compilation of silent films about 1916 and the Anglo-Irish War, *Mise Éire* (1959), with soundtrack by Seán Ó Riada; and Jim Mulkerns, who would go on to make the bilingual short film *Return of the Islander* (1970), narrated by Richard Harris.

In a 1967 letter to Victor, Power commented on a British Arts Council Award, one of only twelve given, which awarded his contemporary John McGahern financial support for a year devoted to writing. He added, "I may say here that I don't altogether regret having to support myself in the civil service. It keeps me in touch . . ."

Notwithstanding his stoicism, two awards won during the 1950s would free Power from office drudgery and deepen his artistic vision. One would lead into the Gaelic heart of Ireland—the Aran Islands, off the coast of Counties Galway and Clare. The second would take him out of the country entirely, to the American Midwest.

4. Letter to James MacKillop, September 1, 1981.

In the first, Power was the beneficiary of grant from Gael Linn (Gaels with us), a nonprofit agency founded in 1953. This was during a decade in which Ireland was still one of the poorest countries in Europe, and funding for arts projects was scarce. Nonetheless, the Irish government established Gael Linn as a nongovernmental and nonprofit agency to foster the Irish language and promote artistic enterprise. One award would ask that the participant travel to the Aran Islands, immerse himself in the language, and produce a book in Irish about being there. According to Victor, the award's first recipient was Brendan Behan, then his late twenties, not yet known as a playwright. For unknown reasons, Behan proved to be an unsuitable participant, and Richard Power was next in line. When Power began his tour, however, Behan turned up on the boat to Inishmore, the largest of the three Aran Islands, and the two writers both roamed island precincts for a short while. Behan did not ingratiate himself to the islanders, which then numbered fewer than two thousand, and soon departed.

The windswept Aran Islands have long played a large role in the Irish imagination. There are magnificent ancient megaliths, but they are not the chief allure. The small, impoverished population eking out a precarious living has long been perceived to be more purely Irish than mainlanders, in part because they were monoglots longer than people elsewhere, and less contaminated by Englishness and cosmopolitanism. This "purity," much esteemed in the nineteenth century, is not supported by recent DNA surveys. As the legend goes (somewhat inaccurately), William Butler Yeats urged John Millington Synge to visit the islands so that he could learn profundities not known in Paris. The resultant poetic travelogue, *Aran Islands* (1907), proclaimed the persistent myth that the peremptory nationalist Miss Ivors uses to hector the insecure urban literary critic Gabriel Conroy in James Joyce's "The Dead." No one had to ask Power to update or refute Synge's vision. The anxiety of influence was ever present.

The narrator of *Úll i mBarr an Ghéagáin* (1958) surveys diverse attitudes toward the islands from within and without, but never argues a thesis. He begins his journal in Galway and observes mainlanders reluctant to visit because they do not know the Irish language after decades of the Irish State's championing of it. More than anything he recoils at the islanders being presented as a variety of cliché "colorful characters." He shares the disgust of a local couple being photographed by visiting Americans. He continually observes individuals unimaginable in Synge: a studiously well-read laborer, a woman who boasts of her visit to San Francisco. Far from being "insular," the islanders enjoy the visits of Spanish and English fisherman. The narrator never condemns, but he rolls his eyes at Ian and Susan from bohemian Chelsea, who see the islands as an artistic arcadia. They dabble at painting, while not being professionals themselves. Locals disapprove of their swimming off the stormy coast and would disapprove more loudly if they knew the two swim naked when no one is looking. The subject of romanticism comes up when the narrator interviews a German engineer contracted by an Irish company for farm equipment. He deplores the waste of government resources propping up the island economy when less money could be spent for greater effect if the islanders—whom he describes as *zahnlos* (toothless)—were resettled on friendlier terrain. Before entering the final section, the narrator embraces it all: "Life in the islands gets at my heart" (Victor Power's translation).

Where *Úll i mBarr an Ghéagáin* departs most sharply from Synge's *Aran* is in the last chapters, in which the narrator leaves the islands entirely and joins desperate Irish-speaking men working on grim building sites in Britain. Power followed this path himself in writing the book, a fate far more likely than drowning as in Synge's *Riders to the Sea*.

Whereas *Úll i mBarr an Ghéagáin* embraces a variety of views and emotions, the tone is much darker in the two works of fiction deriving from Power's time on the Aran Islands—the short story "The Land of Youth" (1960), republished here, and the novel expanded from it, also titled *The Land of Youth* (1964). Observations of landscape, names of characters such as Cóilín, Johanna, and Mairead, appear first in *Úll i mBarr an Ghéagáin* and later reappear in fiction. When Padraic Colum wrote that if romantic Ireland was indeed dead and gone, then Richard Power was a writer for post-romantic Ireland, he was thinking more of *The Land of Youth* than of *Úll i mBarr an Ghéagáin*. The volume never reached a wide readership, but it won the Gaelic Book Club Award in 1959. Victor Power's translation, *Apple in the Treetop* (1980), critically reviled for excess Americanisms, exists only in the single run of an inexpensive paperback edition that failed to garner an extensive readership.

At the same time that Richard Power was painting a bleaker picture of the islands, he also wrote, under the pseudonym Nomad, a tourist-friendly article titled "The Aran Islands," which was published in *Ireland of the Welcomes* (1962).

A second bequest, an Exchange Scholarship, allowed Richard, Ann, and their family to travel to Iowa so that he could pursue a Master of Fine Arts in Creative Writing. Iowa was and is primarily an agricultural state, but its superb universities—in this case the University of Iowa—are well supported by the state legislature. The Iowa Writers' Workshop, which has flourished under different names, was founded in 1922, at a time when no other institution in the world thought that "creative writing" should be worthy of an academic degree. Iowa had a leg up on late-arriving rivals and lured lustrous talent, especially during the tenure of Iowa-born Rhodes Scholar and poet, Paul Engle, from 1941 to 1966. Instructors enticed to Iowa City included Robert Frost, Dylan Thomas, Robert Lowell, and Kurt Vonnegut. Among the fiction writers produced by the program are Flannery O'Connor and Raymond Carver, both masters of the short story.

The Power family spent two years in Iowa City. During his first year Power was a full-time student in the workshop, studying under Paul Engle. Although he was a teaching assistant during his second year, he suffered from a minor speech impediment, and never became a full-time classroom instructor.

While in Iowa Power rapidly came to know a number of literary and academic Americans, some of whom would become lifelong friends, including prominent Irish Americans like Larry McCaffrey, J. F. Powers, and Thomas Flanagan. Power made a less likely friendship with the Kentucky-bred fiction writer Walter Tevis, also thirty years old when he arrived. Initially devoted to science fiction, Tevis had been urged to master the techniques of realism even before he arrived in

Iowa and published his best-known work, *The Hustler* (1959), before he completed his MFA. But he persisted with science fiction, producing *The Man Who Fell to Earth* (1963) shortly after. Both books were made into critically acclaimed films: *The Hustler* (1961) and *Man* (1976).

The short story might have been Power's prime concern while in Iowa City, but he also completed a three-act play, *The Blind Mouth*, under one of his pseudonyms, Desmond Walsh. Set in the present, it deals with commemorations of the 1916 Easter Uprising in which Patrick Pearse himself takes a substantial role. Never produced, the typescript is still on file in the university library. During his time at Iowa, Power also contributed articles for the student publication, the *Daily Iowan*.

Farther afield, he recorded a conversation with William Cotter Murray and Patrick Morrissey on the radio station WSUI in the spring of 1959, titled "The Irish in the Middle West," and rebroadcast on RTÉ that year.

Richard Power's MFA thesis, supervised by Paul Engle, was filed on schedule in 1960. It consisted of three stories—"The Rebels," "The Land of Youth," and "A Province of Rome" (since changed to "An Outpost of Rome")—all of which are included in this collection. Even before his degree was granted, "The Rebels" attracted the most favorable attention. In a move in many ways more significant than the much sought-after Iowa degree, Power published "The Rebels" in volume 1, issue 1, of the prestigious literary journal *Dial* (Fall 1959). The original *Dial* was one of the most significant American serials of the nineteenth century. It was founded by Ralph Waldo Emerson and Orestes Brownson and edited by Margaret Fuller, becoming first the forum of the Transcendentalists. It was published, with interruptions, from 1840 to 1929.

In 1923 the Dial imprint belonged to the aristocratic philanthropist and diplomat Lincoln MacVeagh, who founded Dial Press, intending to be a forum for select authors, a rival to the dominant American house Alfred A. Knopf. Among the authors on Dial's list was the Anglo-Irish novelist Elizabeth Bowen, and Americans Glenway Wescott, James Baldwin, and Norman Mailer. The launch of the new

Dial in 1959, including Power's "The Rebels," was intended to evoke the aura of founders Emerson and contemporaries. Power retained his connection to the company when Dial Press published his first novel, *The Land of Youth*, in 1964, to be followed by a separate London edition two years later.

Meanwhile, "The Rebels" won further acclaim when Paul Engle selected it for inclusion in a crème de la crème selection from the Iowa Writers' Workshop in *Midland: Twenty-Five Years of Fiction and Poetry* (1961).

Upon completing his degree, Richard, Ann, and family returned to Ireland, depicted as an occasion for glee in the uncompleted novel *The Mohair Boys*. Power maintained his connections to literary life in the United States, even decades before the internet. Following a positive review of *The Land of Youth* (unusual for a first novel by an unknown author) in the *New York Review of Books*, arguably America's premier intellectual serial publication, the editors exchanged several letters with Richard Power about possible publications there. Unseen, this correspondence is held in the Power Archives of the National Library of Ireland. In the following year, Power published a commentary on Bloomsday celebrations in "A Literary Letter from Ireland," *New York Times Book Review*, July 11, 1965, 44–45.

When he returned to Ireland at thirty-two, Power was beginning the final decade of his life, raising a family, working long hours in an uncongenial office, devoting what spare time that could be gleaned into strengthening his prose fiction, and advancing his career as a novelist. This meant, among other things, that he abandoned writing for the stage, which had long been a subsidiary interest. Some early successes in the theater must have bolstered his confidence.

Between the completion of *Úll i mBarr an Ghéagáin* and its publication, Power entered the Oireachtas Literary Competition for new plays in Irish. He won—the first nonnative speaker to do so. The prize was not only a financial reward but also a staged production at the Abbey Theatre, under the direction of Tomás MacAnna, one of the most renowned Irish theater directors of the time. Power was still twenty-nine when "Oidhreacht" (Inheritance) opened on March 2,

1958. The one act consisted of three scenes: (a) a Connemara cottage; (b) a Dublin sitting room; and (c) a mail boat going east. Commentators compared the play to John Osborne's *Look Back in Anger*, the most sensational London stage work of the previous two years. But how many audiences in the capital could follow dialogue in Irish? Poet Pearse Hutchinson, an admirer of "Oidhreacht," complained on RTÉ that it was not being properly advertised.

The manuscripts of twelve of Power's plays survive. He wrote the first for radio, "Screen Frame," dated by the National Library of Ireland as 1956–57, predating "Oidhreacht." He wrote a second one-act play in Irish, "Saoirse," which competed for the Oireachtas Prize but tied for first place in 1958 with Mairead Ní Gháda's "Úllghlas Oiche Shamha." Of the remainder we know little, except that Power asked that the manuscripts of all of them be preserved in archives—eleven at the National Library of Ireland in Dublin, and another, "The Blind Mouth," under the pseudonym Desmond Walsh, remains in the University of Iowa's archives, as cited earlier. Power wrote another short story, "A Home for Heroes," under the pseudonym Michael Roberts. Power's other plays written in English and Irish are: "Charon iBponnc," "The Faithful and the Few," "A Green Grace—Aran," "Kevin Barry," "Mo Mhile Slán le Éirinn," and "Songs by Cóilín." The last of these to bear a date is "Cluiche Solo," 1964.

Richard Power wrote Victor in 1967: "I wasted too much time at playwriting." But he took pains that the manuscripts be preserved—an honor not accorded the manuscripts of his more than fifty short stories.

Buoyed by his acceptance in America, Power forged ahead to complete his first novel, *The Land of Youth*, expanded from characters and themes in his short story of the same title, completed in Iowa. The phrase the "Land of Youth" is a translation of the Irish phrase *Tír na nÓg*, the empyrean perceived to lie to the west though not necessarily identified with the Aran Islands. Published first by Dial Press in New York to mixed reviews, the novel appeared in a separate printing from Secker and Warburg in London two years later, persuaded by the significance of the strong supporters and selection by the Book of the Month Club.

The setting of the novel is the fictionalized Aran Island of Inishkeever. Action begins in the summer of 1913 and continues through the Irish War of Independence (1919–21), and after. Protagonist Barbara Nora returns from three years in America to lure young Padraig Mahony away from the seminary and his intended vocation in the priesthood. He is the son of a widow who runs a local store and pub. Barbara becomes pregnant with another man's child and leaves for Dublin, abandoning Padraig. This betrayal sets forces into motion, fomenting turbulent emotions that play out against untamed scenery and physical privation. The narration often depicts dark clouds and implies that isolation makes the islanders distrustful of one another. When Barbara returns to Inishkeever, this time from revolutionary Dublin, she is most unwelcome. Padraig is now an embittered and miserly shopkeeper. Nonetheless, Barbara finds love again, with a young man who gives her son a family name and a decent five-year marriage. Her husband is killed in an extension of the vendetta between Padraig's supporters and those of Barbara. When grown her son dies at sea. Barbara outlives Padraig and takes consolation that the western isles, the Land of Youth of the title, promise her a happy death.

Several reviewers and commentators noted the strikingly different portrayal of the islands and islanders than readers had inherited from John Millington Synge. Bleak as the novel can be, it offers uncanny anticipations of the portrayal of the same landscape in Martin McDonagh's very black stage comedy, *The Cripple of Inishmaan* (1996).

The five years between *The Land of Youth* and Power's next novel, *The Hungry Grass*, were fraught with interruptions. On his return from the Berlin Festival in 1968, where the film *A Game of Chance* was honored, Richard suffered a heart attack. He insisted on being admitted to a Dublin hospital's public ward because he felt no one should be entitled to better care just because one could pay more. He returned to full-time work and full-time fatherhood. His youngest child, Richard Jr., was born in 1966, but Power still scheduled time for writing during each busy day.

When Dial Press awarded Power a $1,000 advance, the family spent it on a new washing machine. Ann Power said it was the most romantic gesture she could image. In the days before disposable diapers, washing cloth diapers required an hour and half of labor each day. At the time of *The Hungry Grass*'s publication in 1969, the chief literary editor at Dial Press was the American novelist E. L. Doctorow, author of *Ragtime*. Publication by the Bodley Head in London was simultaneous.

While based on another story, "An Outpost of Rome," from Power's Iowa thesis, *The Hungry Grass* is an entirely different kind of novel from *The Land of Youth*. The model for the main character, Father Thomas Conroy, was based on Father James Corbett, a widely known figure of Old Parish, County Waterford, where Richard's brother had been a curate before leaving priestly orders. Corbett often attended a nearby summer theater festival, run for a while by Victor; although he never took a role, Corbett commented candidly, often humorously, on the ways lines were read and scenes played. Thc festival drew young people from all over Ireland, including Tomás Mac Anna, Micheal Ó hAodha, and an adolescent girl from Ulster named Bernadette Devlin, and eventually morphed into the Ring Gaelic Theatre Festival. For dozens of young thespians, Father Corbett was a cantankerous but witty observer, a character, if not playing one on stage.

Structurally and tonally, *The Hungry Grass* is far more complex and variegated than *The Land of Youth*, a relatively conventional and somber opus. The action of *The Hungry Grass* begins with the death of the sixty-three-year-old protagonist, Father Thomas Conway, and proceeds through flashbacks and dream sequences, concentrating on the two weeks preceding Conway's death. This framework, which the novel shares with *Lord Jim* and *The Great Gatsby*, is sometimes called an "elegiac romance." The text can be disarmingly humorous and occasionally laugh-out-loud hilarious. The novel is set in the late 1960s; Father Conway drives a Volkswagen bug.

Father Thomas Conway collapses in the upstairs bathroom of a neighboring rectory, right after grace for an otherwise fine but boyish meal enjoyed by priests of the diocese. One mutters that Conway had a "genius for causing trouble." Another quotes French novelist Georges Bernanos that a true priest cannot be loved. The priest whom Conway had preselected to be his executor, Father Peter Mahon, certainly does not love him. Earlier Mahon had taken Conway's place at Maynooth, the prestige seminary. Mahon considers Kilbride, Conway's parish, to be the dunghill of the diocese, and he vomits when he enters Conway's rectory and confronts the stench. What Mahon finds makes little sense to him: pound notes jammed into jars and a letter from an uncle in the Andes Mountains.

The unnamed narrator takes us past the executor's sneering bumblings to the spring and summer before Conway's death, and in flashbacks later in the book to his decision to enter the priesthood and to labor troubles in the years after the Anglo-Irish Treaty. Early in the narrative, Father Conroy passes, disapprovingly, two young priests playing golf, his curate, and a visitor from California, who recommends the formation of a parish committee. The priest is on his way to visit his sister Kate, who married beneath her station into the Kallikaks of the county. Her disheartening husband, Mikie, reminds Father Conroy how anguishing lost promise can be.

Contemporary events, like trying to deny a visiting English Protestant the pony he has won in a parish contest, are juxtaposed with events from the distant past. We learn that Father Conroy never had a vocation in the usual sense but rather agreed to go into the priesthood when an older brother declared that it was not for him. He thus gave up his claim on the family farm. Yet Father Conroy never abandons his commitment to the family, journeying to England in search of possible heirs, the lost children of a dead brother.

Sources close to the author have identified several characters in *The Hungry Grass* as based on certain family members, and at least one is modeled on a public figure. The hectoring Father Evilly, who chides and cajoles the parish, is based on Father James McDyer of County Donegal, a much-admired community developer of midcentury Ireland. Sardonically, Father Conroy responds that the only way to improve the parish is to clear out all the natives and restock the area with Germans, echoing a line in *Úll i mBarr an Ghéagáin*.

Despite Owen Ashe's dramatization of it, the appeal of *The Hungry Grass* is not its narrative but rather the portrayal of its tortured, disappointed protagonist, and his profound if ironic—sometimes uproarious—grasp of his plight. The author's technique relies, in commentator Stanley Poss's phrase, on the juxtaposition of extravagance and banality.

As with *The Land of Youth*, the title *The Hungry Grass* translates an Irish phrase freighted with connotations. *An féar gortach* is grass that causes extreme hunger in anyone who treads on it. Found in the landscape of any county, *an féar gortach* will seize any person who falls upon it until they secure nourishment. Possibly an inheritance of famine times, it exists outside historical allusion. *Féar* (grass) makes a pun with *fear* (man), inviting metaphorical applications. *The Hungry Grass* is also the title of Donagh MacDonagh's best known poetry collection (1947).

Ireland was Richard Power's principal subject. He was certainly influenced by cosmopolitan forces, however; his widow Ann cites his admiration for Thomas Hardy. Power's two years in the United States unmistakably changed him. But except for a few stories set in Britain and the Mediterranean, and one with a biblical milieu, all the rest are set in Ireland, urban and rural, among different classes and in different decades of the twentieth century. He aspired to take his place among Irish writers. As he was born the same year as William Trevor, it is inviting to compare Power with him. As he was working, however, Power paced himself with six perceived rivals of approximately the same age: Edna O'Brien, John McGahern, Brian Moore, Brian Friel, Aidan Higgins, and Benedict Kiely.

In a four-page letter to Victor dated March 2, 1967, Richard focused on those six in an appraisal of more than a dozen figures. Although unwilling to rank them, he unmistakably has the highest opinion of O'Brien and McGahern, both of whom write beautifully. Power snickered at O'Brien's deftness in using the censorship ban to her advantage and praised her remaining Irish in London bohemia. McGahern, Power feared, reacted too wildly to Irish Catholicism as Joyce had.

As for Brian Moore, Power thought *The Lonely Passion of Judith Hearne* a minor masterpiece, but for all the author's craftsmanship, he ranked lower than McGahern. Wonderful as Brian Friel's works for the stage might be, Power felt that his short stories didn't go very deep but were written in the O'Connor tradition of charm. Aidan Higgins, Power wrote, was unrooted and found most of his popularity in German translation. And Benedict Kiely, for all his sheer volume and energy, not to mention his personal kindness to Power, suffered from a grating style.

Richard Power wrote short stories over his entire twenty-year career. He was working on "Night Thoughts" in his last months. The manuscript remained with his family and was treasured by his daughter Frances, who transcribed it for this collection. We have four other sources for the materials published here: (1) the 1960 Iowa MFA thesis, finished texts, all three of which are included here; (2) published stories from the 1950s; (3) manuscripts surviving at the Power household on Convent Avenue in Bray; (4) manuscripts owned by Victor Power, many of which are in Irish.

Several of Power's early published stories are included, even though he was not yet twenty-five years old. Their publication, in finished form, makes it more likely that these texts met the author's standards.

Manuscripts from Convent Avenue, Bray, survived in two discrete trunks, one apparently more favored, the other less so. Manuscripts in the more favored trunk included different drafts of the same story and appeared to be subject to revision even as the author worked on *The Land of Youth* and *The Hungry Grass.* Among these is the manuscript for "The Pill," which from evidence within the story, has to have been written after 1961. Those from the less favored trunk were often on yellowed paper and difficult to read. Some were handwritten.

Manuscripts in the possession of the late Victor Power suffered a sorrier fate. Some, like Victor's translation, "The Tears of Prayer," were forwarded to the editor. Others, although Victor testified to their existence and provided brief plot summaries, have been lost, at least temporarily.

Given Richard Power's lifelong championing of the Irish language, it seems appropriate to honor one his works in the language. "Deór na hAithrí" (1950) might be an early work, but it earned the author his first literary prize. Victor Power's literal translation, "The Tears of Prayer," may suffer from some Americanisms (it was completed in Chicago), but it seems preferable to Richard's revisions of stories originally written in one language or the other, such as "Poblachtánaigh" and "Republicans." With those the details in parallel narratives are not identical, and at this late date we cannot be sure which version came first and which is the translation. The digitizer of "Deór na hAithrí," Mr. Ronan Doherty of Maynooth, has updated some now archaic spellings.

As far as we know, Richard Power never planned to publish any selection of his short fiction. There is no way of guessing what his intentions might have been. The choice and ordering of titles here has been imposed by an American who never met him, more than forty-seven years after his death. Victor Power, one of Richard's rare confidants, suggested that there are probably hidden links between stories that few readers would discern. The Hennessy of "The Threshold," for example, may be the same man as the Hennessy in "Peasants," a very different story. Taking Victor's assertion as a cue, I have juxtaposed stories that invite comparison, such a two stories of boisterous youth, "The Rebels" and "Bringing Home the Bacon," two stories of youthful love, "A Letter" and "Summer Evening," or two stories about Itinerants, the dark " Neighbors" and the jeu d'esprit, "A Pilgrim."

"The Rebels" appears first here because it was the favorite of Paul Engle, Power's mentor, and the most honored in his lifetime. We have no indication that it was Power's favorite, and neither is it the most characteristic in this collection. No other quite resembles its tone. The depiction of barefoot schoolchildren implies that "The Rebels" is set before Power's lifetime. Many of the items early in this collection are either focused on youth, like "Deór na hAithrí," or on the twentieth century, while later works in the collection are focused on more mature themes as in "The Land of Youth." The final selections are set in later times, like "The Pill," and from Power's last year, "Night Thoughts" and "The Mohair Boys."

Frank O'Connor famously remarked that the short story is the nearest thing one can get to the pure lyric poem. It doesn't deal with problems. It doesn't have any solutions to offer. It just states the human condition.[5] His words are more a quip than an aesthetic, and O'Connor was never a writer Power took as a model. Nonetheless, since the time of James Joyce's *Dubliners* many Irish writers have favored lean, pared-down narratives building to a single impression or moment of insight. This would be true of John McGahern's work, although he would otherwise never be classed with O'Connor. The earliest story in this collection, "Deór na hAithrí," can be considered a lyric poem in prose, even with depictions of poverty and domestic tension. Most of Power's earliest stories, from *Icarus* and the *Bell*, would meet O'Connor's criterion. So, too, one of the most affecting, undated stories, "Summer Evening," whose meaning comes from what we infer but is never stated.

Power went to Iowa to study the short story and excelled as a student there, but the three narratives from those years are longer and detailed, hardly lyric poems in prose. Two of the stories, "The Land of Youth" and "An Outpost of Rome," would serve as platforms for novels. The third, "The Rebels," the title story of this collection, could easily be classed as a novella. So could the undated but probably post-Iowa "Neighbors." Thus is this is a collection of short fiction, which includes his short stories.

Throughout his career, from 1950 until his death in 1970, Richard Power worked on short fiction, even as he also produced poetry, journalism, plays, film scripts, and novels. In these works we find a writer of a wider variety of styles, of diverse subjects and surprising sympathies that we do not find in other published work. They are also a plangent reminder of how much we lost when he left us just as his star was on the rise.

5. Phrased differently on different occasions; see *Paris Review* 17 (Autumn 1957); *The Lonely Voice* (London: Macmillan, 1965), 27.

The Rebels and Other Short Fiction

The Rebels

Vincent came down the road from the creamery, carefully scuffling his bare feet in the dust of the cart tracks. I always waited for him because I was his pal. It meant being late for school sometimes, but I never got the stick. Vincent was no bigger than me, but everybody was somehow afraid of him, even Billy Flahavan who thought himself a man. And even the master.

I was the only one who knew that his mother made him wear boots every day. I never let on, even to him, but I had seen him hiding the boots in a hole in the creamery wall and then splashing through a puddle to get his feet looking like everybody else's. I think that was one reason I liked him because of his mother, a terrible woman who would win a martyr's crown for any fellow.

He nodded and said, "*morra*" to me, as I jumped up to join him.

"How's Billy?" I asked. I had heard Billy was in bed after the beating and was probably at death's door.

Vincent shrugged his shoulders, but he knew. He always knew more than we did from the talk at the creamery, but he never let on. It was useless to be asking him.

We stopped at the door of the forge, looking in at the sparks flying in the darkness, while we nibbled away at the jam sandwiches in our satchels. It was Lent, the hungry time of the year, when a fellow doesn't get half enough to eat and the birds go hopping around the dead branches whenever the sun comes out. It was cold, too, even with the sun on our bare feet.

"D'ye think he'll still be mad?" I asked, "the master?" I was hoping against hope for the worst, that Billy was lying in bed, dying or already dead. Only the worst was any use to us, for only the gallows would rid us of the master.

Vincent shrugged as if he didn't care. I noticed, though, that he had a good sod of turf under his arm for the school fire, real hard and black, the pick of the big stack in the creamery yard.

Just then the old smith looked up and saw us. "Off to school with ye," he yelled, "ye little tinkers, ye! D'ye want me to tell the master on ye?"

Vincent tossed a crust in over the half door to make the smith bawl louder, then he began to run. I followed, wishing I could be like him, afraid of no one, not even after the beating.

When we reached the school, we found Chris on his knees by the grate, blowing the embers aflame. He looked up at us with his pink eyes, which were never really dry, waiting for us to toss him our sods of turf. It was Chris who looked after the fire all day, cleaned the blackboard, and gave out the copybooks. He also went out to cut and trim the sticks for the master to beat us with. We didn't hold that against him, though. It was his job, and anyway he had a real gift which he wasn't a bit stingy with—he could cry any time we wanted him to. For a penny, he'd let the tears roll down his cheeks, while we stood around him, looking as if we owned him, watching the amazement on the face of some new fellow. Sometimes the tears began to roll when he didn't want them to and they just kept on rolling until his shirt was wet and we began to get frightened, thinking they'd never stop. Maybe that's why the master never asked him a question. It was just as well, because the poor fellow was very ignorant.

We were sitting very quiet when the master came in. He was a big man, with a gold watch chain on him like the bellyband of a horse and heavy square-toed boots. I never looked much at his face for fear of him noticing me, but it was the color of soda bread and he had a big bald head on him, which used to go all red and shiny whenever his blood was up. We sat reading as hard as we could until he spoke. When we heard his voice, soft and deep, we knew it would be an easy morning. He asked Vincent all the hard questions, just as if there was an inspector there, but any one of us would have got full marks that day. We had taken no chances with our homework. He even cracked a few jokes. When he saw how good the fire was, he said that we must have been keeping the best turf till last. We all split our sides laughing, though most of the fellows didn't know that he was quoting what our Lord said to the publicans, when He was complaining about the wine.

Just before the break, Billy came in. He was the only fellow in long trousers, but even they didn't hide his stiff walk as he went up to make his excuse.

"Him!" the master shouted, flinging out his arm toward Billy, "Him the Almighty Power hurled headlong flaming from the ethereal sky, with hideous ruin and combustion, down to bottomless perdition . . ." He stopped waving his arm suddenly and said, "Milton! *Paradise Lost*, Book One! But I might as well be telling the wall!" Then he asked very serious, "How is it?"

"What, master?"

"Your bottom, boy?"

"'Tis sore, sir," said Billy, rubbing his trousers and cocking a gamy eye back at us, as we pretended to laugh our heads off. Billy always thought it was he who made a joke.

"Sit down, boy," said the master, real solemn, "for your penance, you may sit down."

We all felt Billy's pain, as he lowered himself slowly into his seat. For the rest of the period, we couldn't keep our eyes off those tight trousers, wondering were they stuck to him or was his behind all bandaged up inside them.

Chris went down the road to the master's house to prepare the master's lunch, for the master had no wife. Chris was good at making tea and boiling eggs. He lived with his grandfather, an old soldier of the English army, who used to wander home from the pubs of a Friday after collecting his pension money, muttering to himself, and taking big skelps out of the hedges with his stick. Chris had no mother and no father. Maybe that was why we didn't begrudge him the master.

As it was raining, we had to stay in to eat our sandwiches. We gathered around the fire when the master left, but we kept an eye out for his return. He used to murder us for standing around the fire. He said it made our wits even more sleepy and stupid than God intended.

Billy began telling us how his Da had bet hell out of him, because he wouldn't say what the master had bet him for.

"But, sure, ye might as well be flogged by a fly as by my oul' fella," said Billy. "Jeez, I'd make two of him."

"And what did you do, Billy, tell us?" I burst out. I was killed with the curiosity.

"Nothing much," said Billy, in his hoarse bass voice. He had an open mouth like all the Flahavans and a cowlick of hair plastered down with oil (Flahavan's axle grease, the master called it).

"But you must have done something, Billy?"

"I didn't," said Billy, grinning with that open mouth, "but I might." He stood there, wanting me to keep on asking.

"Go on," I said, "tell us!" I was beginning to get annoyed.

"Ye're too young."

"Was it," cut in Vincent, "a girl?"

"Now ye're talking!"

"But . . ." All sorts of questions were crowding in my head.

"What did you do with her, Billy?" was the only question I could ask, very lamely.

"Nothing! Yet! He caught us walking out the Durrow Road. We'll wait till dark the next time, I can tell ye that!"

"You're not going to go out with her again?" It was first time in my life I'd talked to anyone who had actually walked out with a girl on his own. And who was so sure about walking out again.

"Of course!" He gave me a push. "Go 'way now, little boy, and play!"

"Who is she?" asked Vincent.

"Wouldn't ye like to know now?"

"I knew you were making it up!"

"Did ye now? Well, I'll show ye. Look!" He produced a brown shopkeeper's envelope, creased in two. "She even wrote to me." He took out the letter, a page of a jotter, and folded it to cover the signature. "Go on! Read if ye don't believe me!"

Vincent took it as if he really wasn't much interested. We all crowded round, jostling each other as we tried to read it over his shoulder. All

I could make out was "Dear Billy, You'd better not walk out my way tonight, because my Daddy . . ." Then a shadow fell across it.

"What have ye there?" said the master. He made a lunge for the letter, as Vincent tried to hide it behind his back. His big arms closed around Vincent, lifting him from the floor and twisting him around to straddle him. Then the big black thumbnail levered at Vincent's knuckles, until the hand suddenly opened and the crumpled letter dropped on to the desk. The master laid it out and began to brush it straight with the backs of his fingers.

Vincent's face went red first, then slowly faded to white. "Give it back," he said, his lips all stiff. We backed away from him, staring, backed away to leave him facing the master.

"What's that?" The master's voice was quick, almost frightened. His mouth dropped open a moment, showing the saliva welling around his teeth.

"I said 'give it back.'"

The master's hand opened and closed a few times, as if it had lost its nerve. Then it opened out, flat, and swung against Vincent's face. There was a sharp crack. Vincent staggered back against the fireplace, clutching at his cheek. None of us made a move. We watched him run his tongue into his cheek and spit a blood-flecked dollop into the fire. Then he turned and without a word or a look, walked out of the room.

We had a rough afternoon, but as most of us had learned our stuff off backways and skew-ways and everyway, the master couldn't catch us out. He strode up and down the room, banging his fist into his hand and bawling and looking as if he was going to burst right through the walls. I kept my head down, desperately trying to work out a sum the length of my arm. I was nearly sick inside, thinking of Vincent and of what would happen to him.

We stopped at the forge on the way home. We stared in over the half door, a line of noses sniffing at the thin white smoke of burning hoof as it melted into the darkness. The sledge rang out on the anvil. Our eyes followed the sparks as they were arching up, then quenched themselves disappointingly in the dry, gray, tindery beard of the smith. We were all poised on tiptoe, waiting for him to turn and bawl at us.

When he did so, opening his big spade mouth to show two yellow tusks, we plunged away with squeals of mock terror. We splashed across the stream, then turned to look back at that terrible face suspended in the darkness of the doorway. We weren't really afraid of him. We knew those black hairy hands of his, which rested like legs of mutton on the half door, had never beaten anyone. And even if they had, we would have understood why. We had often given them good reason.

There was nothing else to do after leaving the forge. I was too excited to head for home. I left the boys and wandered back through the village toward the creamery cross. Vincent was up the side road, leaning against an old rusty gate. He was looking into a nettle-grown paddock, where battered churns and slag and packing cases had overflowed from the creamery yard. He kept the red swollen cheek turned away from me.

"You going home?" I asked. I took it for granted he was waiting till the usual time, in case that mother of his asked any questions.

"No." He glanced at me, his eyes cold and clear, as if he hadn't cried at all. "I'm going to get that letter."

"But . . . what d'ye want it for?"

"I want it. That's all."

"How you going to get it, Vince?" I asked after a while. He was looking out over the paddock, as if he'd forgotten all about me.

"In his house, where else? I'm waiting for him to go up to the shop."

We could see the main road from where we were, just the caps and hats and shawls going past and occasionally a cyclist's head flitting silently by.

"What about Chris?" I said. Chris had to put on the kettle for the master's tea and sweep the house out. The master had no other help.

"What about him?" He turned to me suddenly. The master's old green hat had appeared, moving along the hedge. "D'you want to come? Or don't you?"

There was nothing I could say except "yes." My hands began to sweat, though, and the inside of my corduroy pants went warm and wet, then cold.

We waited till the hat swam away over the top of the hedge, then we ran across the fields and vaulted over the fence into the master's garden. I had never been in it before.

I looked around at the little heaps of cinders and the tins and bottles half-buried under the bare, crooked apple-tree.

"Come on," said Vincent, "for God's sake!"

The back door was open. Chris was kneeling halfway up the wooden stairs, sweeping away with a dustpan and brush. When he looked up and saw us, he let a squeak out of him. He tried to draw himself up and away from us, but Vincent caught him hard by the ankle.

"If you open your gob," said Vincent quietly, "d'ye know what I'll do to ye, Chris?"

Chris nodded his head up and down.

"You hear, Chris?"

Chris nodded again, up and down. He looked, from one to the other of us with his little red scared eyes. He was too frightened to talk.

We found our copybooks on the table in the living room. It was dark there and smelt of mildew. A small flame was licking around the fresh sods of turf, but there was no heat in the room. Vincent started looking through the copybooks, while I wandered around, looking at the big dark books on the shelves and stacked on the floor. I picked up a book and shook the dust off it.

"Look at this," I said, "by Dickens! And here's another! Look, there's dozens of them, all by Dickens!"

"I know," said Vincent, "they're classics. They come in sets. My dad's got one."

One the mantelpiece, between some photographs, was another book by Dickens. It was *David Copperfield* and it had words underlined in it and a lot of writing in the margins. It made me feel good to find out what he was reading. I had finished *David Copperfield* months before.

I had a look at the photographs. One of them showed a few people standing around in a play, all dressed up as actors, the men wearing those sissy suits with silk stockings all the way up. On the back, it said "St. Malachy's Training College Dramatic Society in *The Merchant of Venice* by William Shakespeare." Underneath was a list of names.

"Hey, Vincent," I said, "look it here! He did Bassanio." And when I took up the next photograph, I shouted, "Hey, here's the girl that did Portia."

Vincent stopped his searching to come over and look.

"Yeah, that's his wife," he said.

"But . . . I didn't know . . ." I felt aggrieved. Nobody told me anything at home. "And where is she?"

"Gone."

"But where to?" I'd never heard of anyone's wife going away, ever before. Alive anyway.

Vincent just lifted his shoulders. "That's all I heard," he said.

"And what about . . ." I made a great effort to stretch my imagination. "What about his children?"

"She must have them," said Vincent, "that's if there are any."

I was trying hard to think of the master as somebody's father. "But, Vincent . . ." I began.

"Come on, will you?" said Vincent. "We'd better get a move on."

It was then that we noticed that Chris had been standing in the doorway, listening. Vincent went up to him and seized him by the shoulder. "Tell us where he put it," he said. "You'd better!"

"Don't ask me," said Chris, "please!" And the tears began to flow, fast and silent.

"Are you going to tell me?" Vincent raised his hand. And just in time, I found the letter. It was folded roughly and stuck into a tarnished silver jug on the sideboard.

"Give it here to me," said Vincent. He took the letter between finger and thumb. "Where does he sit?" he asked. Chris pointed to a space on the table between the heaps of books and papers. Vincent tore the letter across quickly. Then he tore it again, more deliberately, back and forth into shreds. The little inky scraps of paper floated down over the empty space.

"You're not going to leave them there, man?" I burst out.

"Come on," said Vincent.

"But he'll have your life."

"Come on."

As we went through the kitchen, I noticed the tray that Chris had prepared. There were two cups, two saucers, and two plates on it.

"Chris," I said, "you don't eat here? With *him*?"

Chris nodded. He took up the tray quickly and made for the living room.

"But come here, Chris, tell me . . ."

We heard the footsteps outside the front door, his footsteps. I made a dart for the scullery door. Vincent caught my arm and held me back, pressed into the corner by the dresser. A warm patch began to spread again in my corduroys. I heard the footsteps go hollow in the hall, then go sharp on the lino of the living room. I heard them stop suddenly.

"Who did this?" It wasn't the voice I had expected. It was deep and quiet, as it had been that morning.

"I don't know." Chris almost whispered it.

"You do know. Who did it?" The voice terrified me more than if it had been a big bawl. I thought of Chris and of those tears silently flowing. I made a move toward the room, I couldn't help it, but Vincent's hand dragged me viciously back.

"I don't know," whispered Chris again, "please!"

There was a long silence. Then the quiet voice said, "All right, boy, you may sit down."

As the chairs were drawn in, I heard the scrape of a match and the globe of the oil lamp being lifted. Vincent eased the back door open and next minute, I was out into the air. Vincent led the way round to the front of the house. We crept up to the ivy-covered windowsill. We were just in time to see the master cross from the mantelpiece and toss *David Copperfield* on the table. He sat down under the yellow light of the lamp and began to pour out the tea. Chris opened the book. He began to read, his finger crawling down the page after the words. Every now and then he paused, while the master leant over and marked a word with a pencil. Chris would watch, then look up as the master talked, look up right into the master's face. Once he even laughed, not right out, but he laughed as if the master really had said something funny, that a fellow didn't have to pretend to laugh at. I stood there looking at them. I still couldn't believe what I saw, but I liked looking at them. Something made me turn to Vincent, though. When I saw him there, staring with the corner of his mouth drawn back, I said, "Come on, Vincent, come on, for God's sake."

We had nothing to talk about as we walked home. The hedges on either side of us were alive with small twilight noises. At the creamery cross, we stopped and stood for a while, with our hands in our pockets. I asked Vincent was he going to come to school in the morning, or was he going to mitch.

"Yes," he said and left me before I could ask him which he meant.

He was there before us at the cross next morning, waiting for once. The boys crowded around him, full of questions, then found that they had nothing to say to him.

"Well, lads," he said, glancing around the circle of faces, "so every one of you is carrying his sod!"

Each of us looked at his sod and then looked for Vincent's.

"He'll leather hell out of ye," said I.

"I'm not bringing it."

I lifted my sod and looked at it. It was a good sod to look at, but not so good in the hand, heavy and soft after the winter rains. I couldn't even, for Vincent, throw it down.

"Jeez, man!" Billy always swore like that. He never said the full word because he thought it was a mortal sin. Venial sins he didn't mind. "'Tis not going to stand up to him ye are?"

"The way you did?" asked Vincent.

"D'ye think I'm mad? What did I get anyway, only a few skelps of an oul' stick? That's all."

"Why though?"

"Because I was caught, that's why. But I won't be caught the next time. I can tell ye that."

"There won't be any next time, for him."

"But he'll kill ye, man. Jeez, he'll tear the windpipe out of ye."

"I know," said Vincent. None of us could take our eyes off him. His face was pale. His eyes were like glass with a greenish light shining through them. He seemed taller than any of us, all drawn out. I felt excited inside, but instead of going tall and thin, I went red all over.

"Then," said I, throwing down my sod, "I'm not taking mine either!"

The boys stared at it a moment, then one by one they began to throw down their sods, too.

"Hey!" Vincent was staring at us, real mad. "Take up those sods!"

"No," said I, "we're all in in this together. Come on, lads, drop them."

Only Billy tried to keep his. He began to sidle out of the group, but some of the fellows caught him by the wrist and twisted the sod out of his hand.

"He can't beat the lot of us," I said, as a few fellows looked back at the heap of sods, "he can't. He'd get too tired."

Chris's was the only sod in the fireplace, perched on a nest of crumpled papers and wooden *cipins.* We kept watching it, as the master came in. We couldn't take our eyes off it. That was why he spotted it immediately. The color went slowly up through his face and spread all over the top of his head.

"Step out to the line, the boys who brought no turf."

We all stepped out, trying to look calm, but afraid to look at each other. We were watching that red and shining skull, afraid it would do something, flare out suddenly, maybe, like one of those Japanese flowers that you dip in water. He can't beat us all, I kept saying to myself, please God, he can't beat us all. Oh, God, make him too tired.

He handed Chris a penknife and motioned him toward the door. We knew we were in for it. While Chris went out to cut a new ash plant, we waited in dead silence, twitching now and then, like sheep waiting for the shearing. I was wondering if it was going to be on the hands or on the behind. Please God, make him think the behind is too much trouble. It was too, because he had to hold our trousers tight so that it hurt more. But please God, make him remember that.

He stood at the window, cracking his fingers and muttering to himself, as he watched Chris below in the copse by the stream. When

Chris came back, he grabbed the stick and flexed it a few times between his hands. Then, suddenly, he caught hold of the first fellow in the queue. Without looking to see who it was, he bent the fellow over the desk and raised the stick. The howling began before the first blow landed. With one hand, the master held the trousers tight against the fork of the legs, while with the other, he beat away as if it was and old carpet he had. The howl dwindled into a squeal and then a whimper as the fellow was hauled up and shoved aside. Then the master seized the next fellow.

He worked away like that for a good while, like a red-hot old steam engine. Sometimes, he stopped, gasping for air. Then he was away again on a hack. Gradually, he began to work himself into a good humor. You could see the bald head cooling off. He began to make jokes like "Next, please" and "Step this way, gentlemen," and he bowed to the fellows after he had finished with them. Then he came to Billy.

"Ho," said he, "himself again! Might I recommend, sir, a hair of the dog?"

He laid Billy down with great respect, while we tried to laugh at the joke. Billy was smart, though, the smartest of the lot of us, though you'd never think it. He waited, very quiet, for the first blow, then he lashed out suddenly with his big boot, which caught the master right on the chest.

"I'm sorry, sir," squawked Billy, in his hoarse man's voice, "honest to God, I never meant it. Please sir, listen to me, sir . . ." but there was not need to go on. The master had walked slowly over to the window, hunching his shoulders and raising his knees. He stood there a long time, breathing hard and gradually straightening himself up. He turned suddenly to stare at us. His face was terribly pale.

"Is it trying to kill me ye are?" said he, in a whisper.

We didn't know what to say, without telling a downright lie. We just stared back at him.

"All right," said he, his voice a little stronger now, "go, each one of ye, and bring back your sod of turf. And be here in half an hour."

We shuffled to our feet. None of us wanted to be the first to go.

"And if one single boy comes back in here without his sod," said he, his voice strengthening all the time, "there'll be skin and hair flying. Every mother's son of ye will be bet again and those that I haven't bet yet will be bet twice over. So away with ye now, ye pack of little divils out of hell!" Then he let a bellow out of him. "Well, what are ye staring at? Get out!"

We made a dive for the door. Chris jumped out of our way to let us pass. He sucked his fingers as he looked after us.

The little stack of turf was still at the creamery cross, where we had left it. We jostled around it, each of us trying to pick out the best sod he could find. The thought of Vincent seemed to strike all of us at once. We stopped and looked up. He was there, watching us.

"Come one, man." Billy said, "get yourself a sod."

Vincent just smiled.

"Come on." Billy crowded up on him with that squaring, swaggering stance of his. "Billy Flahavan is not going to be bet twice. I can tell ye that. Not over you!"

Vincent stayed where he was, waiting. Billy's swagger drooped a bit, pretended to be a twitch of the shoulder blades. He glanced back to us for encouragement. "Get the bloody thing, man, can't ye?"

"Yes, get it," I shouted. I felt dirty all over, as if part of me was soft and black as a rotting apple. "We've had enough."

There was a murmur from the lads and they pushed forward behind me. "Yes," they said, "go on, man, get it." Vincent stood his ground, as I was pushed against him. His eyes were staring straight into mine. "Get it!" I said, in a whisper. At that moment, I was all set to hit him. My fists were bunched and I was stiff with all the rage inside me.

Just in time, he turned aside. "Hold on a moment," he said. We watched him run away up the land to the creamery. We began to wonder if we should follow him, to make sure he came back. Then we saw him coming, with three big black sods of turf under his arm.

"Well, come on," said he, running his eyes over us, as he used to do, "if 'tis not afraid ye are?"

"We're not afraid?" I said.

"Bloody sure we're not," said Billy.

"Follow me, then," said Vincent, marching off. We fell into step behind him. We wanted to take our time, to drag our feet in the dust, but we didn't dare in case Vincent turned round.

"What are you going to do, Vince?" I asked, moving up beside him.

"You'll find out!" he said, out loud, so as to lump me in with the rest. "You'll find out, the lot of ye."

The master was at the window, humming a tune as he swished the stick. It was the tune he hummed when he was beating us out of sheer good humor. He used to sing the last line of it, "for you'll remember, you'll remember me," as he brought the stick down hard, emphasizing every syllable. He turned toward us now, as if we had surprised him.

"Ah! So soon, lads? Determined not to miss a good day's sport! Amn't I right, Chris?"

"Yes, master," said Chris, from the seat inside the door.

"Now! Stand out those boys, whose hides haven't yet been properly tanned!"

"Aw! Sir!" pleaded Billy, just as he was easing himself into a seat.

"Aw! Sir! Aw! Sir!" The master swished his stick a few times. "Out to the line, you blackguard!"

"Hey!" called Vincent, who was still standing at the door.

"What's that?" The master turned, staring.

"Don't you want your turf?"

"Sir!" the master shouted. "Say 'sir'!"

"Don't you want your turf?" Vincent was advancing insolently down the room. He stood, weighing a sod in his hand. He had gone very pale.

The master looked at him sharply, snuffing like a bull. He raised the stick and moved forward, his mouth open, spluttering. He ducked just in time, as the sod flew over his head and broke in two against the blackboard. There was silence as the dust drifted down to the floor. Then the master let a roar out of him. He lifted the stick and advanced again.

Vincent's second sod caught him on the forehead, sending his glasses flying. The sharp crack left a thin line of blood. The master dropped the stick. His knuckles dug into his eyes, which were blinded with the dust.

"Look at him!" screamed Vincent, his voice cracking in the middle. "Look at him, now!" He turned toward us. "Come on, lads, quick belt away!"

"Right!" squawked Billy, lifting his arm. "You oul' bastard!" he yelled as he flung his sod straight into the master's blind face, squashing the nose and mouth. "Now you'll remember me!"

The sods bombarded the master's face from all directions.

He sank into his chair, facing us, his hands still at his eyes, that angry line on his forehead, the blood dripping from nose and chin. A sound midway between a belch and a hiccup burst from him. It was followed by a terrible sound, which stayed the hands of those who had not yet fired. It was a sob, a great shaking sob. It tore out of his chest and was followed by another and then another. We lowered our hands and stared. The sobbing eased a little. It became a long continuous moaning sound, like a baby with colic. We drew back slowly.

"Come on, you fools," yelled Vincent, "hit him!" He lifted his third sod. Before he could fire it, he was seized from behind. The sod was twisted quickly out of his hand. Chris flung him aside, then stood back panting, with his puny fists up.

"All right, Vincent!" I got between them quickly, as Vincent flung himself viciously forward. "You'd better get out!"

He stopped, staring at me, as if he didn't know me. Then he took a look at the shocked faces all around. He began to tremble all over. Suddenly, he turned and walked out the door.

The rest of us sat down, one by one. Only Chris went up to stand by the blind, naked, bleeding face. He stood by it, wanting to touch it, but afraid to stretch out his hand. The tears had begun to roll down his cheeks, silently rolling as if they would never stop.

I let the sod of turf fall from my hand. I heard it thump on the floor. I'm sure I heard it. In fact, I know I did. But ever since, whenever I look back, I think that I too lifted it and flung it against the face of the master.

Saving the Bacon

It was a contrary pig. Ever since Father had brought home the kicking, squealing *banbh* in the bottom of the cart we had been in trouble over it—Tom and I, that is, for Father had bought it for us at Carrick Fair. I don't know what possessed him to do it. Maybe he thought he could interest us in something more practical than bird nesting. Anyway, we soon lost our enthusiasm for pig-rearing. Nobody could blame us because the pig spent its time either rooting in the vegetable garden, or trespassing over neighboring farms. Tom and I were held responsible, of course. "They" had a good mind to sell the pig altogether. How would we like that?

We would not like it. Being the owners of a pig gave us a certain prestige at school. We were men of property, even if the property had to be fed twice a day. Usually it was, but sometimes in the middle of a geography lesson, Tom would lean forward to nudge me.

"Pat, I never thought of the pig this morning. Did you feed it?"

And I would answer with a startled "no," which would make old Johnnie look up sharply from his after-dinner nap.

However, in spite of our forgetfulness, the pig managed to get fat and heavy. We had high hopes of selling it at the October Fair when, suddenly, came tragedy. It stopped eating. Just that. At first there was no appreciable difference in girth or in activity. Gradually it grew weaker. It could hardly move about the sty.

Tom and I sat on the wall of the sty and watched it nosing half-heartedly at the mess of skimmed milk and meal I had hopefully spilled into the trough. Tom clicked his heels together ill-humoredly. I could see he was thinking for the pair of us, though I usually fed the pig.

"I might've known it would let us down like this," I ventured, staring sullenly at the prostrate body as if it had deliberately timed this sickness. "We'll never get rid of it now."

Tom was still thinking deeply. Then suddenly his frown of concentration smoothed into that self-satisfied smile I knew so well. He turned to me suddenly, eagerly.

"I'll tell you what, Pat. We'll hold a '25 drive[1] for it. Tomorrow night, say. I'll go see John Joe at the creamery. He'll spread the news in the morning. We'll charge a bob a head. Sure, it's all planned out now."

"If," I said cautiously.

"If what?" Tom was indignant.

"If you can talk Mum around."

"Yerra, that's easy. Just you leave her to me."

I did. I arrived on the scene when the first storm of protests had been overcome and Tom was brushing aside the last feeble entreaties.

"The new carpet, is it? Don't you worry about that?" Tom's voice was soothing. "Yes, I know it'll be a big crowd, but once those fellows get a pack of cards they won't care if they have to play on an upturned bucket in the cowhouse. Muddy boots? Yerra, not at all."

So it went on. I left them to it, knowing that the '25 drive would be held as scheduled.

It was. We were a bit worried at first when nobody turned up. Then a couple of the lads from the cross rode up the avenue and pushed their bicycles into the empty stable. They stood smoking in the yard, looking as if they were in two minds about staying. Soon, however, a mud-splashed Baby Ford swung in off the main road. It seemed only a few minutes before the yard was filled with bustling life as traps were maneuvered into position and bicycles stacked against the stable wall. I unharnessed ponies, held open car doors, and made myself useful outside. Tom welcomed the guests and relieved them of their subscriptions.

He was arranging partners and allotting tables when I looked in for a minute. The parlor was filled already with grim silent quartets.

1. An ad-hoc charity event, often among children.

I never liked cards, so I hurried out to the stable door where there was a more congenial atmosphere. Dan Connors was describing how the row started at the last farmers' dance. Being on the committee, of course, he knew all the ins and outs of it. In the ordinary way a man Dan's age would have done with dances long ago. He was thin and serious, with a bald shiny head. Unfortunately for himself, he was considered very eligible, though the fond mothers of the district had some difficulty in bringing their daughters' virtues to his notice. Although he attended every dance for miles around, it was usually in an official capacity. It's hard to get a man who spends his recreation hours taking tickets at a dance door.

The row was a very involved affair. Dan was just describing how he separated the combatants when he suddenly turned from unharnessing his mare.

"Pat, will ye look at who's coming up the avenue. You'd think the shame would keep them away after the way they carried on in O'Connell's last night."

I recognized the battered trap, drawn by the stumbling pony, as that of Larry and Mrs. Farrell. I had been half expecting them.

"Why, what happened, Dan? I wasn't at the creamery this morning, so I didn't hear about it."

"The old buzzard was found out last night—for once. He and the wife sat down to a game of poker with nothing in their pockets, intending, of course, to play with their winnings. Well, knowing them, O'Connell kept a close eye on the cards, so they couldn't try any hooky dealing. When they weren't getting things all their own way, they had the excuse that they hadn't any money. And the pair of them and they rotten with it! I might have known they'd turn up here tonight. Here, I'm going in."

The pony shuffled to a halt in the yard, its head immediately sagging to its knees.

"How'ye Larry? Evening, Mrs. Farrell." I had to be civil to them. After all, I was host, even if they were paying guests.

"Fair enough." Larry always was a begrudging little fellow with his near eyes and long nose. The wife looked plump and good-humored enough, until you saw her eyes. They were small and mean and seemed out of place above the generous fullness of her cheeks. She stood twittering there like an alert, well-fed sparrow, while I helped Larry to tie up the pony.

"Who's inside?" Larry grunted, as he loosened the girth.

"Oh, a fair crowd." I was casual. "The O'Connells are there too."

I watched his face to see if the information had any effect on him. Divil the bit of it. Larry's features were well disciplined.

"Oh, ay," was his only comment as he jerked the reins into a loose knot and went quickly in after his wife.

It was some time afterward before I followed him. The crowd was intent on the play inside. There were two groups left playing now and the atmosphere in the smoke-hazy room was tense. The heavy air seemed to damp down the conversation to a subdued murmur, broken by an occasional exclamation or by the sharp flick of cards being dealt. Dan Connors was standing with his back to the mantelpiece, obviously ill at ease in his unaccustomed silence. He spotted me with relief.

"Come over here and get a heat of the fire, Pat. You must be perished, boy—out all this time. Well I didn't last long long—met Larry in the first round. Himself and the missus are in fine form tonight. They're winning the semifinal now, and they'll meet O'Connells in the final. Pat, there'll be fun," and then he lowered his voice to what was for him a whisper. "D'ye know I think he passed her an odd card from the bottom of pack. I couldn't swear to it now, but we'll watch them in the final."

The final was begun in heavy silence. We all stood around watching the cards. This seemed to annoy Larry. He swiveled in his chair to stare at the onlookers behind him. They moved discreetly away. Larry and his wife won the first game in perfect unison. Mrs. Farrell lost them the second by dropping a knave too early on. Larry's eyebrows lifted in a slight movement of annoyance. The third game started. Larry dealt. One, two, three, four. He paused. Something clattered noisily on the floor. Mrs. Farrell's chair scraped back as she groped under the table. All eyes were on her as Larry continued to deal. I glanced back just as Mrs. Farrell's card was dealt. I could have sworn I saw that flick from the bottom of the pack. On the spur of the moment I blurted—"Larry, I . . . I . . ."

"Yes, Pat?" Larry's voice was suave.

"Never mind." I was not even sure. Nobody else had noticed anything.

Larry bent down to pick up his wife's spectacle case.

"Look at all the time you've wasted," he said as he tossed the case to her and continued his deal.

Larry seemed to have a bad hand. Even so, the O'Connells were not able to win a trick. Mrs. Farrell steadily built up a neat row of cards in front of her. Came the last trick. O'Connell dropped his card, the three of hearts, a low trump. Larry followed. Not even a trump—a four of spades. All eyes watched Mrs. O'Connell as she laid down the knave of hearts. There was a suppressed sigh of relief. The tension relaxed. We watched Mrs. Farrell almost indifferently. She could hardly win now. With a smile Mrs. Farrell laid down her card. Slowly, carefully, she placed it on top of the knave. We stared, silently, at the five of hearts.

Larry's face relaxed instantly into a tight smile. Then the room was suddenly full of people and talk as if we had become aware of the tension and were trying to shake it off. We congratulated the two Farrells, of course. They did not stay very long. Larry came over to me before he left.

"I'll be dropping over to see that pig in the morning. I hope it's a good one, now."

"Yes, Larry, but I don't know if it's worth all the trouble you went to, to get it."

Larry's near eyes gave me a quick suspicious look. The he turned to call impatiently to his wife.

"Are ye coming? Will ye get a move on. I'm going out to harness the pony."

The atmosphere grew less business-like with the departure of the Farrells. The cards were replayed several times over and then somebody suggested a song. Tom played on the out-of-tune piano. From that it was an easy stage to pushing the chairs and tables back against the walls. The eligible Dan Connors grew fidgety as several couples took the floor. He came over to me, urgency in his manner.

"Listen, Pat, I'll have to leave now. Have to see a fella early in the morning. Sorry now, I can't stay." Muttering something about having to arrange a match for next Sunday, he made for the door. The disappointed mothers sighed as they watched him go.

Larry's cart rattled up the avenue about dinnertime the next day. Larry looked a bit sour as he clambered heavily down. I felt apprehensive about his reactions to the pig. Tom evidently had felt the same. He had gone out the fields after some cattle that had strayed, or so he said. I walked out to the yard where Larry was tethering the pony.

"Morning, Larry. Looking for your pig? Come on round to the sty and I'll show it to you. That's a grand morning now."

"Umph."

"Nice bit of a breeze. I believe we're in for a spell of good weather. About time we got it too."

"Where's that pig?"

Larry mustn't have been feeling too well that morning. I grew more apprehensive.

The pig was lying on its side in the straw.

"Must be asleep," I said.

"Damn funny way for a pig to sleep—with its eyes open." Larry leaned in and poked the pig. There wasn't a stir out of it.

"It's dead a good while. Must have died last night." Larry fixed me with a suspicious stare. I said nothing. I didn't want Tom to reproach me about anything afterward.

"Well, where do we stand now?" Larry tapped his stick irritably on the wall of the sty.

"I . . . I don't know—I think we'd better wait and ask Tom."

So we waited for Tom. He didn't look very pleased when he came in and found Larry still there. I suspected he had seen the dead pig earlier that morning.

"What'll we do, Tom? The pig's dead."

"Dead? Isn't that too bad now. Tough luck, Larry."

This was too cool even for me.

"Yes, but Tom, what about . . ." And I motioned to Larry.

"I'll tell you what, then, Larry. We'll pay you back your bob so's you won't be at any monetary loss. It's just hard luck you know. Could happen to anybody."

I got out of range of the stick, and waited for the explosion from Larry. It didn't come. He was still deep in thought. Finally he smacked the stick on the wall.

"Fair enough, Tom. That'll suit me. I might as well take away the pig all the same. It'll do for the hounds."

I still did not believe it when he drove away with the dead pig in the bottom of the cart.

A few weeks later, just before Xmas, we got a present of a ham from Larry. We had never got anything from him before. He wasn't noted for giving presents. I made the obvious joke about our pig. The same idea had occurred to everybody, so the ham went to feed the dogs.

It was some time before I met Larry again. He reined in his pony on the road.

"How'd ye like that ham I sent you? Damn good pig it came from. Best I ever bought."

"Bought," I echoed stupidly.

"Aye. Matter of fact, I bought it with the money I made on your pig."

"Our pig! But Larry, it was . . ."

"Oh, I know. But you don't catch me wasting good meat on the hounds. I cured it myself and sold it to a fellow I know in the bacon business. Mad to get it he was."

The Threshold

Monnie's bare feet slapped the wet sand. He fingered in his pocket the papered pulp of caramels and the rubber ball Daddy had bought for rounders. The strand was still too soft to play on. Behind him the long, lonely line of his footprints melted into the sand. He had left the boys lying in the rank grass between the huts, talking desultorily, their bare legs waving aimlessly. Monnie had never known the first week of a holiday to pass so slowly. Each day, in spite of its sameness, was still distinct in his mind, but he knew that soon the days would begin to slip past and fuse into one another. Then it would be school again, stiff-paged new books with the smell of printing still on them, a desk carved with strange initials, and the chestnuts falling from the tree outside. In spite of the sun's warmth between his shoulders, Monnie felt the first shiver of autumn.

The sea had left behind it a scurf of tangled weeds, slats, and cigarette cartons. Monnie watched for broken stout bottles, like the one that had cut his young brother. He had bathed the jagged cut in a rock pool, feeling frightened by the trailing wisps of blood—until Ned came along. Ned knew where to press with his fingers so as to stop the bleeding. There was any amount of things that Ned knew. Daddy said he was a real character. He and Johanna were the only people who lived here all year round. In the summer they boiled water for visitors, and Ned collected luggage from the town, three miles away, for people coming to stay in the huts. He had a jennet, which roamed the bog and was always round-bellied and spirited—a terror between the shafts of the rattling cart. Monnie had been told not to sit in the cart, so he compromised with his conscience by sitting on the edge of it, over the shaft. He wondered if Ned was going to the station before dinner. If Daddy was out on the golf links it would be safe to drive the jennet. Monnie's steps quickened with purpose. The loose round stones which blocked the tides slithered under his feet, and then he was on the dusty rutted road.

Beyond the huts he turned right, over a placid stream, and there was Ned's house, standing a little back from the road. The gutters sloped downward from the slates like eyebrows over the surprised windows.

Monnie pushed open the half door and blinked away the Catherine wheel of lights between his lashes. Figures moved in the cool dimness of the room, and several voices jostled each other. Johanna was sitting by the ashes of the turf fire. She was white-faced, shrunken, quiet as a field mouse in the wide-backed armchair. Hennessy, who owned most of the huts, sat hunched over the racing page of the newspaper spread on the bright oilcloth of the table. The light from the window fell on the frayed stiff collar which buckled under the crease in his hairy neck. Near the bedroom door a few shawled woman were whispering. Nobody noticed Monnie, so he sidled behind Johanna's chair into the corner of the fireplace and sat on the three-legged stool beside the machine. Johanna glanced at him vacantly, and then began to rock herself slowly backward and forward, rosary beads slipping dryly between her blunt fingers. Monnie fingered the handle of the machine and then unconsciously began to turn the wheel. As the rumble deepened, the flames stabbed upward through a skin of ashes. Johanna sat up and her eyes brightened.

"Monnie," she cried, "in the name of God, child, what are you doing here?"

The whirr of the bellows slowed into silence.

"I thought maybe that Ned would be going to the station. He might let me drive . . ."

The old woman looked at him and he saw her eyes were red-rimmed. A damp, white rag was bunched in her palm.

"Did ye not know, child? Ned was took bad last night. A *shtroke* it was. He'll be hard set to last the morning. The doctor is in with him now."

She dabbed at her eyes. The gray ashes sheathed the flames.

Monnie had never seen anyone die. He knew he should feel something inside him—like the sick emptiness when he had read in the *Iron Pirate* about the double-crosser being buried alive in ice. But now he felt nothing. He tried to imagine Ned as he had seen him last—the sag of the heavy shoulders, the pale blue eyes set in a web of puckered lines, the white hair straggling from under the cap, the pipe that was like a friendly, interested third person. But the picture would not form and Monnie found himself staring dumbly at Johanna who had begun to whimper softly.

Hennessy grunted with annoyance and squirmed deeper in his chair. He smoothed the crease in the paper with blunt, fleshy fingers on which the nails had been bitten close. Daddy said Hennessy was a *bowsie*. He had been about to tell Mummy why when he noticed Monnie was listening. Monnie was curious. Hennessy must have done something awful bad—like getting drunk or fighting, though he looked too soft to be good at fighting.

"Johanna," Monnie whispered, "what's Mr. Hennessy doing here?"

"Isn't it the least he could do but come," she whispered indignantly, "an Ned an he after giving him his best years. 'Twas Mrs. Hennessy, God be good to her, that sent himself this morning. She always had the soft spot for Ned. But," she added, "sure 'twas good of Mr. Hennessy to come."

Ned would not have said that. "A bloody oul' land-grabber" he had called Hennessy one time. Still, he always returned a curt "*Morra*" when Hennessy's trap passed on the way to Mass. Hennessy owned the land and the shop down the road.

The doorknob turned briskly and the doctor came out, brittle, impersonal, self-contained. The room seemed to pivot around him.

"How is he, Doctor?" asked a woman with a long jaw and eyes that glistened with points of light.

The doctor felt for his coat on the nail behind the door.

"Has he had the priest?" he whispered.

"He has indeed, Doctor."

"Well, I should say about half an hour. . . ."

He nodded toward Johanna who was droning prayers to herself.

"You'll be here, Mrs. Dee, I suppose. Take care of the old woman."

"I will indeed, Doctor, to be sure."

Hennessy followed the doctor to the door.

"This is terrible sudden, Doctor," he said. As his son was up in Dublin studying medicine, he felt he could take liberties. The women inside were listening.

"It is," said the doctor, swinging his bag gently against his thigh.

"Terrible altogether. An' he such a decent, harmless poor man. An' a damn good worker, too. D'ye know, Doctor . . ."

The doctor glanced at his watch.

"But I mustn't be delaying ye. Ye're such a busy man. Yerra, 'tis I should know what a busy time ye have. There's our Tony now up in the city, and he wearing himself to a shadow over his exams. Sure the lad isn't able for it." He sighed gustily. "But sure 'tis a great calling, a great calling, surely."

He stabbed his thumb toward the inner room.

"D'ye think will it be long?"

"Very shortly, now. He's sinking fast."

"That's what I thought. We're busy at the hay this weather and I thought if it was any way long at all . . ."

"Well, you need have no worry about your hay, Mr. Hennessy. Good morning."

"Good morning, Doctor."

Satisfied, Hennessy dragged his chair out to the sunlit threshold. He settled himself down, folded the paper on his lap, and closed his eyes.

Mrs. Dee watched him, then turned to whisper to the other women.

"Did ye hear the doctor? That was a *quare* slap in the face for yer man, an' he too thick to notice it."

She went to the fire, lifted the kettle from the hook, and began to fill an enamel jug. Johanna opened her eyes.

"Is the doctor gone?" she said.

"He is."

"Well? How's himself—is it—is it near over?"

Mrs. Dee bent over the kettle as she framed an answer.

"So, it is," said Johanna. She made as if to rise. "I must go up."

"Stay where you are now. The doctor said."

"Is it him is tellin' me what I'm to do in me own house? Here, give me me stick."

She grasped the stick and leant heavily on Mrs. Dee's arm. Monnie was about to follow, but Mrs. Dee waved him back. The bedroom door closed, but Monnie could still hear the scraping of the chairs and the mumble of voices within.

A pool of greenish light filtered through the glass ball on the windowsill. For keeping fishing nets afloat Ned said the ball was for. It was not often he talked about fishing, although he owned a lovely white boat in the harbor in the town. He had pointed it out to Monnie, one time Daddy had given him a lift in to Mass at the Friary. Sometimes, when his voice was strangely deep and blurred after seeing somebody's luggage to the station, he would tell long confused stories about stormy nights at sea, about torn nets and basking sharks. Monnie was to go fishing as soon as he was tall enough to look over the half door, but he had a couple of inches to grow yet. And now he would never go. He wondered what would happen to the lovely white boat.

The stirrings in the bedroom ceased. A thin voice trickled through the stillness, and then the other voices joined in, flowing murmurously. The rosary, thought Monnie. He wondered if Ned was awake and listening. Suddenly he remembered the time Fr. Joe had been sitting just here in the chimney corner talking soothingly to Ned whose face was raw with anger. Johanna was setting out the gold-rimmed cups on the lace tablecloth that her daughter in the convent had sent her. She was part of the conversation though she only nodded her head at the priest's words.

"It's not only your own good," Fr. Joe was saying, "I'm thinking of. You have your own soul to save. What I'm concerned with is the scandal you're giving missing Mass like this. You haven't done your Easter Duty, you don't . . ."

He stopped when he saw Monnie.

"Hullo, Monnie," he said. "Isn't he getting to be a fine cut of a lad?"

The others were silent.

"Come here to me, Monnie. When are you making your confirmation?"

Monnie looked up and was abashed at the cold eyes set in the smile of the face.

"Next year, Father," he said, and scratched his right calf with his left instep.

"Not till then? Bedad, that'll be a great day for the church. You'll say a prayer for me, won't you?"

"Yes, Father."

"Very good." Abruptly the smile vanished. "Run along now, child. Ned and I have a few things to discuss."

Ned stayed glowering into the fire and refused to meet Monnie's eyes as he went to the door.

Daddy had been talking about it afterward. He said Fr. Joe had been in to see Ned and there had been hell's delights. Mummy said it was no laughing matter, that Ned was a terrible old man not to attend to his religious duties, and look at the mischief he was causing. . . .

Monnie had been a little proud because Ned was different, and because he did not like the delicate way Fr. Joe fingered a teacup, and the way he never fumbled for a word. But now Monnie was frightened because Ned was strange and stubborn and silent and might die like that.

The rosary was finished inside. A chair scraped the bare floor and Mrs. Dee came out to search in the cupboard under the dresser. Hennessy opened his eyes and yawned. He pulled out a gold watch from his shiny waistcoat pocket, opened it, and turned to call into the kitchen.

"Mrs. Dee, how is he?"

"Wisha 'twon't be long now, God help us. Would you not go up to the room?"

"With all them women jabbering? No, not if you were to pay me . . ." He peered in, but Mrs. Dee had gone. "Women!" he turned back to the sunlight. "Can't stand them jabbering." Suddenly he remembered Monnie.

"Are you in there boy? Come on out to the sun."

He motioned to a flat stone shimmering in the haze.

"What book are ye in?" said Hennessy.

"Sixth."

"In the Brothers, is it?"

"Yes."

"Dy'e get e'er a beating?"

"Sometimes."

"Ara, the Brothers aren't what they used to be. When I was a young lad they used to leather the hell out of us. Leather hell out of us, they used."

He turned aggressively for a reply but the boy was silent.

He grunted. In a few moments his eyes closed and his jaw dropped loosely.

A hen raked at the beaten earth and pecked fussily. From the field the voices of the boys pierced the noontide stillness. Monnie could hear the rattle of clubs in a golf bag as some players passed over on the links. Somewhere a bee wandered lazily. Part of the stillness, an eternal undertone, was the hesitant breaking of the little waves on the strand. Everything was the same as Ned was dying. Monnie's heart cried out against the cruelty of it. He longed to tell people, to shock everything into silence. He felt that clouds should band the sun and that the sea should hush its monotone.

Hennessy sat up and scratched himself. He looked at his watch.

"God Almighty," he said, "'tis after dinner hours. Run up, boy, and see how the old fella is."

Ned's eyes were closed but his breath came quietly. His face was dusty white and thinner than Monnie had ever seen it, but the lines had softened. There was a crucifix on the smooth sheet and his fingers trembled upon it. The women were whispering at the foot of the bed, and Monnie closed the door before they saw him. A crucifix! Then Ned was going to be all right. The sun was warm on Monnie's face.

"Well, how is he?" said Hennessy.

"He's all right," said Monnie carelessly. "I mean—he's not dead yet."

Hennessy shifted disgustedly in his chair.

"Yerra," said he, "the divil wouldn't dead that fella."

He laughed, half-ashamed at the boy's shocked face. Monnie suddenly hated him. Hennessy was a vulture, waiting for Ned to die so that he could—yes, maybe that was it—so that he could grab Ned's lovely white boat.

"Are you . . . ?" Monnie said, and gulped as Hennessy's eyes swung round to him.

"Am I what?"

"Will you be taking Ned's boat?" said Monnie in a rush.

"What boat?"

"The boat he used to go fishing in. You know, the white one in the harbor."

Hennessy lay back and guffawed loudly. Laughter furrowed his taut waistcoat.

"Well, isn't he a right old chancer," he spluttered, "to tell you a thing like that? Sure Ned was never in a rowboat in his life, no more than myself. Footin' turf and thinnin' turnips he used be on my place." His laughter suddenly stopped. "Why, what's wrong with ye, boy? What are ye crying about?"

But Monnie did not know.

Peasants

Long before dawn, the air began to fill with the hollow tap of hooves and the long-drawn bawling of cattle. Like the thickening spokes of a cartwheel, the herds converged upon the town. As yet, they moved in units, separated by chalky ribbons of roadway, hemmed in by unpeopled fields, by an occasional closed cottage and the silent mass of a tree. In the pitch darkness, each drover was conscious of the breathing of his beasts, of a sudden quickening of the gait, like the final tip-tap as a cobbler hammers home a sprig. Though he sensed the deeper blackness of the herd in front, he felt more isolated than on his own lonely boreen. Occasionally, a cart creaked past, full of squeals and rustles. A figure hunched high up on the creels called out a greeting and the cart traversed the white strip of roadway and was gone. In blustering defiance of the overwhelming black silence the drover raised his voice and laid his stick to a lagging beast.

Gradually, a watery light diluted the eastern sky. The light flowed over the land, eddied around trees, drowned hedgerows in its colorless depths. It flooded the roadway, which dissolved and blended with the fields. Man and beast fell silent in this merely gray world, in which the only sounds were the monotonous tapping of hooves and the occasional short rasp of a cough.

And then the first bird was up, spinning its quoits of song high into the air. A cock in the distance called urgently, as if it had been caught unaware and was making up for lost time. Its notes sounded blurred through the subterranean light. Gradually, the countryside stretched itself. Twigs stirred in the hedgerows, something scurried past, rustling the roadside grasses. High overhead, a treetop sighed like distant surf. The gray light drained westward, leaving a dull wet shine on each leaf and blade of grass.

Dawn blew the cold tips of the clouds and set them glowing. The perimeter of the drover widened out over the still fields, the sleeping houses. Each individual ribbon of roadway fell into place, became part of a long communal road. Men recognized their neighbors, began to whistle, to shout greetings. Their sticks fell with sharp cracks, driving the cattle forward in blundering rushes. And then the sun laid its red fingertip on the eastern hills.

By the time they reached the outskirts of the town, the herds had lengthened into one loud, irregular, hurrying mass. They swept past straggling lines of whitewashed cottages, then bravely invaded the silent streets. Intimidatingly, the blinds were drawn down the pale faces of the houses. An occasional shop window stared glassily. Rude confined noises rebounded away between the dead walls of side streets. The onrush of men and cattle gained momentum as it approached the Fair Green. Then suddenly, it faltered. A moment of confusion, and it stopped. The great rusty gates of the green were closed. Their spikes impaled the naked sky.

The first herd of cattle bunched against the gates. A crowd of drovers gathered around, loud-voiced, gesticulating, vaguely uneasy. Gradually, they fell silent and waited for somebody to take the lead. The news streeled back and the flow of the herds slowed, then halted. Cattle bunched in the doorways, against the shop windows. The drovers walked forward a little, held urgent meetings, and sent forward delegates to the group at the gate.

Gradually, the uncertainty of the foremost group spread back through the herds. Men tapped idly with their sticks, gnawed their nails, and avoided each other's eyes. Occasionally they lunged forward to beat viciously at strange cattle which blundered into their herds. The cattle snuffed uneasily, pressed more tightly together, then slithered away in a rush. They raised dumb obstinate heads against the blows of the drovers. The strange uncertainty was felt in the houses. Blinds rose cautiously and sleepy faces peered between the curtains. A couple of shopkeepers came out and leant their shoulders against the jamb of their doors.

The leaderless group at the gate still talked and gestured spasmodically. It turned with relief to watch Maurice Kirwan stride forward. He was a tall active man of about sixty. His tweed coat hung loosely on bony shoulders. He had a fine warm farm, but lived sparingly and employed only one man to skim the profits from the land. He drove a hard bargain, had twice gone to law, and on each occasion had been barely justified. A strict religious man who minded his own business, he was not generally disliked. His few enemies were inspired mainly by envy of his extensive conacre and his luck with cattle.

The group of drovers and small farmers parted to admit him. His humorless, bleached eyes surveyed the gate as they offered halting explanations. He interrupted brusquely.

"Where's the marquis's man?"

"Cullen, the herd?" said a voice. "Did anyone of ye see Cullen the herd?"

"Yerra, 'tisn't him he's looking for. 'Tis Mr. Barnivill the agent."

"What are ye sayin', man? 'Tis Cullen have the key. Cullen's the man."

"Where does he live?" demanded Maurice.

The old withered drover pushed himself forward and raised his hand pedantically.

"Come on so with me," cut in Maurice, impatiently.

Followed at a distance by the crowd, the two men passed through the herds and turned down a side street. The old man knocked timidly at the door of a neat brick house which had window boxes of red geraniums. Maurice waited a moment, then knocked loudly and rattled the shining brass letterbox. The window upstairs was pushed up and a thin elderly man in a disheveled striped shirt looked out. His narrow white head rotated slowly as he viewed the street.

"Are you Cullen?" demanded Maurice.

The man's dull eyes gathered toward him, hovered attentively a moment, then widened out over the crowd.

"What d'ye want?" said the man flatly. All inquisitiveness seemed pressed out of him by centuries of routine obedience on the estate.

"I want the key of the gates."

The man's head disappeared and was instantly replaced by that of a stout woman, her cheeks still red from the pillow's warmth.

"The key ye want?"

"Yes," impatiently.

"Sure himself don't keep it anymore."

"Who keeps it, then?"

"Wasn't it your man," quavered the old man, "that stood beside the steward when he took the halfpenny tolls?"

"'Twas indeed, but he'll do it no more."

"What d'ye mean? Speak up, woman," snapped Maurice.

"I mean," she drawled the words. Her eyes were on the staring drovers. "I mean that ye'll pay no more tolls to the marquis. That's what I mean."

"And why not?" Maurice's voice cut through the startled ejaculations of the crowd. The woman paused for silence.

"Because the tolls is sold to Hennessy."

She leant her elbows on the window and looked down with mild astonishment at the uproar.

"You mean Andy Hennessy?"

"Andy Hennessy of Derryabone," confirmed the woman smugly.

Maurice turned away, then paused and looked up at the window.

"And why . . ." His voice was meek now. "And why did he shut the gates?"

She shook her head slowly, prolonging the enjoyment of her own helplessness.

"That's a question ye'd have to put to Hennessy—to Mr. Hennessy," she added with derisive emphasis.

The crowd began to turn away. Her voice rose, harrying the slouching men.

"Faith, ye're the men that begrudged the marquis his tolls. And he only askin' what his father asked before him. Aye, and his father's father."

She paused and added vindictively:

"Maybe ye'll like it better now."

The window closed abruptly.

Back at the gate, Hennessy's man had arrived. His old-young bony face, under smart tweed cap, was impassive to the confusion about him. The farmers knew him slightly as the foreman of the sawmills and as Hennessy's right-hand man in the business of gorging small farms. He was a tool, characterless and efficient. The men, repelled by his indifference, drew back to let him pass. Maurice alone barred his path.

"What's the meaning of this?" Maurice gestured blusteringly toward the gate.

"Mr. Hennessy's orders."

"And is Andy Hennessy to hold up the men of seven parishes with his orders?"

The men around shifted uneasily as they detected a querulous weakening of their spokesman. Hennessy's man ignored the remark and passed on to unlock the gates. He paused with the key groping for the lock and half-turned to say, as if quoting parrot fashion from the contract of sale . . .

"I have been authorized by Mr. Hennessy to collect on his behalf a toll of one shilling per beast."

A moment of paralyzed silence. An old drover said, "Anamundeel," with a sharp sucking-in of breath, like a wave drawing back over shingle. Shouts and threats gathered slowly, surging upward, then crashed clamorously forward. Men's faces lifted with the blood staining on them. Sticks were brandished high overhead and the crowd advanced, stampeding frightened cattle before them.

Hennessy's man stood aloof.

"Burst the gates," shouted someone. But already the crowd was faltering.

"The Guards. Here's the Guards," said a voice in the rear. The crowd broke sullenly apart and three guards passed through. One of them went to speak to Hennessy's man and the other two ranged themselves in front of the gate.

Maurice Kirwan pushed forward.

"I'm damned if I'll pay a shilling a beast to any man," he burst out throatily. A murmur of agreement rose around him.

"Very well, so," said Hennessy's man. "Ye'd best wait till Mr. Hennessy comes."

The men broke into loud, disputing groups which gradually cooled and fell silent. They shifted their feet uneasily and began to feign attention to their beasts. A group of dealers stood near the gates, hands in the pockets of their trench coats, their raw faces set aloofly under the slouch of their hats. A family of tinkers streeled through the crowd. Tight-rolled in her shawl, the woman carried a motionless bundle. Her dark sunken eyes stole glances at the farmers.

Hennessy's big car nosed its way through a cold, hostile crowd, which parted reluctantly for him. It stopped near the gates. Heavily he got out, closed the door carefully after him. His little pea-hard eyes blinked as he faced the crowd. Under the light broad-brimmed hat, his shapeless face had a grayish indoor pallor.

"What's this *raimeis* . . ." began Maurice, then in a deadened voice. "What's this, Andy, about raising the tolls?"

"Yes, the tolls is raised." Hennessy's voice came rich and deep from his colorless body.

"But damn it, Andy, you can't do that. The marquis . . ."

"Ay, the marquis—you drove him to bankruptcy. Times is changed, Maurice."

"But a shilling a beast!"

"'Tis not unreasonable. Look, man, at the price of cattle. Nobody should know better than yourself."

Maurice's voice rose thinly.

"I won't pay it, I won't, I tell ye."

Hennessy's eyes flicked past him contemptuously, played over the staring crowd beyond.

"Very well, so, take your cattle away. And any man here can do the same. No man of you can say he was mad to pay."

Maurice turned away slowly. His lower lip trembled in futile elderly anger. The men watched him intently. Suddenly he paused and his hand reached for a long shabby black purse.

He peeled a note from a wad within and thrust it blindly into the hand of Hennessy's man, the crowd made way for him and he passed through to his own herd.

The foremost drovers paid their money and the gates swung open. Maurice drove his cattle through without looking to right or to left. Hennessy stood at the gate rubbing his grayish jowl with a plump pale hand. He watched the drovers and small farmers go past. His little pea eyes blinked with mild astonishment as they dropped their eyes respectfully and inclined their heads.

The Letter

The wall tapered like a tongue between the open lips of the bay. At its tip curled a red bulbous lighthouse. Beyond, the smooth waters of the river swirled into the wind-chopped waves of the bay.

His tire hissed along the cindery road from the quays like a wind strumming through telegraph wire, thought Tony, as he cycled past the stale-smelling dump and out on to the wall. A breeze riffled across the bay, slicing the heavy air, burrowing under his shirt and down his back. Tony's thoughts raced ahead, anticipating the plunge into clear water, the first free vigorous strokes, and then the slow luxurious pause as he turned to float.

The bicycle jolted toward the lighthouse, which glowed ahead through a faint blue haze. In Tony's pocket was the letter, still unopened. All day he had resisted the temptation to open it, sometimes with thumb tensed under the flap. His heart had thumped loudly, ridiculously, when first he had seen the delicate pale blue square lying on the hall mat. Of course, he had expected it, though some nights he had lain awake, sweating at what he had written, wondering would she laugh, would she ignore his letters. She was so much more grown-up than he, though she was only seventeen, almost a whole year younger.

Hastily, he had picked it up and continued on his way to Mass, feeling it stiff and unresponsive in his breast pocket. The morning sun in the little chapel fell across the tabernacle door, lacing the white altar cloth with splintered light.

"I will go unto the altar of God," went the missal, "unto God, who giveth joy to my youth," and Tony's eyes wandered to the open window. Outside, birds flitted in the green light between the trees. He began to follow the Latin because sometimes his wandering thoughts grated over unfamiliar words, but today the words glided smoothly, sensuously beautiful before his eyes.

With sunlight warm on his face, gravel crunching underfoot to the chapel gate, he had again been tempted to slit the envelope. But just in time he foresaw the anticlimax of breakfast—a stained tablecloth in the digs, cold rasher fat and congealed egg on the plates, a sunless dining room with its sullen furniture. And later, Saturday morning in the accountants' office, the other apprentices discussing some American tournament, typists chattering over coffee, shrilling phones, clacking typewriters. No, he would wait. He would open the letter in some private hour, an hour that he would remember.

Two middle-aged men were sunbathing on the bench against the white wall of the lighthouse. One was peering at a newspaper, his free hand rubbing a bony knee. He nodded at Tony, who wheeled the bicycle past the cool shadowed yard. His eyes were pale blue as if the color had been washed out of them. The other man dozed, snoring gently, his jaw loose. Poor old men, they would never get exciting pale blue letters. They must have such dull sleepy lives. Tony wanted to share some of his happiness with them. Quickly, he slipped out of his clothes and sat beside them.

The newspaper was laid aside with relief.

"That's a powerful day, thanks be to God. Were you in for a dip yet?"

"No, I've just come out of the city. It's stifling in there."

"The water's grand."

The man stretched his thin white arm toward the spiked smoky outline of the city.

"Aren't we right fools to be livin' in there? Here I am, thinking of it all morning. Dust and noise and traffic, crowds jostling in pubs and loud talk in pubs—sure it doesn't make sense. It sucks the bloody life out of a man."

Tony stared at the grimy tentacles that clasped the bay. Would the city do this to him too? Leave him tired and withered and bony. Suck him dry and then cast him aside. And Anne?

"What d'ye work at?" said the man.

"I'm in an office," said Tony.

"Aye, a nice clean life. I'm a baker meself."

But I'll have my own office, thought Tony, some day. And I'll have a car. And on a day like this we'll drive up the mountains and have a picnic, just the two of us. Besides a noisy talkative stream, and Anne will measure tiny cups from the thermos flask, her face intent and serious against the mossy rocks and heather. I will lie there, languorously, watching, feeling happiness like sunlight soaking into warm skin.

"We're the lucky ones," the baker was saying. "Poor man there comes down here every day after signing on at the Exchange. A houseful of kids he has but sure it don't take a feather out of him . . ."

Tony watched the slack mouth of the sleeper twitching. A dirty hand dragged across it. Then a pair of dull brown eyes opened lazily. The man nodded.

"Hullo," said Tony, watching his tongue feeling around dry lips, "Nice day."

"Gran'," The eyes lolled back under their lids . . .

A lazy shiftless fellow, people would say, but Tony was stabbed with anger. God was so unjust, giving some people for life a round of colorless days without hope or memories—

"Ye'd better go and have yer swim, son," said the baker. "The tide's on the turn."

Tony looked confusedly back to the pale blue eyes.

"Oh, yes," he said vaguely.

"Be seeing you after." The man reached for his paper. On the wide concrete terrace below the lighthouse, two men were playing handball. Their muscles flickered as they slapped the ball against the whitewashed side of the lighthouse.

Tony dived in quickly. A gliding greenish moment, and then he was beyond the rocks in the cold waves of the bay. The water flapped in his face as he turned to float. He drifted idly a moment, watching the city lifting over the waves, and beyond the steady mountains unrolling in the distance. As he struck out for the terrace, he noticed that the men had stopped to watch him. He climbed carefully on to the rocks.

"Want a game, mac?" The man's teeth showed white against his shadowed face. "Jim here is throwing in the towel."

"Just as well for you," the other said humorlessly. "I have those minutes to write up, Paddy."

He settled a towel at his back and began to write. The other man winked at Tony.

"A busy man." He tossed up the ball. "We'll start if you're right."

The game was vigorous, interspersed with loud exclamations of disgust from Paddy, whenever he missed a stroke. Tony won narrowly.

"Good man, yourself." Paddy patted him on the back. They sprawled out of breath against a warm rock. The sensations of the day panted in and out of Tony's mind to the drumming of the pulse in his forehead—a white glare beyond his closed eyelids, the sea's murmuring, muffled like an echo from a shell, sunlight stroking his fingers—his body floated lightly on the warm rock as the jerky course of his blood slowed and smoothed, then pressed downward, stagnant and heavy, slowly, overwhelmingly, sinking him into sleep.

Paddy sat up suddenly and nudged him

"Feel like a spot of grub?" he said. "Me and Jim are having a bite if ye'd care to join us."

Tony thanked him, blinking away the sharp points of light between his lashes. The trio sat on the warm concrete and Jim levered the top off a milk-bottle.

"I'm not used to this tack." Paddy held forward a cup. "It's the wrong color."

He gulped it down, then wrinkled his nose in disgust.

"I'll have to disinfect the old larynx tonight after that stuff. I'm not coddin'." He pretended indignation at Tony's laughter. "Not coddin' at all. A few jars at Synnott's. Then maybe a round of the bony fides. Jim, will ye come. We'll make a night of it."

"No thanks." Jim's voice deepened in importance. "It's a meeting, I am afraid. There's signs of a split in the Branch Committee and I want to be in at the kill."

The other man narrowed his eyes and inclined his head knowingly.

"Ye never know," continued Jim, "I might end up on the National Executive . . ."

"Or in the Dáil itself," said Paddy. "If ye play yer cards well."

"*Arra*, have sense, man." But Jim's eyelids flickered over the glint in his eye. The idea was not new to him. Porter and politics. Tony smiled at the thought. Poor fellows, how prosaic they were. Even the loveliness could not kindle their sodden natures.

Gradually the wall levered the sunlight off the terrace. Tony drained his warm sourish milk and tossed the screwed-up wrappers into the sea. Jim lit a cigarette.

"Let's go up to the seat," said Paddy.

The baker was still there, staring at the city, bulked against the reddening sky. He made room on the edge of the seat for Tony. Nobody spoke for a while.

On the left side across the bay, twilight was drawing a blue muslin veil over the twin summits of the sugarloaves, firm and rounded like—like the breasts of a woman asleep. And—there was her slender neck and there, but God, it was a sin to be letting thoughts run on like this—Tony shifted on the warm bench and turned to watch the white shreds of sails flitting in the harbor.

He thought of the letter. Should he read it, now while the sun was still strong and the city so hazy and far away. The day would soon begin to droop, but he sat there savoring the moment, refusing to stretch out his hand for the letter. It lay so noncommittal there half out of his pocket, so impassive. It would not change, no matter what he thought. Would she lay herself bare, as he had, or—suppose, suppose she made fun . . .

With vague surprise, he watched unfamiliar fingers fumbling with the flap. Nobody was looking. The white face behind him swayed, suspended under the sun, like a mole blundering into daylight.

"Dear Tony," he read, "It was nice of you to write. It was such a surprise—"

But he had promised. Surely she remembered.

"Well, everything here is much the same, since you were home—" But it can't be. Nothing can be the same. I mean—

"And it was a really enjoyable dance, but the same old crowd—we missed you—what have you been doing with yourself? Naughty boy, how many times have you whispered those sweet nothings you wrote—?"

A handbreadth of a cloud floated over the sun and the day suddenly darkened, dropping beneath the routine wash of waves against the rocks, the intense white edges of the cloud, the hard-limned sweep of a gull's wings in the blue air.

The baker shivered.

"Near time to be going," he said.

"Did ye bring th'ould fiddle?" asked Paddy. The baker nodded.

"Give us a few bars so, before we go."

The baker brought his fiddle out from the lighthouse yard and sat a long time tuning it with his thin fingers.

The cloud had passed. Old sunlight lengthened along the wall, ridged by the shadows of uneven stones. White sails gathered toward the harbor and somewhere a gull cried wearily.

"God, isn't it a lovely evening," said the baker, fervently.

"Terrific," said Jim.

"I was just thinking," Paddy's voice was hushed. "It's the kind of a day you put away and think of afterward when you say to yourself 'That was such and such a summer.'" He looked around at the others and said half-ashamed but defiant, "Ye know what I mean."

The baker smiled. "'Tis too late for me to lay up things now, but it makes me look back—"

And I pitied him, thought Tony, pitied all of them, the only one to see sadness in all this bounty. He felt a lump in his throat and a dryness behind his eyes.

"What'll I play?" said the baker.

"D'ye know the 'Rose of Mooncoin'?" asked Paddy. In a coarse baritone he began softly,

"Flow on, lovely river,
Flow gently along,
By your green banks I wander
Neath the lark's merry song."

"Aye, ye have it," said the baker, swinging up the fiddle to the hollow of his shoulder. The color seemed to have flowed back into his eyes. What shall I think, thought Tony, of this day that opened like a flower, whose petals now are closing. Perhaps it will seem full of light and happiness.

A cargo boat floated down the brimming river, immense when it blocked the light. A few figures leant on the rail, listening to the thin music of the water. As it passed, the ripple of its wake flopped and fell upon the rocks. Beyond, at the far end of the wall, the glow faded from the sky and darkness stole into the city.

Summer Evening

The boys were to meet on the square in front of the orderly room. Jim Dunne was the first to arrive, his care for punctuality being due mainly to diffidence. For a long time he sat half-astride his bicycle, impressing crisscross tire patterns in the dust with his front wheel. Then Des cycled slowly across the square, one hand stuck in the pockets of his flannels. As usual, his jaws worked loosely on a piece of gum.

"Where are the boys?" he called, incuriously.

"Charlie said something about cleaning his webbing—"

"Huh," Des laughed his lazy sardonic laugh. "A spit and a promise, I suppose."

They waited in silence. The square was deserted, the shadows of camp buildings beginning to lengthen across it. Then the bugler sounded the Angelus. The two boys crossed themselves. Jim's eyes followed as the quiet notes faded away over the intense green of the new-mown airfield toward the distant blue haze of the sea.

"Here's Charlie now," said Des, "Fuss written all over him." He deepened his voice in a rough imitation of Charlie's. "All right, boys, let's get organized."

Charlie came speeding up, slithered to a halt between the two.

"Who've we got? D'ye mean to say that blasted little scut is late again?"

"Looks like it," murmured Des.

"To hell, we'll leave him."

Reluctantly the other two swung into line.

"Look at him coming," Charlie spoke between his teeth. "As cool as you like."

"I hope I didn't keep you fellows waiting," called Tony, "Had to write to the old man. He sent me some dough."

"Uh-huh!" Des raised his eyebrows.

"Course it's nearly all gone already. Poker debts. We had a late session in the hut last night."

He talked over-loudly with an air of assurance which the others resented because he was only seventeen, almost two years younger than they.

"All right, boys, get fell in," Charlie asserted his bogus authority. "Cover off from the right."

The military policeman at the gate glanced casually at their passes.

"A late night, boys?"

"Sure thing," Des laconically shifted the gum in his mouth.

"Don't do anything that'd shock yer Da now."

"We wouldn't know how," responded Charlie brazenly as he swung into the saddle.

Prompted by a sudden boyish rush of excitement, Jim joined in the laughter of the others. Behind him, the spiked gates of the camp held the dusty square, the rows of black huts crouching beetle-like under pallid hangers. The boys swept four abreast along the byroad. Fresh with the green smell of hedgerows, the air flowed past, rounding cheek and forehead. Tawny meadows washed right up around banks and hedges. A tree above a motionless cornfield had assumed a furry solidity. Between the individuated stalks of young corn glimmered a greenish light.

And then they came on the sea. At the end of a white sandy cart track, they saw its deep evening blue, opaque as the light levelled with it. They slowed down.

"We don't need togs," said Tony.

Charlie took command at once.

"Right wheel, boys. There won't be anyone here, I'm sure."

Old sunlight warmed the scimitar of strand. A single long wave turned over on the shore and then the sea was still.

Feverishly, the boys stacked their bicycles and undressed. Their bodies, patched white and brown, cast light spidery reflections as they ran across the sand.

Tony outstripped the rest. He dived cleanly under a wave, then with powerful strokes headed out to sea. Charlie jealously splashed after him, breaking into short chugging strokes. The other boys swam and floated lazily in the warm inshore water.

They ran up and down the strand to dry themselves. Tony attempted a few wobbly cartwheels but desisted when he saw Jim turn a perfect handspring.

"Where'd you pick that up?" he asked.

"At school. We had a good instructor."

"Oh," Tony could express surprise with damaging politeness. He had been to a select English college. "I didn't have much time for the gym myself. When you're on the first fiftccn—"

"Do it again, Jim," called Charlie.

Obligingly, Jim turned a handspring several times in quick succession. Then, panting slightly, he watched the others.

"That's blooming good," said Charlie enthusiastically, a new respect in his voice. Des nodded his appreciation.

They went to dress. Jim was silent, glowing with the warmth of praise struck from the eyes of the others. He pulled his shirt over his shoulders and felt his skin tingle against the stiff material.

The sea had suddenly stirred to restlessness. A spate of little waves came running in, breaking at odd angles and sending thin lines of foam slithering forward. The restlessness spread inland through the quiet evening. As the boys regained the roadway, a handful of startled crows was flung from a distant copse. Overhead, a hawk slithered desperately from a ledge of air.

They passed a thatched farmhouse couched snugly in trees. Beyond was an orchard. Jim spotted the shaded fruit and felt a sudden urge to climb the fence in the excitement of a raid. He slowed down.

"Come on," called Charlie. "It's too risky. We'll try it on the way back."

They began to race along the narrow road, cutting corners, passing and repassing each other with incoherent cries of triumph. They passed a straggling line of whitewashed cottages and slowed down.

"Into file, boys," called Charlie. "Cover off." He mimicked the company sergeant, "Look smart, now. Yiz are marchin' at attention."

Tony took up the mimicry. "Pick up that bloody step." He shouted at Charlie. They all laughed as they passed into the streets of the town.

The warm evening had brought the townspeople out of doors. The men stood chatting at street corners. Groups of girls in light summer dresses paraded the pavements. Des emitted a slow double-toned whistle.

"Eyes front there," called Charlie.

They halted in the center of the town. The tinny strains of dance music eddied down the amber evening air.

"What'll we hit?" Charlie assumed his voice of authority. "The Town Hall or the Classic?"

"The Town Hall's scruffy," Tony spoke up first.

Des shrugged. "All the one to me. The Town Hall's a gas though. They stamp the passouts on the palm of your hand."

"Right," said Charlie. "The Town Hall it is."

As they produced their combs and bunched before the mirror in the Gents, Charlie addressed them.

"Now, boys, every man for himself. And remember—no cuttin' in on each other. There's no sense in it."

The small hall was ill lit. The boys' entrance caused a stir of interest. Their bronzed young faces contrasted with the pallid townies. For a few moments they stood near the door, talking abstractedly and considering the girls sitting by the wall.

"Excuse me, fellows," said Tony, "I see something interesting." He patted Charlie on the shoulder. "See you after, old man."

One by one, the other boys chose their partners.

Between dances, they grouped against a pillar that supported the gallery. They discussed personalities in the camp and laughed extravagantly at Charlie's impersonations. Occasionally, one of them remarked on Des' progress with a synthetic blonde. They watched her face crinkle at his jokes and sometimes they could hear her brittle laughter.

The hall now seemed moist and close. Reacting suddenly from it, Jim was aware of the glistening walls, the husky sweetness of the music, the flush on damp flesh. Bodies relaxed in the warm cloying atmosphere. Cheeks, breasts leant closer, melted together—with sudden revulsion, Jim turned and walked out into the hard green dusk.

He returned in a mood of cold superiority. His glance surprised a tall dark girl watching him. She looked away hastily but a faint smile lingered on her lips. He asked her to dance. She glanced upward swiftly then moved out on to the floor.

She was slim. Her waist, firm and narrow, moved easily under his hand. They began to talk and soon he was telling her about life in the camp. He liked her cool, amused laugh.

In an interval, Charlie whispered to him.

"You're doing all right there. She's nice."

Later, he asked if he could see her home. She hesitated a long moment and then nodded. He realized how much he had dreaded a refusal.

Charlie and the boys were to meet him at the railway bridge. He waited for her on the steps outside. As she came out, her face framed against a high coat collar, caught the glow of a neon light. For a moment he was startled by her beauty.

They walked through the darkened streets. He was talking of what he would do when his reserve training was up. He spoke rapidly, tonelessly, slurring the words. Occasionally, she glanced at him but he could not read her expression.

They turned up a narrow street leading to the old part of the town. Where the road levelled along what had been a rampart, they paused. She leant on the wall and began to point at the river that flowed through the dim-lit town. His eyes stole back along her outstretched arm and fastened irresolutely on her profile. Suddenly, he thought of the stiff-faced blonde and he anticipated the nonchalant boasts of Des. His arm circled the girl's waist and for a moment they both stared out into the darkness beyond the town. Then he drew her toward him and kissed her gently, uncertainly. She remained passive, then after he had kissed her several times, drew back and quietly loosened his arms. Her eyes were darker than the darkness but he fancied she was smiling.

"How old are you?" she asked.

"Nineteen." He sounded surprised.

"Nineteen?" she echoed.

"Well, almost!" He became aggrieved. "Why how old are—" Just in time, he checked himself.

"I'm twenty-nine," she said quietly.

"Twenty-nine?" incredulously. "Good Lord." Then after a pause he blurted, "I didn't think—I mean—"

"When do you leave camp?" she asked hastily.

"Friday next."

"We'll hardly meet again, so."

She was looking out over the town. His arm was still around her. He could see the distant lights of the camp hovering in the middle darkness. A car breasted a far hill and its headlights swept the sky. He was remembering the rush of cool evening air, the slap of feet on wet sand, the whirl of amber light in the streets of an old town. Excitement seized him, renewed the exultation of the evening. Somehow he wanted to crystallize, the moment of re-experience, urgently to perpetuate it . . . Roughly he swung the girl toward him. His lips found her cheek—and then he paused. Slowly, he tilted her head. His wondering fingers confirmed the wetness of her cheek.

Two smooth half-moons guarded her eyes. In the hard streetlight, he noticed the lines arrowing mouth and eyes, distinct as the sinews of a leaf in late summer. He felt the shame of an unwilling eavesdropper. And then she looked up. Her splendid dark eyes forgave him.

Tenderly, his lips pressed her cheek, tasting its faint saltiness. And suddenly, she drew him down and kissed him firmly, fully on the mouth. Before he could realize her gesture, she had patted his cheek, had whispered "Good night." He called out something, but she did not turn. Slowly, he walked down the hill, down to the level of the town.

Charlie was waiting at the railway bridge.

"You were a hell of a long time," he grumbled. He watched Jim mount his bicycle. "Well, how did you get on?"

"Oh, all right." Jim feigned attention to his lamp.

"The boys are gone one ahead. You should have heard Des boasting. And as for that other brat . . ."

Puzzled, he glanced again at Jim.

"I didn't pick up anything myself. Could have, but didn't bother." Finally, aggrieved, he blurted, "Well, aren't you goin' to tell us about it?"

But all through the long hours of the evening, the summer-full years had been drifting down. Jim felt the sad heavy sweetness of their weight. Pityingly, he glanced at the puzzled boy on whom they had yet to fall.

Deór na hAithrí

Risteárd de Paor

Compare the translation by Victor Power titled "The Tears of Prayer," pp. 58-63.

Bhí gruaim ar Bhean Uí Mhórdha agus í ag fágaint siopa Weinrid maidin Dé Luain. An tIúdach plucach beag-shúileach féin a chas léi istigh agus ní thabharfadh sé ach tríocha scilling ar chulaith a fhir chéile.

"Ach, a bhean chóir," ar seisean ag crochadh a lámha reamhra ar a raibh fáinní seodmhara ag spréacharnaigh, "ní fiú an méid sin féin é. Is cuma liom má fuair tú dhá phunt air an tseachtain seo caite . . ."

"Agus an tseachtain roimhe sin agus roimhe sin arís," ar sise ag iarraidh deora feirge agus díomá a cheilt ina glór.

"Agus roimhe sin arís chomh maith," ar seisean ag déanamh aithrise uirthi. Shín sé a mhéar ionsuirthi. "Faigh áit níos fearr muna bhfuilir sásta liomsa ach ná bí 'mo chrá le do ghol. Tá dea-chustaiméirí ag feitheamh liom."

D'fháisc na dea-chustaiméirí a mbeartanna féna n-ascaill agus gháireadar go faiteach nuair a chaoch sé súil orthu. Thug Bean Uí Mhórdha fuath dubh dó ach thóg sí an tríocha scilling.

"Gol," ar sise ag siúl go trom-chosach fé dhéin an dorais, "amhail is dá gcuirfeadh a leithéid ag gol mé. Ní thabharfainn an sásamh sin dó." Thug sí buille nimheanta don pháiste a bhí ag béicigh san pram lasmuigh. "Gol,an ea!"

Reprinted with permission from *Combar* 9, no. 10 (October 1950): 9–11.

Ghluais sí i dtreo an bhaile, an leanbh ag béicigh ní ba ghéire roimpi. Sháith sí an pram isteach i ndoras síor-oscailte Uimhir a Sé, Lána Muire. Tháinig Jimí anuas an staighre lom agus fuadar fé. "A Mhamaí, tá job agam. An gcreidfeá é? Job maith a dúradar san Exchange. Féach nóta puint. Agus beidh tuille agam ag deireadh na seachtaine."

"Cén saghas job é?" ar sise go hamhrasach agus súil aici ar an nóta puint, "agus cá bhfuair tú sin?"

"Job maith é, a deirim. Thíos ar na duganna. Fuaireas an nóta ar cairde dá bharr."

"Allright, ach ná bí á liúirigh ar fud an tí agus an diabhal géarchluasach úd, Bean Uí Bhriain, ag éisteacht laistigh. Tabhair dom an t-airgead."

Thug Jimí an nóta go réidh di agus amach leis ar an tsráid. Buachaill maith é Jimí d'ainneoin an drochshampla a thugadh a athair dó. Bhí tréithe a athar ann agus b'fhéidir gurbh shin ba chionsiocair leis an gcion a bhí aici air. Níor fhéad sí dearmad a dhéanamh ar an bhfear téagartha lán-mheanmnach úd a chaith blianta corracha ina fochair fé scáth an tí seo. Níor fhéad sí fuath a thabhairt dó, cé go ndúirt cách gur mhór an éagóir a d'imir sé uirthi.

D'fhág sí an leanbh san pram san halla gaofar agus chuaigh sí suas an staighre go dtí an cúlseomra clé. Bhí an áit go ciúin toisc go raibh na páistí ar scoil. D'ísligh sí fén líne ar a raibh na balcaisí beaga ar crochadh agus shuigh sí ar thaobh na leapan móire ar na plaincéidí donna a fuair sí ó na "Vincent's men."

Bhí fuílleach an bhricfeasta ar an mbord lom fós ach d'fhan sí tamall ag féachaint ar an nóta ina láimh agus ag moladh Dé. Dhein sí machnamh ar na nithe a bhí de dheasca uirthi. Chaithfeadh sí an fhuinneog a bhris duine de na páistí a dheisiú mar bhí an ghaoth ag dul i ngéire. Bheadh uirthi culaith a céile a fháil ó Weinrid láithreach ós rud é go mbeadh sé de dhíth ar Jimí amárach. Ní bhíodh sé uaidh go dtí seo ach amháin ar an nDomhnach ach níorbh fhéidir leis dul ag obair sna balcaisí a bhí air. Agus—ba bheag nár dhearmaid sí—bheadh uirthi coinneal a lasadh roimh dheilbh na Maighdine Muire ós í a luaigh a géarghá ag doras Dé.

An mbeadh am aici deoch a fháil i bpub Uí Néill sara bhfillfeadh na páistí ón scoil? Bhí an fuacht go smior inti agus chuir an smaoineamh gliondar ar a croí. Ach—bhí an "Vincent's man" ag teacht um thráthnóna. Bheadh ionadh air a aithint go raibh braon ólta aici. Níor chuí dá leithéid sólás a fháil le dearmad a dhéanamh ar chruatain an tsaoil. Ba cheart di dóchas a bheith aici as an saol le teacht agus bheith sásta go raibh carthannas Críostaí ag coimeád splanc beatha ar lasadh inti anso i ngleann na ndeor. Chaithfeadh sí fanacht le deoch go dtí an oíche nuair a bheadh na páistí sa bhaile ag gol agus ag glamaíl is an seomra ag cúngú ina timpeall. B'iad na hoícheanta ba mheasa, mar is ansan a thagadh na seanchuimhní ar ais chuici. Ach níor bheirigh cuimhní ciotal riamh. D'éirigh sí go mífhoighneach chun an dinnéar a réiteach.

Tháinig an "Vincent's man" anuas Lána Muire ag an am díreach ba ghnáth leis theacht gach Luan sa mbliain, ach amháin na trí seachtainí san tSamhradh nuair a bhíodh sé ar a laethe saoire i mBun Dobhráin. Chuir Bean Uí Mhórdha na páistí amach ar an tsráid sara dtáinig sé, óir ba mhinic a cheistigh Bean Uí Bhriain—an cladhaire fiosrach—iad fá gach a tharla eatarthu. Fear meánaosta cneasta a bhí ann, béal bog compordach air. Thaitin sé léi, ach bhí fhios aici nach raibh bua na samhlaíochta ann. Ógfhear a thagadh chuici uair agus d'imíodh sé go corrach míshuaimhneach. An fear seo bhí sé i gcónaí go beoga ardghuthach. Bhí an saol mór eatarthu agus níorbh eol dó é.

"Bhuel, bean an tí í féin! Agus conas tá sinn inniu?" Shiúil sé thart uirthi go dtí lár an tseomra. "Tá súil agam go bhfuil an slaghdán curtha díot agat."

"Tá, a dhuine uasail, go raibh míle maith agat."

"Maith an bhean, maith an bhean."

Bhí fhios aici go raibh sé ag tabhairt fé ndeara fuílleach an dinnéir ar an mbord—sál an bhulóg árain, na braonacha tae ar imeall na gcupán. Shamhlaigh sí cad déarfadh sé ag an gCruinniú.

"Bean dhíomhaoin mhíshlachtmhar. Dá bhfeicfeadh sibh salachar na háite!"

"Bhuel, ar chualais i dtaobh d'fhir chéile?" ar seisean.

"Focal níor chualas, a dhuine uasail. Bhí an 'Cruelty Man' ag caint liom ina thaobh. Tá na poilís in Albain ar a thóir fós ach níor chualathas trácht air anois le sé mhí."

"Nach é an bithiúnach críochnaithe é—a bhean agus a chlann a fhágaint gan taca mar a dhein sé. Béarfar air gan amhras. Beidh sásamh le fáil agatsa as."

"Beidh," ar sise go lagbhríoch. Ba chuma léi fán díoltas dá dtagadh fear a céasta ar ais chuici.

Thosnaigh an cuairteoir ag tochailt ina phóca ar lorg an ticéid a sholáthródh roinnt bia di. Bhíodh sé i gcónaí pas beag tré chéile agus sin á dhéanamh aige—ag iarraidh rud éigin a rá a chuirfeadh i gcéill nárbh é an ticéad seo an Carthannas Críostaí a bhí á bhronnadh uirthi.

"Níl aon athrú, is dócha" ar seisean. Dá cúrsaí airgid a bhí sé ag tagairt. Chuimhnigh sí ar an nóta puint fén gcrúiscín ar an ndriosúr. Chuimhnigh sí ar an job nua a bhí faighte ag Jimí. Ach tháinig taom fuar feirge uirthi leis an bhfear dea—chríoch maol-intinneach seo.

"Ara, cén t-athrú?" ar sise, agus an fhearg dho—mhúchta ina glór. Thost sé agus ionadh air. "Bean ait!" a déarfadh sé ag an gCruinniú. "Bean fhíor-ait. Ní féidir liom í a thuiscint." Bheadh sé carthannach. "An leatrom fé ndear é, is dócha. Ach tá sí ait."

Nuair a d'imigh sé chuir sí an ticéad i bhfolach, laistiar de phictiúr an Chroí Naofa ar an bhfalla. Chuaigh sí ag réiteach an tseomra ach diaidh ar ndiaidh bhí an míshuaimhneas ag brú isteach uirthi. Fé dheireadh chuir sí uirthi a cóta, thóg sí an nóta puint ón ndriosúr agus thug sí aghaidh ar an tsráid.

Bhí sí díreach ag dul isteach ar thaobh—dhoras an phub nuair a thug sí fé ndeara go raibh Bean Uí Bhriain laistiar di. Lean sí ar aghaidh gur shroich sí an séipéal. Isteach léi agus í ag lua mionna móra i dtaobh fiosrachas na mban agus i dtaobh fiosrachas Bhean Uí Bhriain go háithrid.

Bhí an dorchadas ag ísliú ó shíleáil an tséipéil agus na scátha fada ag leathnú idir na colúna. Chuir loinnir na gcoinneal roimh an altóir crutha aite ag corraí ar na fallaí. Chuaigh Bean Uí Mhórdha go neamhchinnte fé dhéin dealbh uaigneach na Maighdine Muire a bhí tar éis éalú ó thine—chnámh na gcoinneal. Las sí coinneal agus thosnaigh sí ag guí.

"Go mbeannaítear duit, a Mhuire, atá lán de ghrásta . . ." Tháinig na focla go líofa chuici ach níor fhéad sí breith ar na smaointe laistiar díobh. D'amharc sí ar aghaidh na deilbhe ach bhí sí fuar neamhthuisceanach.

"A Naomh-Mhuire, 'Mháthair Dé . . ."

Uaireanta agus í ag guí mar seo, thabharfadh sí an leabhar go raibh cuma éisteachta ar an aghaidh gheal chré úd. Seafóid ab ea é, gan amhras. Nár mhinic a dúirt an tAthair Ó Conchubhair gur chreid na Págánaigh bhochta a leithéid. Ach, nuair a bhí solas bog na gcoinneal ag dathú an aghaidhe bhí sí cinnte go raibh an Mhaighdean go lách ag tabhairt airde uirthi, mar a bhí sí an oíche úd nuair a d'iarr sí job le haghaidh Jimí.

D'éirigh sí go corraitheach ar chuimhneamh di ar Jimí agus an cuairteoir agus an ticéad laistiar de phictiúr an Chroí Naofa. Choisric sí í féin agus thug sí aghaidh ar an mbaile. Bhí na páistí ag súgradh ar an urlár roimpi agus Jimí ag léamh an pháipéir.

"A Mhamaí," ar seisean, "an dtiocfaidh tú chuig pictiúr? Tá sár-phictiúr iartharach sa Ritz."

"Pictiúr!" ar sise agus ionadh uirthi, "an bhfuil tú dáiríre? Agus . . . agus cá bhfuair tú an carbhat sin?"

"Sin! Ó sin ceann a cheannaíos inniu. An dtaitníonn sé leat? Ní shásódh aon ní na leads ach iasachtaí a thabhairt dom nuair a chualadar go raibh an job agam. Nach iad atá flaithiúil? Ach, tar chuig na pictiúirí. Is fada an lá ó bhís sa Ritz."

"Ní raghad. Caithfidh mé dul amach arís."

Chrom Jimí ar an bpáipéar a léamh. Buachaill maith é. Chuir sé a athair i gcuimhne di agus é ag léamh an pháipéir ar fhilleadh dó ó obair an lae. An folt rua—dhonn céanna, na guaille . . . D'ardaigh sí pictiúr an Chroí Naofa go réidh agus fuair sí an ticéad. Amach léi ar an tsráid.

Bhí an cruinniú ar siúl fós i Halla Uinsionn. D'fhéad sí glórtha sámha an mheán-aicme a chloisint laistigh ag dordán agus ag dul i dtreise nuair a bhí argóint ar siúl. Uaireanta chuireadh ráiteas greannmhar ag gáire iad agus uaireanta bhíodh sos cainte ann. Bhí fhios aici ansin go raibh socrú éigin déanta acu agus go raibh ainm clainne á scríobh nó á stracadh amach ar an liosta díobh siúd lena raibh an carthannas á íoc.

Fé dheireadh tháinig a cuairteoir féin amach. Chuir sí forán air agus sara raibh caoi aige labhairt, dúirt sí:

"An ticéad seo! Ba cheart dom a rá leat inniu nach raibh gá agam leis. Tá job faighte ag Jimí agus ní bheidh an ticéad ag teastáil uaim níos mó. Seo duit é!"

Agus d'imigh sí roimhe síos an tsráid. Ghlaoigh sé uirthi ach chomáin sí ar aghaidh, gan fhios aici go raibh sé ag áiteamh uirthi an ticéad a choinneáil. Bhí fhios aici nach ligfeadh an náire di bualadh leis arís ach smaoinigh sí ansin nach mbeadh uirthi sin a dhéanamh. Nach raibh job maith faighte ag Jimí—agus nach raibh sé ag feitheamh anois le í a thabhairt go dtí na pictiúirí. Bhí an saol go maith agus bhí Muire ag tabhairt airde uirthi.

Bhí Bean Uí Bhriain ina seasamh ag doras síor—oscailte Uimhir a Sé. "Dia duit," ar sise, agus ba léir óna dreach go raibh scéal nua aici agus fonn uirthi é a insint. "Bhí na poilís anso," agus d'fhan sí go fiosrach go bhfeicfeadh sí an scéal ag dul i bhfeidhm ar an mbean eile.

"Na poilís! Cad ina thaobh, in ainm Dé? Ó—ag lorg m'fhir chéile, an ea?"

"Ní hea. Jimí a bhí uathu. Bhris sé isteach i siopa aréir agus ghoid sé timpeall caoga punt. Shíl na poilís go bhfuil baint aige leis an Lotts Gang—gur ball nua é . . ."

Níor chuala Bean Uí Mhórdha ach an glór fuar ag caint is ag síor-chaint. Bhí an staighre an—ard agus an—dorcha. Gol, an ea! Ach, a Mhuire, cad ina thaobh? A Jimí bhocht! Guigh orainn ár bpeacaí anois.

Chuala sí an gheoin san tseomra. An leabh a bhí ag screadaíl gan fáth.

The Tears of Prayer

A Translation of "Deór na hAithrí" by Risteárd de Paor

Translated by Victor Power

Mrs. Moran was upset when she left Weinrib's shop on a Monday morning. The plump, small-eyed owner himself waited on her and he would only offer her thirty shillings for her husband's suit.

"But, my good woman," he said, splaying his fat hands that glistened with jeweled rings, "It's not even worth that much. I don't *care* if you got two pounds for it last week . . ."

"And the week before that and the week before that again," she said, trying to conceal the tearful anger of disappointment from her voice.

"And before that again as well!" he said, mocking her. He pointed an accusing finger at her. "Find another place where they'll give you better satisfaction if you're not happy with my offer. But don't be bothering me with your tears. I have my regular customers to deal with!"

The regulars gripped their parcels tightly under their arms and laughed in embarrassment when she turned her gaze on them. Mrs. Moran gave the owner a black look of hatred but she accepted the thirty shillings.

"Tears," she said as she trod heavily toward the door, "As if this sort of thing would make me shed tears. I wouldn't give that fellow the satisfaction." She slapped her crying infant in the pram, still upset. "Tears, he says—"

She headed home, the baby bellowing even louder in front of her. She pushed the pram into the ever-open doorway of Number Six, Mary's Lane. Jimmy came running down the stairs, shaven, and in a great hurry.

"Mammy, I have a job. Would you credit it? A good job, the Exchange said. Look! A pound note! And I'll have more than that at the end of the week."

"What kind of a job is it?" she asked doubtfully, staring at the pound note, "and where did you get that?"

"A good job, I'm after telling you! Down on the docks. I got this quid on credit for it."

"All right. But don't be broadcasting it all over the country and that sharp-eared divil, Mrs. O'Brien listening outside. Give me the money."

He gave her the money readily enough and out with him to the street. She reproached herself for how sharply she had spoken. He had his father's traits and perhaps that was the reason why she felt so guilty about him. She was never able to remove for long from her mind the image of that good natured, foolish man who'd spent those homey years living under her roof. She could never bring herself to hate him though everybody said that he had done them a grave injustice.

She left the infant in the pram in the windy hallway. She made her way upstairs to the back room on the left. The place was quiet because the children were at school. She ducked under the line from which the washing was suspended and she sat down on the side of the big bed, on the brown blankets which she'd been given by the "Vincent's Man." The leavings of breakfast were still on the table but she sat there staring at the pound note in her hand. She began to think of the things she had to have. The windows needed fixing—the breeze came blustering through the cracks. She would have to redeem her husband's clothes from Weinrib's at once for they'd be needed for Jimmy tomorrow. He never needed them until now—except on Sundays but there was no way he could go to work wearing his old rags. And—she'd almost forgotten it . . . she would have to light a candle to the Blessed Virgin for it was she who interceded for her at God's door.

Would she find time to steal out to O'Neill's pub before the children came home from school? The cold was eating into her bones and the thought lightened up her heart. But—the "Vincent's Man" was coming this evening. Such a devout volunteer would be scandalized by the smell of booze. His kind wouldn't understand consolation without remembering the toughness of life. She should be thinking of the life to come and to be grateful that Christian charity was keeping a spark of life, with pious injunctions, alight in her soul in this vale of tears. She would have to wait devoutly until night when the children were crowding the room that was closing in on her. The nights were better but that was when old memories came lashing back at her. But memories never boiled a kettle yet. She got up impatiently to prepare the dinner.

The "Vincent's Man" came down Mary's Lane at the exact same time he came usually every Monday of the year, except for the three weeks in the summer when he went to Bundoran on his holidays. Mrs. Moran sent her children out on the street before he came for it was often he quizzed Mrs. Moran—the inquisitive bastard—on everything about them. He was a neatly dressed, middle-aged man with a soft, comfortable mouth. She liked him, but she knew he was in no way imaginative. A young man came once and he left in a moody, unsettled frame of mind. The regular man was always loud-voiced and lively. A great wide world separated them but he didn't know that.

"Well, the woman of the house herself! And how are we today?"

He advanced on her to the center of the room. "I hope, ma'am, that your cold is better."

"Indeed it is, sir, thank you very much."

"Good woman! That's the good woman!"

She knew he was taking in the leavings of the dinner on the table—the crumbs from the loaf of bread, the drops of tea on the rim of the saucers. She could imagine what he would say at the weekly conference:

"A lazy, good for nothing housekeeper. If you only saw the dirt of the place!"

"Well, any word about your husband?"

"Not a word did I hear, sir. The 'Cruelty Man' was talking to me about him. The Scottish police are still after him, but nobody heard a word from him in six months, sir." It was none of his business.

"Isn't he a right animal—to leave his wife and children with no support? But they'll catch up with him, don't worry. You'll get your satisfaction yet from him."

"Indeed," she said weakly. She didn't care about revenge so long as her man came back to her again, the poor mixed-up fellow!

The man began to dig in his pocket for the ticket that could be exchanged for a little food. He always was a little embarrassed as he did this—searching for something to say that would imply that it wasn't this ticket but Christian charity that he was bestowing on her.

"There's no change at all, I suppose?" he said. Money matters he was referring to. She thought of the pound note concealed under a jug on the dresser. She thought of Jimmy's new job. But a cold, sudden fury took hold of her toward this lighthearted, glad-handing volunteer.

"Ara! What change?" she asked, the anger buried in her voice. He stopped, silent, wonder in his face. "An odd woman!" he'd report at the conference, "A really strange woman! I can't understand her." He would be charitable. "Neurosis! That's what it is! But she is very queer!"

When he left, she hid the ticket behind the picture of the Sacred Heart on the wall. She began to tidy up the room but again and again a strange uneasiness took hold of her. In the end, she put on her coat, took the pound note and went out on the street.

She was just about to enter the side door of the pub when she noticed that Mrs. O'Brien was already ensconced in there. She kept going until she reached the chapel. She went in and she was muttering swear words about inquisitive women and the inquisitive Mrs. O'Brien in particular.

The dark was thickening from the ceiling of the church and the long shadows were lengthening from the pillars. The flickering candles were throwing strange shapes on the walls from in front of the altar. Mrs. Moran went uncertainly to the lonely statue of the Blessed Virgin that was eluding the fire-glow of the candles. She lighted a candle and commenced to pray.

"Hail Mary, full of grace, the Lord—"

The words came readily enough but she was unable to grasp the thoughts behind them. She looked up at the face of the statue but it was cold and remote. "Holy Mary, Mother of God—"

Sometimes, when she'd be praying like this, she would swear by the book that there appeared an expression of keen listening on the bright clay face. Imagination, it was, no doubt! Didn't the priest often say that the pagans believed in that sort of thing. But, when the soft light of the candles colored the face, she was certain that the Virgin blurred its hard lines into an attitude of attention, just as happened that night when she'd prayed for a job for Jimmy.

She got up restlessly thinking about Jimmy and the visitor and the ticket behind the picture of the Sacred Heart. She blessed herself and headed homeward.

The children were playing on the floor and Jimmy was reading the paper. "Oh, Mammy," he said, "will you come to the flicks with me? There's a great picture on at the Ritz, fabulous—"

"Pictures?" she said with wonder. "Are you in earnest? And . . . and where did you get that tie?"

"Oh that? Oh, I bought that today. See? Do you like it? The lads were jumping over one another today to lend me things when they found I had a job. Isn't it marvelous how generous they are? But, get ready and come along with me to the pictures—"

"No—no, I won't. I have to go out again!"

Jimmy bent over his paper, reading. It reminded her of his father and he after coming home from work. The same reddish-brown hair, the set of the shoulders . . . She straightened the picture of the Sacred Heart and after slipping the ticket into her pocket, she headed out the street.

The conference was still going on in Vincent's Hall. She heard the pleasantly modulated voices of the middle class from outside the door, rising and falling when an argument would go on. Sometimes, a funny anecdote would set them off laughing and sometimes again, there would be silence. She knew then that some determination had been made and that the name of some family was written down or that some family name had been struck from the list by those who dispensed charity. In the end, her own visitor came out.

Going on the offensive, she said, before he could say a word, "Here's my ticket. I—I don't need it. Jimmy has a job. Here. Take it. Take it, I'm telling you . . ."

And she went directly down the street. He called after her but she didn't pay any attention, not knowing that he was telling her to keep the ticket.

She knew her shame would never allow her to meet him again—but, after all, hadn't Jimmy got himself a job now, and wasn't he waiting at home for her now to take her to the pictures? She hurried home.

Mrs. O'Brien was standing in the ever-open door of Number Six. "Hello," she said, and it was clear from her expression that she had some new story to tell and a great desire to pass it on.

"The police were here," she said, and she paused, inquisitively, to see how this story would affect the other woman.

"The police? Why, in the name of God? Looking for my husband, were they?"

"Oh no! Oh not at all! Looking for Jimmy they were. A shop was broken into last night and a thousand pounds was stolen. The police thought that your young fella might have something to do with it, and that he's a member of the Lotts gang—"

Mrs. Moran heard nothing except the cold voices going up and down. The stairwell was very steep and very dark. Tears, is it? But, Mother of God, why? Poor Jimmy! "Pray for us sinners now and—"

She could hear the rumpus in the room. The infant was crying again, for no reason . . .

Republicans

It had turned out a grand day for the funeral. Everybody said so, especially the womenfolk, who were dressed for spring. Had it not been for them the occasion might have been overlooked altogether. In almost every case, it was the wife who had picked up the morning paper, seen the notice in the obituary column.

"D'you know who's dead?" she had said, pausing portentously while her husband bolted toast and marmalade. "Poor Jackie Dempsey."

"Is that a fact? Show me." A moment's silence. Then, "My God. Jackie Dempsey."

It hurt, this stab of memory, which brought the old days crowding tumultuously to the breakfast table.

And that was why they knelt now, middle-aged men and women, while the priest moved in his black vestments before the bare altar. In the front seat, was a minister of state; beside him, a manufacturer of boots and shoes, and beyond a lawyer who had built up a remunerative practice in politics. Behind sat lesser dignitaries, a district justice, an army officer, a higher civil servant. At the rear in shabby black were members of the family, some still bewildered, others barely restraining their tears, one or two shaking silently.

A few elderly women moved around the bier, clutching prayer books to show that they were lingering after an earlier Mass. There was rustle of leaves as they read the cards attached to the wreaths. One, more daring, pushed aside the mass of flowers to examine the plate on the mean coffin. The tall candles flanking the bier had long since flickered out.

When Mass was over, the priest, wearing a black cope over his stiff white alb, came down from the altar. The people crowded around as he read the absolution. A cold draught came from the doorway. "*Libera me, Domine, de morte aeterna*," said the priest. He had been fasting since seven o'clock Mass and his voice was dull, fumbling as with cold, over the stark phrases. The little altar boy methodically chipped the grease from the candlestick he was holding.

There was a pause when the priest had finished. Nobody moved for a moment. The men looked uncertainly at each other. There was a whispered consultation and then some of them crowded around the coffin. They pushed the wreaths aside and lifted it on to their shoulders. It swayed as they bore it through the doorway and out on to the street. The crowd followed, breaking up into little groups, telling each other how sad it was and how sudden. Poor Jack Dempsey! And the poor widow! How terrible for her. But wasn't she blessed that she had her family reared. And how resigned she was to the will of God.

She walked out on to the street and paused, blinking in the hard spring sunlight. Black did not suit her. She looked shapeless in it, her high color, her swollen eyes incongruous, even comical. She seemed unaware that she was the central figure, as if she moved in a calm deadened world of her own. The minister approached her to offer his sympathies. She listened, smiling vaguely, then shook his hand as listlessly as she shook that of her next sympathizer. The men approached her one by one, repeated their formulas, and escaped with a feeling of relief. The women lingered around her, noting who was present and talking in that half whisper of shocked gravity that they reserved for funerals.

Her son was looking after the carriages. He was a big raw-faced lad who would later be good looking in a heavy indolent way. Not half enough carriages had been ordered so that he was forced to leave some of the important people standing on the pavement. Eventually, a relative, a dapper little man, impatiently took control and found places for most of those remaining in the private cars.

The family sat in the first carriage. The younger son, in a corner seat, was wiping his spectacles, his eyes all puckered up. He was like his brother but thinner, his features more refined. The man beside him pressed his arm gently.

"Are you all right now?" he said. The boy nodded and smiled gratefully. He had been quite self-possessed until the crowd moved out into the sunlight and this man had met him at the door. Then suddenly, unexpectedly, the tears had come in a blinding rush. The man had led him, stumbling, to the carriage.

"It's nothing to be ashamed of, boy," whispered the man. He had been a friend of the family as long as the boy could remember. Everybody called him Fitz.

"I don't know what happened," said the boy. "It must have been you standing there and everything so ordinary—"

"I know, I know, but sure you're all right now."

Fitz took off his hat and ran his hand through his thin, white hair. He was about to say something to break the silence in the carriage but then he changed his mind. Instead he twisted his thin, agile body to talk to the stout overcoated countryman beside him. They discussed families they both knew in the country. Fitz exclaimed every now and then at the news of a death or a marriage or a farm that had changed hands.

The funeral followed the road by the canal, a calm blue in the sunlight, past a pair of swans drifting beyond the rushes. It turned left over a bridge. Somebody in the minister's big car, searching anxiously for a suitable topic, mentioned the recent motor accident at the bridge. As it had been difficult to strike a note somewhere between gloom and frivolity, the theme was seized upon with relief. When the accident had been described and everybody had had his say, the minister said that there was far too much carelessness on the roads nowadays and that what was wanted was more stringent measures. To this everybody agreed.

There was some confusion at the gate of the cemetery where the cars and carriages halted. The drivers in their shabby top hats clambered down from their seats. Doors slammed, horses stamped, and people sought each other frantically. The hearse continued through the gateway. The crowd, gathered in animated groups, now drew together. They followed the hearse along the rutted path under new-leaved trees, whose branches were lucent with cold sunlight. Grass carpeted the graves underneath and the tombstones were half swathed in damp moss. The green quiet was broken only by the chafing of wheels on the path, the throbbing song of a thrush, the murmur of conversation from the rear of the cortege. An occasional gardener straightened from a freshly disturbed grave to watch the funeral go past.

The hearse halted in the new part of the cemetery, scarred by graves on which young shoots of grass already grew. The coffin was carried over the soft upturned clay and rested a moment on the edge of the grave before being lowered in. A priest came hurrying down the path, twitching his surplice into shape. He read the prayers over the grave and the crowd murmured the responses. The undercurrent of men's voices sounded unexpectedly strong and deep. The priest blessed the grave and, as at a signal, the first shovelful of earth drummed on the coffin-lid. There were muffled sobs from the womenfolk. Gradually the sound deadened as earth fell upon earth. Then the green sod was rammed down and the workmen scraped their shovels and hurried away.

The place had lost its individuality, had become another scar on the field. The funeral of Jackie Dempsey was over and the mourning would now be private in the hearts of a few. Gradually the crowd drifted away.

The minister turned to go. He glanced at his watch and remembered that he had to see a trade union deputation in the afternoon. He suddenly felt the warmth of the sun on his heavy dark overcoat. The dim memories of the dead man that he had been dutifully summoning up during the ceremony, faded out of his mind. He noticed that the boot and shoe manufacturer was trying to break away from the tiresome district justice in order to approach him. Going to bother me again about that damned import quota, he thought. Quickly, he turned and walked briskly down the path toward the gate.

His breath misted slightly on the clear air. He was aware of the bursting buds, of the sap of spring rising in the earth. He breathed deeply and swung his arms. A man in front paused to turn over a dead bird with his shoe. Something in his quick nervous movements seemed familiar. He straightened, turned around, and the minister met a pair of faded blue eyes in a thin, lined face.

"My God, Fitz!" said the minister.

"Tom, the hard Tom!"

They clasped hands firmly.

"It must be years . . . Where've you been, Fitz?"

"Where I've always been, Tom. It was you who left . . ."

"Ah, now, no recriminations," said the minister good-humoredly. "Not on a day like this."

"Fair enough, Tom. How are you keeping?"

"Oh, can't complain. It was terrible about poor Jackie."

"Yes."

"If I'd only known he was so bad . . ."

Fitz's eyes were intent on the dead bird. He toed it idly.

"In fact," said the minister, "I'd been meaning to look him up for a long time. Both of you, in fact. We might have had an evening together in Kavanagh's, the three of us."

"That would have been nice."

"Yes, it's a pity, but sure . . . ," he said resignedly, "we know not the day nor the . . . By the way, Fitz, we could drop in there now for a chat. I feel like a drink."

"But sure, you're a busy man, Tom?"

"Oh, I can spare half an hour," said the minister modestly.

At the gate the minister's car stood waiting, its engine purring. The driver was stifling a yawn as they approached. He got out quickly and held open a door for them.

"Yerra, no," said Fitz. "We'll walk it. Sure 'tis no distance."

"Very well, so."

The minister instructed the driver to call for him later.

"You could do with some walking, you know," said Fitz, as the minister took his elbow affectionately.

"The same old Fitz," the minister laughed. "Will you never learn tact?"

They bantered each other about the onset of age all the way to the pub. The minister exclaimed at the changed name over the door.

"They've let the light in at long last," he remarked, pushing open the new swing doors.

"Aye," said Fitz. "Bad cess to them. Remember the comfort there used to be here—the partitions of dark wood, the brass rails, and the spittoon beyond the corner, the dirty ceiling, and the prints of the '98 rising . . ."

"But, isn't this a great improvement?"

"Ah, I don't know now."

"What are you having, Fitz?"

"A pint."

"Begod, I'll have the same myself. It's just like old times, Fitz."

He ordered two pints of stout from the curate, a young man dressed in a stained gabardine pants and a two-tone waistcoat.

They sat on two stools before a mirror which reflected bottles and polished glasses. The pub was empty except for a couple of paint-spattered laborers who had slipped in from a nearby building job. In the shadows at the end of the counter was a little man in a bowler hat and stiff white collar. His crabbed face was underlined by a tawny moustache.

"Yes," said the minister, settling his bulk comfortably on the stool. "There's no doubt it's a great improvement. The country has looked backward long enough. It must go forward now. We've had our share of improvements in the last thirty years . . ."

"At a price . . ."

"Oh, granted," said the minister lightly.

They were silent a moment.

"Jackie always said this place hadn't changed a bit since Emmet's day," said Fitz.

"Ay, poor Jackie," the minister sighed gustily. "Poor fellow." He watched the curate draw the pints from an iron barrel below the counter.

"That's a new contraption . . ."

He stopped, noticing that Fitz's eyes were over bright and that he was fumbling for a handkerchief.

"D'you remember . . ." said the minister desperately, pushing a pint in front of the other man, "d'you remember the time you hid the hand grenade in Jackie's stout?"

"What?" said Fitz, blowing his nose vigorously. "The hand grenade? Oh yes." He smiled. "That was a good one."

"God, I'll never forget the cool way you walked in on Jackie and me that day with the Tans on your heels almost, searching the street."

"And d'you remember the face of the Cockney sergeant who searched Jackie? He was no match for Jackie's lip."

"No, what's this Jackie said as the sergeant went out the door. It was damned good if I could think of it. Ah, no matter."

He raised his glass. "Well, here's to Jackie and the sergeant, wherever he is and to all of us."

"To all of us," echoed Fitz.

The minister set down his glass and folded his lips, frowning thoughtfully.

"But you were always the cleverest of the three, Fitz. It's a wonder you never . . ." He paused in embarrassment.

"Did better for myself than a warehouse clerk? I could have, I suppose . . . by reneging . . . like the rest . . ."

"Ah, now, Fitz, that's a hard word to use. Sure who believes in it nowadays. It's only a myth, Tone and Emmett and the rest of it . . ."

"Well, according to your speeches in the papers, you . . ."

"Ah, you can't go by that. It goes down well when you've nothing else to tell the crowd. I suppose I even believe it myself in the excitement of the moment. But when you step down off the platform and into the comfort of your car, then, well, you begin to wonder . . ."

There was silence a moment while he drank. Fitz toyed moodily with his glass.

"Yes," continued the minister. "Idealism was all right in its own day, but now the country wants sound practical men."

"But you remember the old days, Tom?" Fitz burst out.

"Remember the way we believed . . . the bond between us. We knew each other through and through . . ."

"We were young then. We had no sense."

"You came to your senses, though Tom." Bitterness filtered into his voice. "But Jackie and I—we're the failures. Jackie drifting, drinking a bit, and me—a bitter old diehard."

"Not at all, man. You have plenty of time before you yet. Look, I could easily put in a word for you—fix you up maybe in the . . ."

"Yerra, be quiet, man. What respect would I have for myself?"

The minister spread out his hands.

"Please yourself, so," he said indifferently. "But I think you'd be a fool to refuse. A damn fool."

"I'd be in good company," said Fitz lightly, "with the fools."

"Maybe." The minister was slightly nettled.

Yes, good company, thought Fitz. Pearse, who despised the wise men, the lawyers with their keen faces. MacDonough the poet—and Jackie.

"Look at poor Jackie," said the minister, sorrowfully, as he poised his glass before drinking.

Dispassionately, Fitz remembered the mild-mannered shabby little man whom everybody had called "poor Jackie."

"D'you remember, Tom, the bashful way he used to produce those poems of his, scribbled out on scraps of paper?"

"Yes, yes, I remember." The minister laughed heartily.

"You used to read out the patriotic ones and Jackie would be half ashamed and half proud . . ."

"Yes," said the minister shortly.

The laborers were having a heated argument about greyhounds, and the barman, his elbows on the counter, threw in an occasional word. The old man at the end of the bar querulously contradicted something. In the shadow, his eyes showed a dirty white.

The minister had turned his head to listen.

"There was one poem you used to like reading out," went on Fitz musingly. "Something about the rising . . . that it wasn't just the Indian summer of a nation's spirit . . ."

“What?” said the minister as if impatient at being interrupted. “Oh, that. No I don’t remember how it goes.”

He rose from his stool and stood, buttoning his coat.

“You’re not taking the offer, so,” he said casually.

“No, Tom, thanks all the same.”

The minister hitched the heavy coat higher on his shoulders. He’s still a fine figure of a man, thought Fitz, a bitter little smile playing around his lips. I suppose he will come to my funeral and allot himself an hour or two for melancholy reminiscences.

“Well,” said the minister, glancing at his watch, “I must be off. Why not drop out and see us, Fitz, sometime? We’ll have another chat over old times.”

He pushed open the swing doors and they walked into the sunlight.

“Give me a ring, sometime. Be sure now.”

“Of course,” said Fitz.

They shook hands.

The car was waiting down the street. Fitz watched the minister walk toward it, noticed the ponderous walk, the neck thickening above the wide collar, the solid unimaginative slant of the hat.

The words came suddenly to his lips, surprising him because he had hitherto reserved them for the dead.

“Poor Tom,” said he, “God have mercy on him.”

Neighbors

The bungalow was a mile beyond the last city light. Fields of oats and barley surrounded it and there was no sound at night but the trickle of a stream and the barking of dogs on a distant farm. It was a place where a man could do great work—which, of course, was why they had bought it.

They had come from the heart of the city, from a one-roomed flat filled with a stove, two cots, a studio couch, and the only item they owned outright—a tall, Victorian office desk—which Michael had picked up in the auction rooms. It had been noisy there above Baggot Street; the traffic was never ending, but they had never noticed it, not even the last buses bucketing over the canal bridge, or the ambulances wailing all night to the hospital.

Here, they were being continually surprised by the silence. Sometimes, as she pegged out the clothes, Margaret would feel it touching her, like a sudden isolated drop of rain. Or Michael would notice it, as he stood at his desk, and would look up to see the mist hanging in the hedge. Or perhaps they would both sense it together, as they lay sleepily in the dark. It seemed full of promise, their silence.

At weekends, friends came out from Baggot Street, jackknifing out of old cars, waving guitars and cartons of beer. Parents and relations came seldom, if at all. Her family, prosperous legal people, had found him hard to take—"a draughtsman of some kind," her mother had been overheard to say—with an accent, it might be added, which was far from Dublin drawing room; Margaret's course in the art of the quattrocentro, had not shown much of a return. However, to give them their due, they did try, after the wedding, to make contact, but

Michael was suspicious of any show of friendliness. As for help, he rejected it like charity.

His parents still lived in the small, red-brick terraced house off South Circular Road. He had begun to lose touch with them during his last years at school. Then, the art scholarship which he insisted on taking, the beard which he grew, the casual way in which he lived for three months with Margaret, in sin, put him altogether outside their tidy, pious lives.

He did not miss his parents or she hers. In fact, it was even a relief on Sundays when their friends went and the house was quiet once more. As time went on, the friends came less often and then hardly at all. This was just as well because there was not much money to spare, not like in the Baggot Street days when there always seemed to be a few shillings for a bottle of wine from the off-license. There were so many other things to spend it on now, things that could not be put off, like mortgage repayments, ground rent, and fire insurance.

They did not regret buying the house, although it did seem more continual a burden than they had realized when they put down all Michael's prize money as a deposit. That had been a moment of triumph for him, not only because of what it brought him and because it "showed his in-laws," but also because secretly he had not had great hopes of bringing off the fellowship. He suffered from the dour suspicions of the self-taught that merit really counted for little. "Wheels within wheels" was a phrase of his father's, which he often mentally quoted.

Besides, competition was unusually keen that year and even when he was called before the board, he gathered that the final decision was still to be made.

"The judges were impressed," the secretary told him. "Yes, they seemed to like your work very much." At which, the other gentlemen nodded solemnly. He was timid before them. They were men of affairs who knew what and what not to buy—and, although he could have made fun of them in the right company, here they had him in their power. The decision they made could either send him into exile, like most of his friends, or give him a piece of Ireland in which to live. Of course, Margaret's people would have been only too glad of the opportunity to put in a word for him—they were good at that—but he had received their hint with scornful silence. He would win on his merits, or not at all.

The chairman, who had not greeted him, was leafing through some papers, like an old and disillusioned lizard searching without much hope in a drift of leaves. "Aha!" he said at last, breaking in on the polite questioning, "So you went to school in the Green? The Brothers?"

"Yes?" Michael stiffened. Were they going to throw this at him, that he hadn't been at a "good" school?

"When I was a boy at the Green—" The old man paused and looked around the table with a faint grin, "I was marrying a gun!" And as they looked down, embarrassed, or made little vague congratulatory murmurs, he gave a high-pitched, gleeful laugh, "I'd killed my first Tan before I left school. Yes, indeed." He glanced around the cowed faces. "Matter a damn what they say, it's a damn fine school, the Brothers' in the Green." He narrowed one eye at Michael and then swept the papers down the table to the secretary.

So Michael won. Even in the first moment he guessed it, he was nagged by the thought that he had not fully won (but that was a common affliction in a country where not even the gun had ever won a war outright). "What d'you want, you old worrier?" Margaret asked him as he brooded over his victory, "Bonfires on the hills?" But no, he hadn't wanted that. He would have been satisfied to know that the piece of Ireland which he had been given had been properly paid for. "All that's wrong with you," Margaret told him, "is that you're a joyless, guilt-laden, urban Irish peasant." For which piece of abuse, he tumbled her happily into bed, as she had expected.

Still, he continued to feel that his right to win had not been proved. He got the opportunities to prove it—he had no complaints about that. All the first summer, he was kept hard at it, standing all day at his desk in the small, bare room that looked out over the field of oats. His only relaxation was to play with the children when Margaret went shopping. He enjoyed them, as he had never done in the flat, when they made his work so difficult. They rarely fought now; each had room to grow, to be himself, and to be loved for that reason. They played together by the hour in the sandpit he made for them or on the swing he had built.

On fine evenings, when they were in bed, he worked in the garden with Margaret. He had never seen things growing before—they hadn't even had window boxes at home—and the vigor of growth in his garden was a continual delight to him. He planted trees, a hawthorn and a weeping birch from the wood nearby, planted them quite out of season and they took root. They seemed to stake out this piece of Ireland for him, to make it more securely his own.

Once a week or so, he took the bus into Dublin to call on the printer or to see a client. What he liked most about going in was the pleasure of coming back again, walking in the twilight up the hill, between the burgeoning fields, to his home. There he would find the children washed and in bed and the supper tray set out on the hearth in the light of the fire. Margaret had the gift of making frugality seem like plenty; it was a gift to which the puritan in him responded ardently.

On his way home one evening, he saw in the grove of trees below his house a small fire burning. A man knelt by it, kindling it with twigs, a ragged man with a hat pulled low over his face. When Michael bade him good evening he barely looked up to say, "Evenin', boss." Then he snapped another stick across his knee and the sound echoed dully in the wood.

As Michael turned in the gate, he met a young woman coming out. She went past quickly, a shawl about her head, so that he could not see her face. He greeted her too, but she made no answer, or if she did, answered him so low that he didn't hear her. He found that she had just been to the house to beg for food and old clothes. In fact, so persistently had she begged, that Margaret had given her things which he still needed, for instance, the heavy boots that he used for gardening.

"But they're worn out, Michael. They don't owe you anything." Maybe not. But he owed them something. In his hosteling days, he had tramped the roads of Ireland in them, climbed any mountain worth climbing. He couldn't tell her that; she had a sharp ear for sentimentality.

She was pleased by the visit, excited that she should have been asked for help. He, however, sulked because of his grievance, resenting her pleasure. After supper, for the first time since they came to the house, he had to draw the curtains before he could begin work. Later, he stood a while at the bedroom window and looked at the distant light of the fire. When the wind brightened it now and then he could see two seated figures outlined against it. Occasionally they leaned closer together and obscured it.

Were they going to sleep all night on the ground? It was September, quite chilly, and there had been rain all the afternoon. Surely they didn't have to, he thought, as he turned away impatiently, crossed the uncarpeted room, and began to lay his clothes neatly on the kitchen chair at the foot of his bed. They were both very silent that night, lying a little apart from each other and not making love.

Next day, the couple was gone, the only signs of their sojourn some tins and a milk bottle in the trampled grass beside the embers of the fire. One of Michael's boots lay further on by the roadside, with its lace gone. He picked it up and flung it angrily into the ditch. Going back to his desk, it surprised him that such a small thing should upset him. It seemed that he really did dislike waste.

On a morning in October, he woke to find a village of flimsy green tents spring up beside the copse. Carts with uptilted shafts stood about, draped with tarpaulin to serve as living spaces. Several fires burned and the roadside grass as far as his gate was trodden flat by children, dogs, and grazing ponies. A man rested on his arm beside one of the fires, with his hat on the side of his head, quite motionless. From the copse beyond him, several women and girls were gathering armfuls of sticks. The scene seemed not quite real, its details smudged, as if it were behind a screen—and indeed, the copse was filled with the blue haze of smoke from the fires.

There was knock at the door as Michael sat down to breakfast. He went to answer it and found a little girl standing there with one hand already outstretched. She muttered an entreaty, rapidly as if to have it all said before the door shut on her. She was about six years old, dark, with hair hanging in strands over her face.

"Gie us a penny, mista, will ya?" She raised her eyes a moment and let them rove sharply over him.

"A penny?" He looked at the flowered dress, which drooped below her knees, at the red, plastic boots in which her chapped legs were rooted, and which seemed to be wellingtons cut down to size.

"E'er a thing at all?" She wiped her nose with her sleeve and looked past him into the kitchen. "A bitta bread and butter. A suppa tay." She swept the hair back from her face in a very adult gesture and looked him in the eye with a sudden access of dignity. "Go on, mista, will ya? I'm hungry."

He turned away and brusquely called his wife. As she came eagerly out, exclaiming at sight of the girl, he went back to his breakfast. Margaret, he had discovered with some irritation, enjoyed dispensing charity.

Another knock came later in the morning. He let Margaret answer it and could hear her come back into the kitchen and lift the lid of the bread bin. He refused to let himself be distracted. He was busy on a booklet for an international travel agents' conference to be held soon in Dublin. It was important to deliver it on time—he had hopes of designing a forthcoming book on early Celtic art for the Cultural Relations Institute. Before giving him the commission, it was probable that the institute would enquire about him from the conference organizers.

The third call came just before supper. As Margaret moved out from the kitchen, he waved her back and went to open the door. A youth in a tight-fitting jacket and jeans stood posed on the step. As Michael stared at him, he put a cigarette butt to his mouth, drew on it nonchalantly, and took it away again.

"Evenin', boss." He nodded his head and one uncombed greasy ringlet fell over his eye. "Anything you can spare us? A bitta bread and butter? A suppa tay?"

"This is the third tine today . . ."

"Anythin' at all, boss, any oul' clothes or a pair of oul' shoes—"

"No."

"A few pennies, mista."

"No. Go away."

The youth drew on the butt, then took a slow, surly look up at Michael from under his eyebrows. For a moment Michael thought he might be attacked. He felt the blood rush to his head and wanted to hit back at the fellow, hard.

"Go away!" he shouted, and moved suddenly forward, out on the step.

"For the love of God, mista!" The suddenness of the change was alarming; the youth seemed suddenly to crumple. "Give us somethin' for Christ's sake, mista. I'll say a prayer for ya."

"No!" The suppliant pose, the whining tone, were more than he could bear. "Leave us alone, d'you hear?" He came in and slammed the door, then stood, trembling with rage, with his back against it.

Margaret said nothing when he told her to answer no more calls. She finished her meal in silence and took the supper things out to the scullery. "All right," he called, "I'll send something to this bloody committee. I'll send them £1." Yes, he would send £1 out of his next check. The Itinerants Settlement Committee was probably a collection of bourgeois do-gooders, but at least they were organized, they had a plan. Better to make a decent contribution than to dribble the money away in casual charity. He said all this to Margaret, but she made no reply as she clattered away with the washing-up and he did not press the subject further.

The calls suddenly ceased. At least, they ceased while he was at home; while he was away, he was not so sure—an occasional milk bottle outside the gate, or a half-eaten loaf were evidence that the calls were better timed. He said no more to Margaret; they were both astute at avoiding occasions of quarrels, but it was a continual irritation to know that his scanty wardrobe and his larder were there to be drawn upon and squandered. Out of his next check, he sent £l to the committee and told Margaret, so that she could, in future, shut the door on their neighbors with an easy mind. However, she just went on with her work and made no comment.

He was raking leaves, one afternoon, around the side of the house, when he saw the little girl going out the gate with something under her shawl. He threw down the rake, intending to have it out at last with Margaret, for breaking their implied contract. Just as he reached the door he heard a little cry and saw the tinker youth who had called on him leap out from the hedge in front of the girl. He hurried to the gate, thinking the girl was being attacked, then saw that they were playing a game. As she backed away, the youth followed her saying, "I'm the big man with the beard." He mimicked Michael's walk and tone, as he went on, "No, go 'way. What d'you want? Go 'way."

"Stop it!" she said.

"Go 'way," he chanted. "What d'you want? Go 'way."

"I don't like that game," she said. "Play another."

"What'll I play? The fox?"

She giggled and said, "Yes, I like that. I'm the rabbit."

The youth crouched down and began to walk stealthily in her direction. "One step, two step," he began, as she backed away in nervous little runs, "This is the way the big fox went out hunting . . ." He took a long, loping stride, stopped, lifted one paw, and sniffed the breeze.

Seeing his face full on, the close eyes and twitching nostrils, Michael thought . . . God, he really is a fox. Then the young man looked up, suddenly straightened and turned away, pushing his hands into his pockets.

"Come on," the little girl called impatiently, "Be the big fox." But when she followed the youth's gaze and saw Michael watching, she turned and began to run away.

They intrigued him, made him restless so that he found himself going often to the window to watch the camp. He tried to talk once to the small children, the toddlers, but they fled from him, shrieking, and then pursued him at a distance with cries of "Gie us a penny, mista, will ya? I'll say a prayer for ya."

He was attracted and repelled by their disorderly minds, but he hated the devastation they created around them. Plastic bags and papers blew into his garden and flapped against the back door. He swept as far as the gate every day and then stood brush in hand, looking at the appalling mess they had made outside. Discarded clothes hung on the hedges, dogs and ponies had left their droppings on the road, ponds of trampled mud stood around every tent. He wrote to the Guards, to the county council, but received only noncommittal replies; the official agencies had got too much bad publicity when they evicted the tinkers from a field near the housing estate and now they wanted to leave well enough alone—he was the only one discommoded and he had only one vote. He wrote a letter to the newspapers, then tore it up when he thought of his in-laws. He could not bear to have them set the political wheels turning for him.

His worst experience was when he laid out a lawn so that he could take his work outdoors next summer. The night after he raked it smooth and spread the seed, the ponies broke in and trampled the place into a quagmire. Raging, he went down to a young tinker who lay by the roadside, where the ponies were grazing. The man never looked up while he shouted, hardly moved at all, until at last, removing the straw from between his teeth, he muttered, "Not my ponies, boss," replaced the straw and refused to talk again.

Michael went back to his room and tried to work, but found it impossible to get started. All the morning, the tinker lay by the roadside, chewing the straw and waiting for his woman to come back from her begging to minister to him. Margaret brought in the morning coffee and Michael drank it, standing at the window, not yet having set pen to paper. His work seemed onerous and purposeless. Was it for this he had studied so hard and so long? To produce this booklet for skeptical, over-sold travel agents, who would flick through it in the hotel lobby between sessions of pep talk? Only the faith that something better must result brought him once more back to his desk to try again. He had a great faith in determination.

It wasn't misplaced, his faith, on this occasion at least. The book for the Cultural Relations Institute came his way after a number of interviews and lunch meetings. Celtic art was not particularly his line, but it was closer to what he wanted to do than a soft sell to travel agents. Besides, it was a prestige job and he would have a percentage for seeing the proofs through the printers. The advance was more than he and Margaret had handled before in a whole year. What should they do with it? Furnish the house? That was what Margaret wanted, but to him the house seemed less permanent now than it had been. He wanted to buy her clothes, to go to an expensive restaurant, have a weekend in a luxury hotel (like all people who mind the pence, he had an exaggerated idea of the staying power of pounds). They compromised at last by buying a secondhand car; it was a long walk to the bus, fares were going up, and there would be frequent visits to the printers at the far side of town. Besides, they were marooned out here, at the back of beyond, with only the tinkers for neighbors. And Margaret was expecting again.

But somehow the car did not end their isolation. They seemed to be drawn more and more into the tinkers' world. One night, there was a fight in the camp, bodies rolling over and over between the wheels of the carts, women shrieking and running as the combatants rolled right through a fire, scattering it in a flare of embers. Rigidly, he lay in bed, listening, conscious of Margaret rigid beside him. They didn't speak even when he got up to go and soothe one of the frightened children.

One afternoon, he brought his eldest boy for a walk through the fields to the hilltop. They were crossing a stile when a yelping trio of tinker youths came out of the wood. The leader—the one who had called on him—held a greyhound by a roughly knotted rope. As they reached the stile, the leader waved at Michael and shouted some epithet which Michael couldn't understand. The others stopped and looked at him, jeeringly, then at the tug of the rope, they vaulted the stile and set off running by the hedge. Minutes later, they reappeared on the slope of the hill silhouetted against the winter sky—three thin figures leaning upward, drawn by the straining hound, like a print out of some ancient scene of the chase.

Both the fight and the hunting party would have made perfect illustrations of Celtic art, so Margaret suggested. Michael was pleased, but because he knew that the institute's ideas were limited to the eighth-century concepts of intricate whorls and tail-eating snakes, he did not mention the suggestion for fear of causing more delay in getting the project off the ground. He had enough problems as it was. A panel of experts had been appointed to advise him and he had to sit through several meetings while historians, archaeologists, and civil servants argued fiercely over points of detail. Sometimes the arguments spilled over into drinking sessions, where the qualifications of absent panelists were scathingly reviewed, and any discreditable anecdotes brought to light with joyous Dublin malice. Listening to them, he gave thanks that he was a man who worked alone and provoked no envious wits to exercise themselves on him.

He did not feel easy about the drinking, though. As a student he had been no better than the rest at parties. He had got drunk carelessly, without giving a thought to it. Here, he was alarmed by the determined drinking of the elder men and also by the expense of a round of drinks (the place they frequented considered it vulgar to serve a pint of stout.) He usually managed to escape with only two or three whiskies inside him, but even so, he drove home afterward with great care, clutching the steering wheel tight, hunched over it as if to inhibit the demon within him from taking over.

He was always very quiet when he got home, rather sullen because there was no possibility of working after a few drinks. The only thing to do after he got the car into the garage was to go to bed and sleep off the effects before supper. Even then, of course, the night might well be shot if Margaret came up to waken him—the house quiet and the children asleep—and delayed too long by the bedside. *That* was the only thing he would sacrifice an evening's work for, gladly without an aftertaste of guilt, but of course, he would make up for it by getting up earlier next morning.

He impressed the panel more than he realized, sobriety to them being synonymous with sense of purpose. They were glad of him because they could continue to argue about the side issues, knowing that he was getting on with the work. They withheld any admission of appreciation because it might be quoted against them later, if things went wrong. They were old hands and praise no longer came naturally to them.

The work progressed until at last the book was ready to be put to tender. The designs looked well and Michael got some satisfaction in watching the attentive faces of those invited to file past the exhibition stands in the great Georgian room. Some members of the panel were there, obviously preparing to carry him off to the usual place. He managed to evade them; he wanted to get home, to go for a walk with Margaret in the country, as they used to do in the old days when some great plan was afoot. The best part of this job was done, and well done . . . He was restless now. He wanted to talk of his next job, to wonder whether he might, at last, try something on his own. He was uneasy, too, wondering whether he had left it too late, because of the house with which he was burdened and his increasing family.

On his way home, cold sober, he was driving not dangerously but just a shade faster than usual, when the little girl ran out from the tinkers' camp. He had no time to swerve. She ran right into him, disappearing suddenly in front of the bonnet. She made no sound and he remembered thinking, as he hurried back to the little bundle of clothes that lay on the side of the road, how surprising the silence was.

His own self-possession surprised him too, looking back. Of course, it had saved his life, as everybody said, because they could easily have killed him during the first few minutes. Their shouts brought Margaret running out. She saw the wild faces of the men gathered round him and without hesitation she pushed her way through them until she stood at his side. Michael at once shook himself free from them, went down on his knees, and began to lift the body in his arms. The shouting suddenly stopped as he shouldered his way through them to the car.

Margaret ran ahead and held the door open while he reached in quite calmly, and laid the body along the backseat. She stood back and watched him sit in and drive away. She did not realize the danger she was in until she became aware of shrieking and saw the woman sitting on the grass verge with her head thrown back, like a dog in pain. The knot of men standing where the child had been, were staring, not at the woman, but at her. She turned away, very slowly, and walked, trying not to hurry, in through the gateway. Every step of the way up the path to the front door, she waited for the rush of feet behind her, but none came. Looking back as she closed the front door, she saw the men still standing there, staring after her.

Michael's collapse came later when he sat on the hospital bench and saw the young house surgeon come out of the door marked CASUALTY and head toward him. Although he had known that the child was dead the first time he touched her, before the men surrounded him, it was only now that he began to tremble all over. They gave him sedation, kept him an hour or so, then sent him home with one of the sisters.

It was dark when he got back. The Guards were there. He watched them measure the road, running their torches up and down the length of the skid marks. Over at the camp, the men sat at their fires, watching. The accident had now become public property; it no longer concerned them. When the Guards moved among them, asking for statements, they shook their heads. One old man blurted out a brief, halting description of what had happened, a Guard took down the statement as best he could, then shrugged at his companion and turned to go. The men still stared, as if they felt incredible that the death of the child could occasion such ceremony.

Of course, thought Michael, they must be used to losing children. One often read of their infants being suffocated or burned inside the tents, at night, by a change of wind. Perhaps their children didn't mean a great deal to them. Perhaps there wouldn't be any great fuss after all.

Everything was quiet after the Guards drove away, but, later, when he had taken a sleeping pill and was almost asleep, he heard crying from the camp, a woman's voice crying. It went on and on and seemed to follow him as he was dragged down into sleep.

Next morning, Margaret went out after she had got him his breakfast, without waiting for her own. She did not say anything, but he knew she was gone down to the camp. He stacked the dishes in the sink, sent the children out to play and waited for her. From his window, he could see her standing among a group of women and children. One woman sat on the ground, clasping her knees, with her head downcast. Although the others seemed to refer to her from time to time, she never lifted her head or made any move. The men, to Michael's relief, had taken themselves off somewhere.

She came back, busy with arrangements. The funeral was to be the following day. They had already taken the body to the cottage of some relations up near Glenbride, where it would be waked that night.

"I said that we'd drive them, Michael, from here, any of them that wanted to go, but they said to me, the men have arranged for hired cars to come. Oughtn't we to offer to pay for them, Michael, don't you think?"

"I don't know. We'd better be careful. It might look as if we're admitting liability."

"Yes, of course." She looked away, then looked back at him, a little flushed. "To tell you the truth, Michael, I did tell them we might pay. They wouldn't hear of it, though. They seemed to want to pay for it themselves, but I thought since we . . ." She glanced at his face and went on, "But it doesn't matter, Michael, really. Whatever you think best. I suppose we should go to the funeral anyway."

"Yes, I'll be expected to go, I suppose."

"If you don't mind, Michael, I'd like to go too. Yes, really I would. I'd feel better about it if I could go."

"Of course. If you want to."

And Michael turned back to the window to look out at the camp, where the woman was sitting on the ground. He did not turn when Margaret's hand pushed its way into his.

"It's not your fault," she whispered.

"I know, Christ, don't I know!"

"It's not theirs either. So don't—" She slid her hand free and they stood, apart, looking at the bowed figure, which seemed to be growing out of the ground. Then one of their children came banging on the back door and she had to take him in, feed him, and clean him and put him down for his midday rest. Michael stayed at the window, unable to find any reason to move, to go back to the work he had to do.

A ramshackle van stopped at the camp that evening and people scrambled into it, first the men, then as many women as would fit. The rest of the women and the children were called for next morning by a large, black undertaker's car, which sped smoothly away, leaving the place deserted.

When Michael arrived at the cottage with Margaret, they found both car and van, together with various traps, carts, and old trucks, drawn up on the muddied verges. Although it was raining hard, several men stood at the gable of the cottage, drinking bottles of stout. Small clutches of bottles nested here and there in the scutch grass of the garden. Margaret stopped when the men waved and shouted what seemed to be an invitation. They looked wildly drunk; their clothes hung soddenly from them, stained with wet patches. Water ran from the brims of their hats when they tilted their heads to drink.

Michael tried to make her go back to the car, but she shook her head and followed him into the crowded porch. Nobody paid any attention to them. They pushed their way through into the kitchen, then recoiled, but it was too late; the crowd had closed about them and they were caught in the confusion, in the squirming crush of bodies. Faces turned upward to them and fell away, eyes dulled, stupefied with drink. The smell was overpowering, but not altogether unpleasant; it seemed not the smell of human sweat, but of wet clay overlying a faintly rank, animal smell.

Michael pressed toward the door of the inner room, got it open, and pushed Margaret in before him. The quiet within was startling. Two nuns sat on the only chairs. Around them, the women and a few older men knelt or squatted on the bare floor. Out of the corner of his eye, Michael saw the child's body laid out on the bare mattress. The nuns had begun to rise deferentially to their feet.

"No, no, sit down," he told them.

"Are ye from the settlement committee?" the older one asked, looking at him over thick glasses. She had a long face, intersected by deep, straight lines. "We came out just now from the hospital," she went on, as he shook his head. "'Twas the mercy of God we did, because ye can see the way they have things arranged. There's no one turned up with the coffin yet. What's keeping him, Anthony, in heaven's name?"

The gray-haired tinker kneeling beside her waved his hand several times in front of his face. "He do be a bit late, sister," he murmured.

"Late is right." She turned to Michael. "We had everything in order here last night when we left, the child properly laid out and the women saying the rosary. Listen to them now! Go out, Anthony, like a good man, and see if there's any sign of him."

Anthony rose slowly to his feet, swayed drunkenly to get his balance and then headed for the door.

"That's the father of the child," she said. "Poor fellow, he doesn't know whether it's coming or going he is."

Michael had not expected the father to be so old, but then, tinkers looked much older than their age. He waited defensively for an accusing look, but the man fumbled the door open, then stood in the doorway, bemused by the crowd outside. Slowly he began to put on his hat, fitting it down over his head, pulling it into place. He drew the door carefully behind him, without once looking at Michael.

Margaret had drawn close to the bed and was looking down at the child. Her eyes were brimming. Michael followed her, slowly drawing near and for the first time in years, made the sign of the cross, a quick, shamed gesture. As he looked down at the child, she turned to him quickly and whispered, "She's lovely, Michael."

"She's gone straight to heaven, of course," the older nun said, in a matter-of-fact voice.

"Oh, I'm *sure*!" Margaret burst out.

"What's vexing me, though, is they have Father O'Meara waiting up there by the graveyard, in the pouring rain." She looked around at the men who were watching her intently. "And only for me, I may say, he wouldn't have been up there at all today. You men forgot to tell him to come."

The men shifted and dropped their eyes. "Anthony said . . ."

"Oh Anthony said! Hadn't poor Anthony enough on his mind? Couldn't one of you men have gone up to tell the priest instead of sitting here drinking?" She winked suddenly at Michael. "I declare to God I'd sooner be teaching a class of four-year-olds. Wouldn't you, Sister Claude?"

The young nun looked at the lowered heads of the men and then glanced up quickly at Michael. "I don't know, Sister." She blushed. "I never taught a class."

"Well, you'd know if you had. But it wouldn't be as bad as looking after these gents."

The door burst open and Anthony stumbled in, feeling for his hat to take it off. Next, came a young tinker, carrying a roughly made box of heavy wood, which he bumped over to the bed and lowered on the mattress beside the body. He stood back then, wiping his unshaven face with his cap. The expensive sheepskin jacket was soaked with rain and his suede boots were muddied. He smiled at the people around, as if well-pleased with himself.

The older nun rose to her feet, horror on her face. "Merciful heavens," she whispered. "You couldn't even do that right!"

"What is it, Sister?" the other nun half-rose apprehensively.

"Look at what he got! The coffin!" She turned on the young man, who backed away from her. "Well, honestly you'd vex a saint. Sure, 'tis too small."

There was a wail from the women. The men jumped to their feet and crowded around, shouting exclamations.

"Stop it," the nun called. "That's enough, now. Stop the racket! Outside now, all of you! Go on, leave us alone here. We'll have to see what we can do." She looked to Michael. "Would you help us, sir, get them out? We can't keep the priest waiting up there in the rain."

He moved them out, easily enough, last of all the gray-haired father, who was sobbing quietly. Outside, he stood with his back to the door. The crowd in the kitchen was silent, staring at him, waiting. Only then did he realize that he had left Margaret behind with the nuns. He turned to go back to fetch her, but could not bring himself to open the door. Awkwardly, he stood waiting. All the time, the tinkers stared at him, as if his indecision made them uneasy.

At a knock on the door, he turned quickly and opened it a few inches to see Margaret motioning to him to come in. She seemed quite calm. "Sister says would you call in the young fellow to help you."

"To help me?"

"Yes, to carry it out."

They took hold of each end of the coffin and lifted it. It seemed so light that, for a moment he wondered whether there was anything in it at all or whether some vanishing trick had been done on the body. Just as they moved toward the door, an old woman stumbled in past them and made for the bed. Michael stopped and, still holding the coffin, looked back. She bent over the mattress, over the place where the girl had been laid and began to feel with her hands as if to caress where the face had been. Was it some last tinker ceremony, he wondered with a prickling of his skin, some magical dismissal of the spirit? But no, he realized with disgust, as the old woman gave a little, sick whimper and fell drunkenly on to the bed. The women around immediately began to pull her roughly out.

Rain lashed the coffin lid as they pushed out through the porch and half-ran toward the van. They bundled it into the back and shut the door. Then Michael ran to his own car, in which Margaret was waiting.

"Let's go!" he said.

"Where to?"

"Home."

"We can't go home, not now."

He looked at her, for the first time wanting to strike her. "Yes!" he shouted. "We've done enough!"

She said nothing, just looked ahead at the misted windscreen. A car zoomed past, a little red Fiat. From its window, the younger nun smiled in at him and lifted her hand in a small, timid salute.

As he looked at the gray glass in front of him all the anger went out of him, leaving him cold and empty. "Oh, Christ," he whispered and leaned forward to switch on the ignition.

The gate of the graveyard was locked and a few young women stood leaning against it, holding their shawls over their heads. Margaret stopped suddenly at the sight of them.

"Come on," he said, as he reached the stile. "What's the matter?"

She motioned toward the women who had turned slowly to look at them. "I can't."

"What's wrong?"

"It's . . . bad luck."

"What? What's bad luck?"

"So they say. It's bad luck to go in, when we're—the way we are." And she put her hand lightly on her belly.

"Oh, for God's sake—"

"I'll wait here."

He looked at her, standing under her red umbrella, very slight and straight, among the other women.

"No, not there," he shouted. "Go back. Go on back to the car." And as he watched her go, he wondered why she should have angered him so much.

He took the path which had been trampled through the long grass to the graveside. The priest stood waiting there with a prayer book in his hand. Over his head, the older nun held an umbrella. As Michael joined them, she turned and raised her eyes to heaven. "Will ye look at them!" she murmured. "They couldn't even dig the grave properly. Sure, that's not deep enough at all."

Two young tinkers were still digging in the grave, standing waist deep below the mound of wet clay. Clumsily, they wielded their shovels.

"Come on," said the priest, "'twill do, 'twill do. We can't be here all day." He waved abruptly at the young men and they climbed out, shamefacedly, and went to join their companions at the far side of the grave.

The priest began the prayers in a loud voice. The umbrella wavered over his head so that every now and then rain splashed on the pages of his prayer book. He found it hard to turn the pages and had to stop sometimes in mid-sentence while he unstuck them. At last, he was finished. The men looked at one another, waiting for someone to make the first move.

"Go on, let ye!" urged the nun and the two young men lifted the coffin into the grave. They covered it with sods and then, lifting up the shovels, began to throw in the clay.

When the grave was nearly full, the mother pushed past them and, with a cry, flung herself down into it. She lay there, facedown, twitching and shrieking.

"Oh Lord, oh Lord!" said the priest. "Take her out, some of you." At once, several men jumped in, and lifted her out and set her on her feet. Wet clay covered her from head to foot. Her eyes showed white and from her red mouth came short, breathless shrieks. The women led her away to the far corner of the graveyard and the shrieks gradually died away.

But not altogether. A low, moaning sound lingered on, like the wind humming in telegraph wires. It grew stronger and stronger until it seemed to fill the air. Looking around, frightened by it, Michael saw that it came from the mouths of the women gathered near.

The priest and the two nuns blessed themselves and began to hurry away toward the stile. As they climbed out on the road, the sound sharpened into a wail, lost, empty, desolate. It thrilled through Michael so that he stood rooted in the muddy ground beside the grave unable to move.

The men filled in the grave, bent down and beat their shovels hard on the clay. It was then Michael noticed that the rain had stopped. Looking up, he saw the clouds drifting apart. They grew fainter and fainter until at last the white disc of the sun showed through. The bare branches of the beech tree gleamed in its light, as did the wet gray headstones that leaned this way and that. Green fields brightened down the valley. The sound rose higher, so sharp that it hurt, but sure of itself, exultant. Only when the sun burst through the last faint remnant of cloud, did it die away.

He turned and walked slowly back to his car. And there, behind the bright misty windows, he took Margaret in his arms, still smelling the wet clay in which he had stood.

A Pilgrim

The tinker lay on his back, contentedly, looking up at a blue sky that was bare of cloud. All his worldly possessions lay about him on the grass, a little tent that seemed to have no resistance to rain, a black kettle, a frying pan, and a pair of torn blankets that had not been washed since he had bought them two years before. His little donkey grazed quietly fifty yards away. On the road beside the field, an occasional car passed, and slowed down as it approached the customs barrier. The tinker had reason to think of that customs barrier with distaste, for only that morning a surly RUC sergeant had told him to get to hell out of Northern Ireland and not to show his face there again. Bloody lot of Orangemen, he thought to himself, they think they own the country. So here he was now, midway between the northern and southern customs—a no-man's-land—he reflected bitterly. He was not going to let himself be worried by the morning's incident; oh, no, it had happened too often before. He would stay where he was until he felt like moving—he might go to Cork or even to Dublin—neither place had ever been graced by his presence. He plucked a blade of grass and chewed it meditatively, as he shifted to a more comfortable position on the grass.

The sound of footsteps on the road made him sit up sharply. He peered through a hole in the hedge and saw two men approaching. They both carried knapsacks on their shoulders, and one of them carried a rolled-up tent under his arm. "Hikers," the tinker said to himself. "Maybe I can touch these boyos for a couple of bob." This was more in hope than anything else for their appearance was not indicative of great worldly prosperity. He pulled himself through the hole in the hedge and jumped on to the road.

"Hello," he said as the two approached. They glanced suspiciously into the field as if expecting an ambush by a clan of tinkers. Satisfied, they stopped a few yards away.

"Hello," one of them said.

"Going far?" the tinker asked cordially.

"Oh, we're trying to get to Dublin by tonight," the other hiker answered.

"Is that so?" said the tinker, becoming interested, "and how in the name of God do ye expect to get to Dublin tonight the way you're going?"

"By hitchhiking," said one of the men.

"And what's hitchhiking?"

"Oh, you know, getting lifts in cars or lorries."

"Ye mean to say," said the tinker, "that ye just walk along the road and get a lift in any car that comes along?"

"That's right," said the two together.

"But supposing no car stops for ye?"

"Well," said one of the hikers, "we've been traveling all the week that way without any difficulty. As a matter of fact, we're just after getting a lift from Lough Derg in a big American car."

"*Jakus*," said the tinker; he was learning something new every day, "well tell us, what's this place Lough Derg like?"

"It's tough enough," said one. "You get nothing to eat while you're there except dry bread, and you get no sleep at all the first night."

"Cripes, that's murder," said the tinker, "and how do ye feel after it—beat-out, I suppose?"

"Well, I feel great, anyway," said the younger of the two, "soul refreshed, you know."

"Mm," the tinker didn't know much about souls, "I might try it meself sometime."

One of the hikers was watching a car approaching and as it came near he waved his thumb in the hitchhiking style. To the tinker's astonishment, the car stopped and a man leaned out of the window.

"Want a lift?" he asked.

"Sure," said the two and climbed into the back of the car. "Good-bye now," they shouted to the tinker as the car moved off. Nice lads, the tinker decided as he got over the hedge to his camp—nothing superior about them like you'd expect from city people.

As he prepared his tea, the tinker pondered over all he had learned that evening—hitchhiking and Lough Derg. Wouldn't it be nice now if he could try his hand at both of them—just as an experience. He ate his meal, the while debating whether or not he would have the nerve to go to Lough Derg. This business of not eating anything would kill him surely. But on the other hand he would have great stories to tell the tinkers the next time he met them. Dammit, he said, I'll go out this evening. His donkey and camp would be all right where they were—no one was likely to steal anything from a tinker. Having made up his mind, he set about preparing himself for the journey. The suit he had on him would have to do him (he had no other) so he tried to clean it of the stains that had accumulated since he bought it. He placed all his belongings inside the tent and with a final look around, climbed through the hedge and started walking along the road. As soon as he heard a car coming, he stopped and hitched with his thumb—but with no result. Ten cars passed without stopping during the next hour and the tinker began to despair of ever getting a lift, until at last a small van stopped for him and he was invited to hop in. He chatted gaily with the driver, a farmer who lived near Lough Derg. It was the first time the tinker had ever been in a motorcar and he enjoyed the experience to the full.

Darkness was falling as the tinker approached the bleak shores of Lough Derg. He was just in time to travel on the last boat from the mainland to the island of penance. His heart beat with a certain amount of trepidation, for he knew not what was before him. The pilgrims were greeted cordially on the island, and were shown to the cubicles where they were to sleep on the second night. A list of instructions, which he was to observe faithfully, was handed to him, but being unable to read, he tore it up and decided to do what everybody else was doing.

The night passed without incident. All during the following day, although half-dropping with a lack of sleep, the tinker carried out the necessary exercises. This was a new and wonderful experience for him. He was treated as an equal, he could converse with rich and poor alike, people listened when he aired his views. He discovered that he was popular, that he had personality. Several offered to drive him back to his camp when the retreat was over, and so it was with feelings of regret that he left Lough Derg. His second night's sleep had refreshed him considerably, and although undeniably very hungry, he was, he decided, a new man.

The driver of the car that he had picked for his return journey stopped at the Éire customs post and the tinker decided to walk the short distance to his camp. As he peered through the hole in the hedge, which was his front door, he received a rude shock. His donkey and tent and all his belongings had disappeared—only a circle of trampled grass indicated that the camp had ever been there. Worried, he ran back to the customs post and burst into the little hut.

"Where the hell is my camp?" he cried.

The customs officer looked at him coldly.

"It has been impounded by the state. You ought to have known better than to leave your belongings unattended on the border."

The tinker clenched his fists and his face reddened. But Lough Derg had chastened him. His hands dropped to his sides and he sighed.

"Let God's will be done," he said, and walked slowly out the door.

The Land of Youth

When Padraig and Bairbre set out to destroy each other, we made no move for a long time to come between them; we wouldn't have been able to, even though on a small island like ours we live, you might say, in each other's minds. We knew from the start that whatever had driven them apart had driven them away out of reach of the rest of us.

It was not until he tried to use our own children against Bairbre that we did at last interfere. We had never told the children about Padraig and Bairbre, for we thought that silence would be the best end for their story. We would of course have told them if we could only have guessed what was in Padraig's mind that day, as he came in from the hooker with the island stores.

Most of us were down at the slip, as usual, watching his currach crawling in, heavy with coal and oil drums and sacks of meal. He jumped awkwardly ashore, careful not to wet his boots. Holding the gob of the currach, he turned and called to the group on the slip, "Here, men! Give us a hand here!" Two of the men reluctantly left the group. They ran silently down in their rawhide slippers and waded knee-deep into the water to lift the currach ashore. Then they walked away up the slip and rejoined the group. Padraig shut his lips tight, glanced after them from under his fox-terrier eyebrows, then looked around for more help. He saw a few schoolboys hitching their satchels on their backs as they turned away. "Here boys!" he called, "Where are ye off to? Come down here to me."

They went down to him. They rolled up the oil drums and sacks of meal. Then they turned the currach over and shouldered it all the way up the slip. With their bare white legs moving in step underneath, the black currach was like a strange beetle crawling up on the land. They trooped back then to carry up the oars and the baler. They didn't mind working for Padraig. They were hoping he would let them drive the horse and cart up to the village and maybe ride the horse down to the well afterward.

Quickly, then, they returned to stagger up the slip with the island stores. We called them the island stores, though we still had to buy them from Padraig at a price which he justified by reason of the service he gave. No one in his senses, he said, would ever have thought of running a shop at all in such a place. Not that he ever had to justify himself to us. It was Father Kiely who had done all the complaining, the time he was held on the island by a storm and refused to pay the price that Padraig put on a packet of razor blades. As both of them were obstinate men, the priest had to return to the mainland with a ten-days' growth of beard. Still, we called the stores the island stores because Padraig was one of us and would always be.

When they had Padraig's cart loaded up, the boys all climbed in and started off sedately for the village. Padraig walked along behind, looking into our fields and gardens, stopping to peer over the walls to see how the potatoes and rye were doing, putting a price to everything, his price. When he reached Bairbre's shop, he walked straight past without looking to right or to left. Bairbre's son was there, striding up and down the stone-fenced garden at the back of the shop, talking away to himself, and wiping the dribble off his chin with the back of his hand. As always, he wore the white town shirt, which she changed on him twice a day as if he were a great gentleman. There was no great desire on Padraig to be looking on that sight.

The boys drew away from Padraig as they went up the hill. They stealthily nudged the horse into a faster pace. On the far side, they lashed it into a gallop and went belting down into Padraig's yard with a rattle of oil drums and with the boxes of groceries bouncing about as if there were live things inside. Quickly, they jumped down to unload the cart and untackle the horse, so that they could ride it down to water, the lot of them, and be well on their way before Padraig arrived. But just as they slipped the collar off, Padraig came hurrying into the yard. "Tie him up there, boys!" he called, out of breath, "and come in here to me!"

They followed him into the cold kitchen and sat down in a row on a wooden bench, facing the fire which wasn't there.

"Let ye wait a minute," he said as he went to open one of the big cardboard boxes. They waited, lifting their bare feet off the stone floor and rubbing them nervously together, like a line of flies. He took out a bottle of boiled sweets and went along the line, carefully shaking two sweets into each outstretched hand. "Now!" said he, pulling up a chair opposite them and holding out his narrow red hands, as if to shield himself from the glow of a fire, "tell me, how d'ye like them?"

They nodded their heads, their mouths too full to talk. They had stuffed both sweets in, in case there were more to come.

"I'll have sweets here now, from this out," said he, "all kinds of sweets, licorice allsorts, caramels, marzipans. Let ye tell them all below at the school."

"How much?" asked one of them cautiously. Little Jimín it was, from the post office, cracking a sweet in two to let the words out.

"They'll be cheaper than ye'll get in the other place."

"But how much?" Jimín was his mother's son.

"Fifteen a penny them are," said he. The boys sucked their sweets in silence. In Bairbre's shop they got only twelve a penny.

"Well, now!" said he, rising up, "I'm keeping ye from yer homework. That wouldn't do now, would it?"

The boys hung back on their way to the door, hoping that there might be another sample going free, but Padraig was already opening his packages and checking the stores against his invoices.

"Can we take the horse to water?" asked Jimín, when he saw that it was the only thing he had a chance of getting.

"No," said Padraig. "Be off with ye!" When he was working at his invoices, with the steel spectacles clamped on the end of his nose, he'd nearly refuse a man a pint of stout and that's one shilling and threepence worth. We'd have to wait till he was finished with the books before we'd order a drink, as we'd wait for a priest to finish reading his Office.

"All right," grumbled a big boy with a breaking voice. A couple of free sweets had made him too bold. "We might go on buying Bairbre's sweets, so we might."

Padraig looked up at him quickly, with those sharp eyes of his.

"What are ye doing here," he said, "with the children?"

"I'm not doing anything," the big fellow muttered, backing away.

"Get away and leave them alone," said Padraig, following and aiming a slap at him. "*Gach aois a chomhluadar féin*—every age its own company: Don't ye know that?"

"I do," the big fellow said.

"Well, then, how many times have ye to be told it? Now, get away with ye. And if ye don't mind all I've said, I'll talk to the master about ye."

That was enough to send the big fellow scurrying off with his ears reddened for him. The children stood looking after him, as if they had been caught out in a shameful thing that no one would explain rightly to them. They always did look that way, when Padraig made use of his *piseog*. He had them to suit every occasion. They all went to show what a great order there was in the world of men, from priest, teacher, postmaster, and shopkeeper all the way down to the rest of us common people. And woe betide the man or boy who put his foot outside the place laid out for him.

That was how Padraig made the children take the bread out of the mouth of Bairbre and her son. They kept their own counsel for a long time, as our children do, for "every age its own company" is a true saying on the island, though we'd never think to make a law of it, the way Padraig did. The children might never have turned their backs on Bairbre, had they not been as bad as the rest of us for getting value for their pennies. Even then, though, when they had left her, they used to miss slipping into her shop for a pennyworth of sweets, missing most of all the sight of the son sitting quiet in the darkness of the chimney corner. He'd sit there all day, with cushions snug about him and he slumped the way she sat him, like a rag doll. His eyes were like those speckled stones the children would pick up on the beach. On those quiet days of his, he'd look tame enough for them to pet him. Not so the dog lying against his feet. It would open an eye every now and then, like the cover of a keyhole drawn back, then silently it would bare its teeth. All of us in the island were afraid of the dog. We'd almost swear it looked out at us with those same speckled stone eyes.

The children, of course, had never heard us speaking of that son of Bairbre. We rarely spoke of the creature even among ourselves; he was born on the day that she had cursed Padraig and some said that the birth was a judgement on her. None of us had any wish to remember her standing on the rock as the bodies of her husband and her two sons were brought in all naked and torn to the slip. While the waves still played with the slats and crumpled canvas of the currach, Bairbre turned around toward the village, toward the fine slated roof showing over the brow of the hill.

"*Múchadh is báthadh ort*," she said in a loud even voice against the tearing gale, "May you never see the glory. May you die with the scream of the dawn!"

Some of the women took hold of her and led her home. But none of them could ever persuade her that it wasn't Padraig who had robbed her of her flesh and blood that autumn evening. Father Kiely, a young man at the time, came over specially from the mainland when he heard what had happened, but even he could not make her understand.

"Yes, but in the name of God, woman," he said, "can't ye see that Padraig had no evil in his mind? Maybe he did offer your men double the pay to bring the engineer back to the mainland. What harm was there in that?"

"Yes, but why would he offer it? Tell me! Why?"

"Why, because . . ." but Father Kiely thought it better not to go spreading gossip. He knew as well as we did why Padraig wanted to oblige the engineer; it was a matter of a grant from the county council for the extension of his store.

"Does it matter why?"

"He sent them out because a storm was blowing up. He knew right well they'd be caught on the way back. He dared them to go."

"Nonsense, woman!" but the priest looked taken aback, "Ye don't think the man would do a thing like that?"

She said nothing. She just looked at him.

"But tell us here, woman, what's all this about anyway?" Father Kiely was an obstinate man. He never rightly understood what was going on on the island, but he'd keep a tight hold of a rumor till he'd worry some kind of a meaning out of it. "What's between ye? Will ye tell me that?"

She never told him, but he asked a few questions elsewhere and he went away with a few answers. God knows what queer notions the poor man has of us ever since, that is, if he judges us all by the way Padraig carried on over Bairbre, when 'twas just a question of taking a wife, not to mention the way Bairbre herself behaved when she came back from Boston, Mass. A right pair of them there was in it!

She was a wild slip of a girl then, with a great show of American clothes, white gloves, and summer hats, and satin dresses, which she wore with an air before all the girls of the island. She hadn't over much of the heavy pennies, though, that she should have been putting toward her dowry the three years she was away. However, she had no want of looks from the men's side of the church of a Sunday, but looks of that kind cost nothing; she got very few offers. Those that pleased her vexed her father and those that pleased him sent her into fits of laughter. The offers came either from snug old bachelors or from men whose holdings barely held the grazing of a goat.

Her father, a sensible man, was all for packing the girl back to Bostonmass until she got some sense for herself. It was then that Padraig made his proposal. It seemed a good match, better than her father could ever have expected. It pleased her too, not because Padraig would come in for the business and a wealth of money when his mother died, but because the other girls had never dared set their caps at him. He was a student for the priesthood, home for the holidays after four years in the seminary. Though the people said the mark of a spoiled priest would be on him for evermore, Bairbre paid no heed, nor, in their hearts, did the other girls of the island. They could only think how fine his quiet priestly ways were compared with the rough ways of the young islandmen. It was what the girls thought that maybe counted most with Bairbre.

Padraig's mother fought hard against the match; she had set her heart on making a priest of her son. Unless he went back to the seminary (so she told the men who crowded the counter of her shop every night), she would never again look her neighbors in the face. The tears would creep in to her voice as she resorted more and more frequently to the bottle hidden in the cupboard of the kitchen dresser. The older men would shift their glasses uneasily on the counter, while a few of the young fellows would grin and nudge each other at the thought of how her tactics would overrule Padraig. They were wrong, though. For the first time in his life, Padraig faced up to her. Neither tears nor threats could move him until at last the match was finally made.

That night, all the people of the island gathered into the *cleamhnas* party in Bairbre's house. It lasted all next day and the better part of the following night as well. Some of the women have photographs which show Padraig and Bairbre standing side by side in the sunshine. They look stiff and a little nervous, but happy in different ways.

In the middle of the second night, when all the company was very quiet, listening to a young girl giving out a song, there came a clatter of boots on the flags of the street. In trampled the captain and crew of a Scottish trawler that had been driven into the sound by a rising westerly gale. The man of the house made them at home, as was right and proper. He plied them with all manner of drinks, until they'd be in form to join in the singing and the dancing. They were gamy lads, the strangers, and it wasn't long before they were in form, too good form—the men of the island thought. Padraig and some of the islandmen had to go down to the shop to bring up another barrel of stout. While they were gone, and later, while they were tapping the barrel out in the hallway, the trawlermen began to make free with the girls. A few of them gathered around Bairbre.

"Goddamn that westerly wind," said one of them, "that it didn't blow us in here a day sooner."

"Maybe," said the captain and he winking his little blue eye at them, "it got us here soon enough." And he slipped his hairy arm around Bairbre and rubbed his bearded chin against her cheek. She pushed him aside, laughing at his impudence, but when she discovered that he too had spent a while in Boston, she turned to him as if she had met a friend in a distant land. The men stayed around her, laughing and talking. When nobody was looking, they made her try a few sips of cognac they had bought off a Spanish trawlerman. She had never touched strong drink before and she sent them into loud guffaws with the things she said. Poor Padraig was all this time filling mugs and glasses for the crowd and listening to the old people who came to call down God's blessing on his marriage. It was Bairbre's father who at last went up to the trawler captain and said, "Ye know, stranger, this is the girl that is to be married!"

"Indeed then," said Bairbre, "I'm the girl they say is to be married." And she had eyes for no one else but the trawler captain the rest of the night.

The trawler stayed in the sound for the best part of a week. The only man who never knew why was Padraig. He was still fighting hard against his mother, who was all set to put off the wedding as long as possible. He never guessed at what had happened till one night several weeks later when Bairbre left the island. Three young lads—they thought she was Helen of Troy or some woman of the songs—rowed her across the nine-mile sound to the mainland. Off with her then to Derry to meet her trawler captain.

It wasn't long afterward until she was back. She hadn't a word to say for herself. The rumor went around that the fellow was married, but no one could ever say for sure. All we did know was the kind of game the fellow had been up to; we soon saw signs of that. Padraig nearly went out of his mind when he was told of it. He came straight down to the slip, where the men of the island were gathered to mend a currach. We were sitting on the ground, our backs against the stone fences, watching the smoke drifting around the big black pot and the bubbles of tar bursting at its brim. He stood before us, like one of us in his homespun tweeds and bawneens, but that long priestly face of his as pale now as that of a dead man. He wanted us to rise up on the instant and make an example of the girl, to tar and feather her as some of the mainland people do. He talked of tying her to the old pagan pillar in the gap by the churchyard, as our people did with those who stole the Indian meal in famine times. None of us made a move to follow him. We're not like that on the island and never were. We men, some of us, have taken our chances too, though not with our own women. We let the girl alone, as Christ did with Mary Magdalene, but there's little credit due to us for that. The man that would have lifted a stone against Bairbre would want to have been born both blind and deaf.

Coilín Shéamuis married her before her time was come. No one was put out to hear of it. Girls were scarce on the island at the time and several men a lot younger than Coilín would have been glad to have her. They knew at the very least of it that they wouldn't be getting a barren wife, which is the greatest cross of all.

They were a good match, Coilín and Bairbre. He had just come back after a spell in England, where, as he said himself, he'd been selling his sweat for long enough. He was a big burly fellow with a terrible temper when he was roused. Himself and Bairbre had it hot and heavy a few times, but she gave as good as she got. Indeed, it would be hard for any man to best her, for even in anger she had a voice that would tease the birds off the branches. Coilín himself had no sense at all when she was about. We used to watch him, letting on to be working when the women would be gathering in the seaweed to spread out on the land. Bairbre would be standing out in the cold sea, swinging her *sprong* with the best of them. She looked smaller than any of the women, but she had enough life in her to do for any two of them. Poor Coilín would lose the strength of his arms and he watching her, with her black hair drawn smoothly back, the red flannel petticoat kilted up, and the waves breaking white around her thighs. Many's the joke was made about him over the pints of stout in Padraig's shop, though we took care that none of them reached his ears, or Padraig's either.

She had some trouble with her second child, Coilín's first. For nearly sixteen years after, they thought that this was to be the only fruit their marriage was to have. However, the day the bodies of Coilín and her two sons were brought ashore, she was carrying her third child in her womb. It was born that selfsame night and she was to rear it for the madhouse in Ballinasloe.

Coilín had not left her over-endowed with the world's goods (though God knows why she and her little creature had to go on living). The King of Graces, so we have it, is like a friends' house, which no one need leave but by his own free will. And so, we set her up in a snug little sweet shop. We all contributed the money when the curate called for a collection, all except Padraig Mahony. We weren't surprised at this. We hardly expected him to help set up another shop on the island, even though he sold no sweets in his. The least he might have done, though, was to pay the woman her rightful debt, the fare he had engaged to pay to her drowned man. It was the one debt he never paid. Maybe he set it off against what he thought she owed him. He had a very strict conscience about debts, but it worked like one of his ledgers, always in his favor.

Bairbre was no shopkeeper. She was content to make a living and that was barely as much as she made. As the little son grew up, she used to talk of sending him to school, as if that would cure him. When the time came, she never did; even she knew. Oftentimes, when the children would come in to buy sweets, they'd find her sitting at the counter with the creature in her lap. He'd have a steel-nibbed pen in his hand, which she'd be guiding across the page of a penny jotter. Even the smallest children would be loath to look at the sight of that.

Maybe that was why, as he grew older, that she drew in on herself more and more. She stopped going down to the well when the women would be there, talking and singing and whiling away the time till their men would be home from the fishing. She seldom spoke to them, only when she'd want one of them to get her stores for her (for she never again darkened the door of Padraig's shop). Even her nearest neighbors got out of the habit of dropping in on her to pass the time of day. On a small island like ours, it's strange how seldom people see each other when there's no great desire on them to meet. That was why, when Padraig made the children take their custom from her, that we never heard anything about it. She had got out of the habit of talking to us.

It was a good long time before the women noticed that her sweet jars remained empty and that the toffee bars and chocolates in her windows had faded in the sun. Then they noticed that the smoke from her kitchen didn't have the smell of a turf fire. They said nothing, for no woman wants to say something, which one day she might hear said of herself. One evening, though, on their way home from the milking, a group of the women met Bairbre crossing a field in the dusk. She had a sack on her back and we knew then, for sure, that it was the dried dung she was burning. We began to ask a few questions and we soon found out the whole story. On our island, there is no greater sin than to take away a person's livelihood. We told Father Kiely all about it on the following Sunday.

"I'll go talk to him this very minute," said Father Kiely, pushing out his jaw and tugging the wet beret off his head, as if he was going to fling it down at our feet, "I'll go straighten his legs for him."

"Don't say where ye heard it, Father," said one of the old men. We hadn't expected the priest to act that quick, before Mass and all. But then, Father Kiely always was very contrary on an empty stomach.

"Good God, are ye men at all?" said he, drawing back to look at us. We turned away. It was all right for him to talk. He hadn't got the next season's stock of oats and rye and salted bream promised to Padraig. He wasn't up to his neck in debt for his meal and his oil. And he was a priest.

Padraig was coming out the door of his shop with his missal in his hand when the priest came up, pushed him back in, and shut the door. We left them to it. It was none of our business. We felt in a way as if it was one priest talking to another, for Padraig it was who led the prayers for the dead and kept the book of baptisms and marriages. To tell the truth, he had more of the look of the priest about him than had Father Kiely himself, whom strangers often took for an islandman. If Father Kiely had given his white alb and chasuble to Padraig and let him come out on to the altar, I don't know but that we wouldn't have genuflected in the right places. Maybe that was why Father Kiely always spoke to him in a loud voice, like a man shouting back to the people on the land.

We saw who had the best of it, when Father Kiely swept out in his vestments and crossed himself with a great flourish at the foot of the altar. Padraig edged into the back of the church. When we passed out after Mass, he was still kneeling there, the two red patches still in his cheeks. Not only had he to give up selling the sweets. That evening, he sent little Jimín down to Bairbre's with the whole stock he had on hands. He told Jimín not to tell anyone, but he might as well have told the island as to tell the son of our postmistress. Especially when the news was that Father Kiely had avenged himself at last for those razorblades.

We thought everything was nicely settled when the children began to deal again with Bairbre. We had reckoned without Padraig, though. He began writing to people on the county council, who were well in with the government up in Dublin. We heard about the official letters going back and forth, but we didn't know what was going on till we heard that he had been made a peace commissioner. We were pleased to have a commissioner on the island, though it was seldom enough that any of us wanted documents sworn. The last thing we expected, though, was that Padraig would use his new power against Bairbre. In fact, his main purpose was to have her son certified and sent away. The island was up in arms on the instant, but Padraig no longer cared what anyone thought of him. He told a deputation of the men to clear out of his house. Now that he had the official power behind him, as well as the power of the purse, no one could shake him, not even Father Kiely himself.

The day Bairbre's son was sent away, we all gathered at the boat slip, not to see the poor creature off (for we might as well have seen off his old sheepdog), but to look at a woman who now had more than her share of earthly trouble. God forgive us, not one of us made a move to help her. But what could we have done? She had lost husband and sons all over again; that was what the creature meant to her.

The dog was the only one to cause trouble at the slip. Bairbre stood by herself on the rock above us, her face hidden in the folds of her shawl, as she watched her son being lifted into the currach. Beyond her, up in the village, the dog was howling. We could hear the distant thuds as it hurled itself against the door of her shed. When it fell silent suddenly, we looked up the road and there it was making straight for us.

We scattered on all sides as it plunged down the slip and into the water, right under the prow of the currach. It rose, splashing and choking, and hooked a paw over the gunwale. The men beat it down with their oars. The currach pulled out from the slip and rose to the first wave that came rolling in from the sound. It left the dog there in the water, the waves reaching up for its muzzle, it barking resounding off all the cliffs of the island, until the din lifted the wild seagulls into the air.

The barking ceased when Padraig's currach came crawling in from the hooker. The dog shifted its ground uneasily, its eyes still on the hooker which swung around slowly as the sails caught the wind. The dog let out a couple of deep troubled bays across the widening stretch of water. Then, as the currach ground against the slip, Padraig lashed out at it with his oar, forcing it to retreat away up the slip. It stopped to shake itself, whimpering and trembling all over, then turned and made away up to Bairbre. It pressed its sleek wet body against her skirt and turned an eye down on the man standing below in the overloaded currach.

Padraig clambered ashore. Holding the gob of the currach, he took a quick glance up at Bairbre from under his eyebrows. Then he turned to call the men on the quay to give him a hand. All the time he was unloading the currach, Bairbre stood staring out to where the hooker's brown sails were flitting along the distant blue coast of the mainland. We were afraid she would lay another curse on Padraig. Afraid we were. We try to forget that a man has been cursed, so that we can live on the same island with him. To tell the plain honest truth, the reason that we were so afraid of Padraig was that we could never forget that about him.

This time, Bairbre said not a word. When she turned to go, she came slowly down by the wall of the slip, past the cart which Padraig was busily loading. He kept working away, but he was watching her out of the corner of his eye. She stopped beside him, looking him full in the face. "*Muise, a Phadraig, nach tú an trua Mhuire*," said she, "'tis Mary's pity ye are!"

Not a word did he say as he swung a half barrel of porter up on the tail of the cart.

"Everything I had ye've taken from me," she went on. "Would ye not say to me now 'I forgive'?"

"Hold up!" Padraig bellowed, as the horse edged forward to reach for a tuft of roadside grass. He tugged viciously at the reins and the horse reared up with a rattle of chains. "Mind out there!" he called to Bairbre, as the white teeth grazed her head. And that was all! Bairbre turned away from him and began the long walk up to the village. The dog followed on her heels, turning those speckled stone eyes on us as it passed.

After that day, Bairbre seemed to lose all taste for the business. She sold off the stock she had and made no move to refill those empty sweet jars. No one said anything to her, but we did take it amiss, for after all it was our money which had started the shop. She took to spending long hours in the old ruined church that the monks from Rome had built in the time of the Saints. Walking up and down the mossy chancel, she'd spend her day telling her beads over and over. Now and then, she'd glance up at the sound of a thrush in the bushes that grew out of the chapel walls. She'd stop a long time watching him giving out his song and he swelling out his breast in the sunlight.

She was seen at dawn a few times, hurrying across the fields before the island was awake, moving with that quick graceful gait of hers, which made it so surprising to look into her face and find an old woman. Then one day, she was seen out west under the cliffs, climbing down over the black wet rocks to gather *feochans*. It's a sure sign of the bad times when a person goes to gather *feochans*, for it's barbarous food, shellfish, and fit only for the nourishment of hens and ducks. A few of the women called in to see her one night, to see what they could do for her. They stopped a moment in the doorway, watching her before they said, "God be within!" She was sitting on a stool, away out in the middle of the room, as if she could have been anywhere. The place was smoky and untidy (for like all who spent a spell in the boardinghouses of Bostonmass, Bairbre was never noted for tidiness). She seemed to be listening from a great distance to the tick-tock of the old clock over the hearth. Her hands rested happily on her knees. There wasn't a stir out of her until the dog suddenly moaned aloud in its sleep and she cocked a bright blue eye over at it. "Wisha, isn't it bad ye are!" she said with a humorous lift of her lip that drew all the lines of her face into a smile.

She rose up when she saw the women and made them welcome. She put down the kettle and wet a pot of tea. The women sat there all the evening, drinking cup after cup of tea and talking of this and of that. They might have been sitting there yet for all that they found out about Bairbre.

They dropped in several times after that. Bairbre always made them at home and talked politely with them, but they felt somehow that they were intruding on a gathering of her friends. They began to time their calls for when she'd be out saying her prayers in the old church. They'd leave in a few eggs for her, or a salted pollack or a loaf of fresh soda bread. Next time they'd come, they'd be surprised how little of the food was gone. It was only when we heard her great news that we realized that it was maybe because she had no need of mortal food.

A fine evening in spring it was when she told us. The men had come in at night setting out their spillets. They had tumbled dead tired into their beds, leaving the sea empty of boats and ships.

Bairbre was out gathering dung for her fire. She had wandered as far as the lonely western shore, when all of a sudden the slanting sun shone out as strong and as bright as at midday. She straightened up, amazed at the hush that had fallen on the waves and all the little birds that nested by the cliffs. There before her, lay a green and lovely island. She stood looking at it, at the sheep on the hills and the smoke curling out of the houses and the fat cows grazing in the pastures. It was so near that she could see the waves turning over on the strand. Men were walking there, dressed like great gentlemen in white town shirts. Behind them, the meadows shone as if each blade of grass was lit by the light of the sun. It was the brightness of it all which at last brought a tear to her eye. She blinked it away, but, alas, when she looked again, there was nothing. The late sunlight lay along the green tops of the waves, riding smoothly in to burst below the cliffs with the boom of an empty barrel. The twilight songs of the small birds broke out again from the short rough whispering grasses. The island was vanished away.

The light and stillness of it were still with Bairbre when she came to tell us. First, she paid a visit to the church to thank Almighty God for this promise of a happy death. Her story roused the men from their beds. It was many years since anyone had seen the land of youth and the island had talk of nothing else. The men gathered in the pub, soberly drinking Padraig's black stout. They listened to the old men talking of those in days gone by, whose eyes had been opened in the same way to the mercy of God. Padraig took no part in the talk. The scratch of his nib behind the counter made the men lower their voices to a whisper.

At the legal time, he rose up and began to close the shop. Seamus Rua, a big lump of a fellow home from England, refused to leave.

"Go on, now!" said Padraig, taking the glass that stood before Seamus, "'Tis the legal time and right well ye know it."

"A lot that ever worried you," said Seamus, "as long as there's drink to be sold and money taken in."

"'Twill be the legal time here from this out!" said Padraig, "I'm thinking that there's a great want of law and right thinking here on this island." He looked around at the silent faces of the men. "I never in all my born days heard such nonsense as was talked here tonight."

"Ye're not doubting Bairbre's word, man?" Seamus said, laying his two big hands down on the counter, as the men behind him murmured among themselves.

"I can't doubt what I never believed," said Padraig.

"*Anam 'un Diabhail,*" swore Seamus, grabbing hold of Padraig's jacket and twisting him nearer, "if I don't . . ."

"Easy," the men said, "easy now!"

Seamus drew the man tight up against him, then sent him spinning back against the shelves behind the bar. A bottle of whiskey crashed to the floor, a full bottle, still wrapped in tissue paper. Padraig stared down at it, fumbling at his jacket and trying to pull it straight.

"So ye're going to teach us law and order!" Seamus said, coming around the end of the counter and trailing his fingers along the black wood as he came.

"That's right," said Padraig, as the other man caught hold of him again, "I'll knock the nonsense out of yer heads, so I will. I and Father Kiely!" He brushed the hands off his jacket, roughly. "Now get out of here, you! And don't come back until you have proper respect for this house!"

That quietened Seamus for the night. It quietened the rest of us, too. We had no wish to let Father Kiely know anything of Bairbre's vision. Being a priest and a man from the mainland, we knew he wouldn't understand.

Padraig meant every word he said, as we found out the following Sunday, when he called the priest aside on the way to Mass. We knew from the way Father Kiely flounced out on to the altar, that he was only barely holding himself in till he got to the sermon.

"Are ye Christians at all?" was the first thing he flung at us. His angry blue eyes moved over us, back and forth, as if he was daring one of us to answer. Then he launched into his sermon. It was his best ever. We were all shaken after it, but deep inside us, we felt glad. We had judged him right. A priest and a mainlander would never understand us, not in this world anyway.

Padraig had a little smile on him as he left the church. He was pale, though, and his face was drawn as if he hadn't slept. He never looked any other way in the weeks that followed. He became a changed man. Every evening, he changed a little more, always in the direction of strictness. He closed his shop at the legal time, though there was no one on the island to set the law on him. The prices of the island stores came down little by little, until they were the same as those on the mainland. He kept a close watch on the men when they were in drinking, to make sure that no one drank more than was good for him. He even took the glass out of old Tom a'Gabha's hand and sent him home to milk his cow and have his supper with his daughter and son-in-law and their children. Old Tom would never again set foot inside the door of the shop, no matter what thirst was on him.

On Sundays, Padraig took to meeting Father Kiely at the boat slip. "What's the matter with ye?" the priest asked, as Padraig helped him ashore, for all the world as if he had been sent straight to us from

Rome, by order of His Holiness himself. "Is it gone in the hoofs ye think I am?" and the priest jumped ashore, as nimbly as a young lad.

Padraig was always first in the line for confessions. During the month of May, it was he who gave out the rosary in the church every evening. He gave it out, as if he was directing every pater and ave beyond the blue-veiled statue of Our Lady, beyond the great crucifix of Our Lord itself, away out the windows to the darkening summer sky. Afterward, he stood in the shadow of the porch, to stop the girls from making their dates with the men over the holy water font. In spite of it all, he lost little by little that upright priestly look. His shoulders began to stoop. His cheeks sagged out until the tiny blue veins barely held them. His hair began to go, until he had the look of an old scalded crow that a gale would sometimes carry over to the island from the mainland. The man was dwindling before our eyes, as if the very kernel was withering inside him.

He began to leave his light on all night. Those going the road would sometimes hear his voice raised in the litany of the saints. He chanted the responses to himself in Latin, like a chapter of priests. Seamus Rua, who was a bit of a rover after the girls, heard him late one night intoning the "Tantum Ergo" and then going through the whole ceremony of benediction. The hoarse rough voice gave Seamus the idea, God forgive him, that the poor man had drink taken. We all got the same idea when we saw Padraig upset the currach on a calm September day by clambering out of it in a panic and throwing himself into the sea. Only for the men on the slip, he'd have lost his life that day and maybe the best part of the island stores as well.

It was when he collapsed at the door of the church on a dark, wet Sunday in November, that we began to think that it wasn't the drink but the man's health was at him. Father Kiely hurried around from the vestry in the middle of his unvesting. The men lifted Padraig out of the puddle in which he lay and stretched him out on a fallen headstone. He was frothing a little at the mouth. The veins on his forehead stood out like cords that someone was trying to tear away, skin and all, from his skull. Father Kiely, who had some medical learning (he had to, for he crossed that sound in seas that no doctor with any sense would stir out in), examined the chest and pulse. When Padraig came round, the priest told him that the best thing he could do would be to see a specialist in the big town.

"But I can't, Father," said Padraig, "what about the island?"

"Ye'll get someone to look after the shop for ye."

"But 'tis not only the shop, Father . . ."

"'Tis all ye should be looking after," said the priest. "the island has been here long enough, God knows . . ." said he, with that mainlanders edge to his voice, "and 'twill be here long after . . ." and then he stopped himself. He was never a great man for tact, Father Kiely, no more than most men from the mainland.

"I can't, Father. I wouldn't know what would be going on."

"Please yourself, then." Father Kiely pulled the purple stole off his neck and pursed his lips to it, as he folded it, "only I won't be thanking you some dirty night when I'm dragged out of my bed to come over to you."

Those were hard words from a priest, but they had their effect. Padraig went away in the hooker the next time it came to the island. He left Jimín, a big lad now, in charge of the shop. He couldn't have made a better choice, for Jimín took to the shopkeeping as if it were second nature to him. And so, maybe, it is with some people.

Padraig hadn't been in the big town since he was a young lad. We wondered how he'd fare there, but we knew that he wasn't one to give us an account of his travels and the strange ways of the people he'd meet. A cousin of the weaver's, however, has a public house in the town and it was he who told us afterward what happened. After Padraig had been in to see the specialist, he came straight to the public house and ordered himself a large brandy. He hardly opened his mouth all day, except to order more drink. Even when the woman of the house came downstairs, hotfoot, for news of her people on the island, Padraig had nothing to say for himself. He even had a bit of a dispute about the bill when he was leaving. "But don't ye know, man," he said, when he was charged the usual price, "that I'm a shopkeeper, too?" He thought his state in life entitled him to drink at trade prices.

"If I charged the way you charged, ye'd be paying as much again," the publican replied. Padraig didn't let that go. He argued the toss for a long time, but he met his match in the publican. When it was time to go down to the harbor, he left the house with more drink inside him than was good for his pocket or for him. And he looked more out of sorts with the world than he ever was, even when sober.

It was a different man altogether that arrived back to us on the island. He came up the slip, flapping his red hands at us, as if he was motioning us to kneel down for his blessing. The men in the currach tossed his homespun coat and his blue town suit out on to the slip after him. He let them lie there at the water's edge. He was looking at us, smiling and swaying his head from side to side, as if he were waiting for silence. Then slowly, he folded down on to the slip. A wave reached up and almost touched the tips of his black boots.

We carried him to his house, laid him down, and forced brandy down his throat. He opened his eyes wide and stared at us, from one to another of us, men, women and children crowded into his bedroom. Some of us began to drift toward the door before those hot yellow eyes swung around to us and marked us out.

"Where's Bairbre?" he asked in a whisper. The women crossed themselves, thinking his mind was wandering.

"Bairbre!" he said.

The men withdrew to the kitchen to decide who was to go for the priest. They could hear him repeating the name over and over again, his voice falling away to silence. Then suddenly, as if he had been jerked awake, he shouted out, "Listen! Let ye all tell her. I saw it, the land of youth!"

The men came crowding back to the door. There was a great hubbub for a few minutes, then everybody went quiet, watching him. Not one of us had any doubt but that he was telling the truth. One look at his white face was enough and it staring past us into the glass of death.

We told him we were sending for the priest.

"No, no," said he, "what do I want with him? 'Tis Bairbre I want."

But we insisted. We were afraid of what Father Kiely would say if we didn't. We sent three of the fastest oarsmen off to the mainland.

The men went back through the kitchen to the shop. They sat on the benches around the walls and Jimín served them with stout. They tossed the money into a pint glass on the counter. Then they sat back, watching that glass, wondering which of the many cousins of various degrees would empty it and run the coins through his fingers. They could hear the drone of Padraig's voice from the bedroom, as the women prepared him for the last sacraments. Telling them of the vision he was, repeating the story over and over, like a man talking in his sleep. Toward evening, when he was washed and shaved and tidied, a candle was brought in and he fell silent. He lay on the white bed under the flickering light, his narrow hands clasped together on his breast. A little smile touched his face, which was as white as if it had been dusted with flour. He looked like a man readied for the coffin.

It was the quiet time of the day. The weak western light had faded off the dark stone walls and the white fronts of the houses. Suddenly down the street came the quick patter of bare feet and the shriek of the children, who all the afternoon had been constrained indoors. They came with wide-eyed faces, their voices wild. They could feel the night coming over the sea from the east, slipping from wave to wave.

The mothers in the bedroom made a move to go quieten them. They had hardly risen to their feet when they stopped all of a sudden at the sight of Bairbre in the doorway. She had her shawl about her face and her head bent, as if she were waiting. Padraig was roused by the silence in the room. He raised himself on his elbow. He was laughing, great gulping sobs of laughter. He pointed his long finger at Bairbre in the doorway.

"There she is now!" said he, "the divil's own liar!"

"Don't, Padraig," she said, "don't take it from me."

"Liar!" he screamed. "But I've seen it. I tell ye, I've seen the land of . . ." His eyes went hard. His mouth shut tight, then fell open loosely. We heard the death rattle as the women eased his body back on to the bed.

"The land of youth?" asked Bairbre. The women nodded their heads. "Oh, thanks be to God," she said, as she sank on to her knees.

She began the keening. The sound was taken up by all the other women. The harsh measured wailing filled the room and brought all the men in the kitchen silently to their feet. It passed out over the litter of the yard, the crates and empty casks. It filled the street and mingled for a moment with the voices of the children, making a strange harmony. When the children turned in silence to face it, it rose above them, taking wing into the dark. Away out on the sea, four men in a currach heard it. The three oarsmen stayed their oars and crossed themselves. The man huddled in the stern raised his head and said in a loud voice, "*Requiescat in pace.*" Then the sound died away over the dark moving waters.

Padraig was buried after Mass the next Sunday. Six men came out from the crowd at the door of the church, went quickly beneath the bier, and swung it up on their shoulders. The white-draped coffin moved away over the heads of the crowd, swaying as it passed through the church gates and down the rocky path between high stone walls. The sun shone on the shawls and the red flannel skirts of the women walking two by two with their men. It shone on the girls in their wide blue skirts, lowering their eyes and smiling as they passed the stares of the young men at the gate. It shone on the bare-legged boys, whose hands were joined in prayer, but whose eyes were alert as the eyes of sparrows. We were all there, following this man, who had once for all his faults been one of us. And after us all, her eyes cast down, her lips moving in prayer, came Bairbre.

On the way to the graveyard, the funeral passed Padraig's house. The bearers laid down their load and wiped their faces with their caps. We knelt down to say a decade of the rosary, then moved on again. The graveyard was before us on a sandy hill, headstones pressed into its summit like a crown of thorns.

Father Kiely was waiting in his white surplice beside the hole in the ground. He said the prayers and the coffin was lowered in. The women sobbed, as they do whenever any human clay is given back to the earth. There was no keening now, for Father Kiely was there. All around could be heard the murmur of Christian prayer.

Two cousins of Padraig took up shovels, spat on their hands, and sent the sand and light clay drumming down on the coffin lid. One of them was getting on in years. The crowd watched him weakening, as the sweat ran down his temples into his eyes and blinded him. The young man worked away like a machine. When they were finished, they threw away their shovels and stooped to lay down the top sod. Father Kiely closed his book, blessed himself, and turned away.

The crowd broke up. They moved through the long grasses to find the graves of their own people. They knelt beside the headstones. A few flung themselves sobbing on the ground, as if this new death had brought back memories of the other deaths. Bairbre was the only one to stay by Padraig's grave, a rosary beads twined around her withered hands.

She rose when the dog pressed itself against her. It whined a few times, very softly. Its head moved from side to side, making its eyes glint in the sun. When it moved forward to root in the fresh clay, she called out sharply and it turned to follow her.

We looked after them as they went step by step down the path. Below them, the surf beat against the barren cliffs. Beyond, stretched the dim and empty sea. Thinking we were of Bairbre and of the man that was gone. Nobody had told her and we knew that nobody would ever tell her of the terrible vision he had seen. For the land he had seen was as rocky, black, and treacherous as our own. And it was set across the sound from Bairbre's land, on the dark and sunless side.

An Outpost of Rome

"Yes," said Father Conroy, "we have the good here and we have the bad. Just like anywhere else. But I'll tell you one thing about them." Suddenly rapping his pipe against the empty grate, he shot a baffled glance at the shining shoes of the young man who sat drinking his whiskey. "I'll tell you one thing. The truth isn't in them!"

The young man stirred, as if the remark had been aimed at him, as indeed it had. He shifted his gaze to Father Tobin, the curate, and eased himself back as far as the visitor's chair would allow.

"What's the shooting like this year, Father?" he asked brightly.

"Haw?" Father Tobin had been leaning forward, staring at the glass of lemonade between his palms, as if there was something wrong with it.

"I bet there's any amount of grouse in these hills?"

"Oh, 'tis fair. The shooting is fair." The wrinkles tightened again, lifting the eyebrows back into the bald forehead. "So they say."

"You don't mean to tell me you're not a sporting man?"

"Haw?"

Father Conroy rose at that, thrusting his pipe into his pocket. "I think we might go up . . . Oh! Don't let me rush ye." The young man had hurriedly raised his glass. "How about another?"

"No thank you, Father."

Whiskey! thought Father Conroy. When the fellow said sherry, I should have told him I kept it for the lady friends. But that would have proved nothing. It's so easy to shock even the Catholics nowadays.

"You're not coming, Father?" he told his curate. God knows what Father Tobin had blurted out on the way up from the curate's house in the village.

"No, Father." The hands shifted on the lemonade glass, but the long body still leant out of the hard-backed chair, supporting that wrinkled, downward-gazing brow. "There's a few things I should rightly be getting at."

Yes, thought Father Conroy, my typewriter! By the look of him, he's thinking up another letter to the papers about the army of occupation up north. "True Gael," how are ye?! As if I didn't know!

Father Conroy waited by the door, as the young man came drifting across the room, the heavy briefcase his ballast.

"After you, Father!"

"No, after you, Mr. Bourke!"

Bourke! thought Father Conroy gloomily, as he watched the cavalry-twill-clad legs out-distancing each other down the hall, like a pair of fumbled calipers. He felt for the small business card in his pocket, confirming the worst. It was the "o," which had first sounded the warning. Burke, now, was a good name, one that could always be relied on. But that "o" . . . It had been added back in the darkness of the Penal days by the branch that had defected. Still, one could never be sure of a name these days, the way the Catholics aped the affectations of the others.

The kitchen door opened behind him, noiselessly, but he knew it had opened. The whole house felt warmer, brighter, richer with the smell of stew. He knew she was standing there, akimbo, on her own private drawbridge.

"Father!" He came to a halt, like a well-drilled squad, one, two! "Will ye be wantin' him," a jerk of the thumb toward the legs now gliding down the front steps, "for lunch?"

"I don't think so. No! I don't think so."

"Better be sure, Father." Misunderstandings had happened before.

"No," he said.

"Very well, Father!" On his own head be it. He felt the door closing behind him, leaving the house in outer darkness.

"Shall we drive up, Father?" The young man's hand waited on the door of his car (a well-used Austin, model of three years back. Firm can't be doing all that well, thought Father Conroy. Serve them right, trading under false colors. If they are!)

"Drive? But sure 'tis only up the hill here!"

The young man hesitated before he slammed the door shut, just long enough to give Father Conroy a brief glance in at the dashboard.

"It's no trouble, Father. I assure you."

"I walk it a dozen times a day," snapped the priest. He had duly noticed the silver St. Christopher badge dominating the dashboard. "Unless you want to."

They can't be doing business with the Protestants anyway, with that up. Dear Lord, he thought, could I be wrong after all? A sin against charity it would be, to judge a man on so little evidence. He walked on ahead, afraid that the young man would guess at his shame.

"I'd say I'm right all the same, Father." The young man suddenly caught up with him.

"How d'ye mean?" He could never stop the color rising when someone stared directly into his face. It flowed into the pockmarked cheeks as unexpectedly as if a withered old crab apple were suddenly to redden.

"I mean about the grouse."

"Oh?"

It was the young man's turn to blush. His eyes were feverish. He seemed to be stuck in a conversational bunker, flailing away as he tried to get back on the fairway. His tumbler of whiskey had been generous.

Now's the time, thought Father Conroy. But the subtle questions eluded him. His tumbler had also been generous and he wasn't used to whiskey before lunch. "You shoot, yourself, then?" was the best he could come up with.

"Oh, no, I don't get the time usually, though I have been out a few times with my principal."

"Ah!" Father Conroy saw his chance and leaped in. "That's Mr. —?"

"Mr. White."

Baffled! The name was as interdenominational as you could get. Father Conroy tried again, a shot in the dark.

"How did you get time for that?"

"Oh, well, I get back to the city weekends, Saturdays, I mean." He ran on recklessly, "Mr. White, of course, wouldn't go shooting on—"

"Yes, I see." Proof positive! Or almost! What Catholic layman would dream he was desecrating the Sabbath with a shotgun? None that Father Conroy had ever met. He shook his head as he trudged on. Maybe it was the lowest tender, but it was thumbs down.

At the brow of the hill, the young man was stopped by the view of the bay. Father Conroy pushed open the churchyard gate and waited.

"Are they from your parish, Father?" He was pointing to the little boats rocking slowly in pairs, away out on the gray sea. Father Conroy's sharp eyes scanned the boats. He nodded.

"It must be nice having fishermen, Father?"

"Why so!"

"They're such good people. Honest people!"

Father Conroy glanced quickly at the overlong sideburns, the yellow tie, the tapered suit somewhat ruffled at the rear by the car seat.

"Ye get all kinds," he said and stopped. Maybe they were that simple, city people, in spite of their extraordinary getup. Maybe the lad was a genuine poor fellow, that one of his own parishioners could run rings around. Father Conroy glanced at the young man affectionately. He had a soft spot for simple innocent people, he met them so seldom. It was a great pity about the religion, though. And then, he thought of the St. Christopher badge. He looked away uneasily at the bay. He felt like a judge before whom both prosecution and defense had laid a cast-iron case.

His uneasiness grew when the young man followed him out from the vestry and casually bobbed a knee before the altar. Having surveyed the altar in silence, the fellow opened the briefcase and laid out the plans on the altar step. A propelling pencil suddenly appeared in his hand.

"Well, now, Father, it won't be hard to improve on this. I take it you've decided on the Carrara?"

"No, the Sicilian," said Father Conroy austerely. He had written to his sister, a retired nurse up in Dublin, asking her which was the better value for the money, Carrara or Sicilian. Her reply had begun: "Dear James, What memories your letter brought back! I remember well the day I accompanied poor Mr. Humphreys (the Englishman—heart) to view the marble quarries at Carrara. The sun was shining beautifully as we reached our destination and all along the railway line, the slabs of marble were gleaming as white as snow. We were taken, first of all, to a charming little village called . . ." and so on for two pages to "your ever-loving sister in J. C., Eileen." A postscript followed. "I can't tell you anything about the Sicilian, James, as poor Mr. H. would never go there. He thought the people were not very nice." Repelled as much by Anglo-Saxon prejudice as by the thought of a blazing white sun altar in his church, Father Conroy had plumped for the Sicilian.

"The Sicilian, Father?" said the young man, pursing his lips. He reached into his briefcase. "In that case, you'll probably be interested in a slightly different design I have here. It's very up-to-date, the latest thing, in fact, and not quite so—severe. We've found it to be very popular all over the country."

"With whom?" asked Father Conroy, hopefully.

"With people who know, Father. Why, only the other day, I got a contract from the Ursulines for their school chapel, a smaller altar, of course, but—"

"Yes," said Father Conroy, losing interest. You could never go by the nuns.

"Now, in the plans we submitted to you, as you'll see here—" The young man was well out of the bunker now, driving confidently down the fairway. Father Conroy watched him glumly. "This, of course, would be somewhat more expensive than the one we tendered for, but when I show you this photograph, Father, I think you'll agree—"

"Yes," said Father Conroy. How were nuns, poor things, to recognize a Freemason if they saw one? But did Freemasons place their cars under the patronage of St. Christopher? Maybe they did? How was one to know these things, never having met one of the breed before?

"Yes," he said angrily, as the young man looked up at him with a query. What difference did it make whether "Church Requisites, Limited" was a Masonic outfit or not? He would be accepting the lowest tender in good faith. And anyway, a small Protestant profit was probably better in the sight of God than an exorbitant Catholic one. Still . . .

"Yes, he nodded, as the young man laid out the more expensive plan and quickly put out of sight the one tendered for.

Still, at the back of his mind, he had a picture of a group of parish priests, swaddled in sweaters and gaberdines, stamping their feet at the first tee. As he approached, he could see one of them turn his face aside to mutter something. The others hid their grins as they lifted their clubs in practice swings. He had a good idea what the joke would be. "Hey, fellows!" the wit would have said, "watch out for Conroy's masonic grip!" Or, maybe, "Don't let him talk you into a cut-price altar. He gets them through the Brotherhood!" Father Conroy stirred with dislike for his colleagues. Sheep, that's all they were . . .

"No," he said suddenly, interrupting the flow of sales talk.

"I beg your pardon, Father?"

"No, I've got to think this over."

"As you wish, Father. But when you compare this with the other design, I think you'll find that for the extra money—"

"I mean the whole business."

"What?" The young man's face was blank. "But you accepted our tender, Father—"

"I didn't mean, I—" He hadn't signed any contract, not yet.

"But, Father, I'm afraid—" The young man hesitated, unwilling to utter anything so unpleasant as a threat. Yes, thought Father Conroy, I did accept it. Maybe they'd have a case. "The Masons v. Father Conroy"—he saw it all headlined. Dear Lord, what a mess!

"The diocesan inspector wasn't in favor of sanctioning this at all," he muttered. That was true, the first time the inspector had called.

"I think you'll find, Father," the young man surveyed the drab, off-white timber structure, something in the style of a kitchen dresser, which the village carpenter's grandfather had made, "when he sees it, that he'll agree that it's in bad shape."

"Maybe," said Father Conroy. "In bad shape" were the words the he himself had used the second time the inspector had called, this time to be shown a number of small holes, which had appeared beneath the Gospel side of the altar. Pat Lacey, the village carpenter, had diagnosed them to be "the worm," against which even a diocesan inspector had no argument. (Father Conroy had heard through his sources that Pat had changed his mind on hearing that the new altar was not to be of timber. He was going about the parish, saying that his grandfather's altar was good enough to see Father Conroy into the clay, hinting too that the holes were not wormholes at all, but had been drilled by some unknown person, meaning Father Conroy.)

"Let me talk to him," said the young man eagerly.

"Oh, no, no. 'Tis too much trouble."

"I can easily call on him on my way back."

"No, no. I think I can maybe—talk him round."

"Good!" said the young man. "Now, Father, if you'd mind casting your eye over this!" The propelling pencil hurried away over the plan, drawing Father Conroy's eyes after it. "As you can see, I'm going to face the risers with Midleton."

"Yes," said Father Conroy sullenly.

"Oh, it's the latest thing, Father. I have a sample here to show you."

Father Conroy looked at the miniature slab of marble, white kidneys in a background of dried blood. "Yes," he said, hopelessly.

"It got great praise, Father, when we used it for the Franciscans' new church at Drumcannon."

The Franciscans! thought Father Conroy. What did they know of the world, who was a Mason and who was not? You could never quote the Franciscans.

"I guarantee you, Father, you'll have crowds coming here just to have a look at it."

"I don't want crowds."

"You could sell them souvenirs, postcard photos. That's what the Franciscans did."

"No," snapped Father Conroy.

"Of course, you're right, Father, to think of your own people. After all, it's for them you're getting it."

Yes, thought Father Conroy. And hard enough it would be to coax the money out of them. If they knew it was put up by the Masons! If Pat Lacey ever found out! He watched the young man resolutely checking the dimensions of the sanctuary. There must be some way of getting out of it.

"It'll do wonders here." The young man folded his rule and patted it back into his hip pocket. "I really mean it, Father." He strode back enthusiastically across the sanctuary, stopping just in time to bob his knee before the altar. He picked up the briefcase and stood, swinging it against his thigh. "Unless you'd care to see another design, Father? I have it here, though it may be just a little expensive for your taste."

"No, no," said Father Conroy, moving toward the vestry.

"Well, I don't want to be taking up any more of your time, Father." The briefcase was set firmly on the vestry table. A fountain pen had appeared in the hand, the gold-mounted comrade of the propelling pencil.

"Let's go down to the house," said Father Conroy.

"But, Father—"

"Stay and have lunch."

"That's very kind of you, Father, but—" The fountain pen reluctantly disappeared. "Are you sure it will be all right? With herself?" So he was used to priests' housekeepers!

"Of course!" lied Father Conroy.

Outside, at the gate, the young man paused, head upraised in a city man's pose. He sniffed eagerly at the sea breeze, which stirred the branches of the oak trees around the churchyard.

"It's a fine situation, Father. A situation—and a church—like this deserve a good altar. The best that money can buy!"

"Let's go!" said Father Conroy.

Approaching the house, Father Conroy thought he heard the clatter of the typewriter. He went up the steps to the hall door, two at a time. Father Tobin, however, was abstractedly refilling the glass of lemonade. "All set, Father?" he asked, slowly lowering himself into the hard-backed chair.

"Not quite." Father Conroy looked suspiciously into the china-blue eyes.

"We've decided the other altar would be more suitable," the young man put in, answering Father Tobin's look of inquiry.

"Oh? How much will that be?"

"It's the better altar." The young man was curt. Evidently used to dealing with curates too!

"More expensive?" asked Father Tobin.

"Naturally. As it's better."

"I see," pursued Father Tobin, "but how much—"

"Father Tobin," said Father Conroy, "would you mind telling Katie that Mr. Bourke is staying to lunch?"

"Oh?" Again that curious glance, which Father Conroy quickly quelled. "Right you are, Father."

He returned a moment later, jerking a thumb in the direction of the kitchen. "She wants to see yourself, Father."

Katie waited at the far end of the hall, one hand on the door of her kitchen, the other on her hip. He knew the pose. She said nothing until he approached and halted to await his interview.

"Ye want him to stay for lunch, Father?"

"That's what I said."

"Ye didn't say it to me, Father." On any other day, that might have been the last word.

"I'm saying it now," he burst out. "Now get the lunch. And quick!"

"Mercy on us!" The hand flew to the breast, to ward off any assault. As he turned on his heel, the kitchen door slammed shut behind him.

"The father of Irish republicanism!" Father Tobin was saying, "Surely, ye've heard of the great John Mitchel?"

"John Mitchel!" The young man was bluffing valiantly. "Yes, of course, Father, but my history is a little—"

"John Mitchell was the man who—" Father Tobin, long arm draped over his chair, was about to get into his stride.

"Father!" said the parish priest sharply. Father Tobin slumped back into his chair, called to heel.

In the long silence, Father Conroy poured himself another drink, a stiff one. He motioned the decanter toward the young man, who shook his head. "Come on!" said Father Conroy, roughly. He splashed the whiskey into the glass reluctantly extended toward him. Father Tobin rose to go.

"You stay too, Father." He might have need of an ally, even Father Tobin.

"What about—" Father Tobin motioned toward the kitchen.

"Tell her you're staying too," said Father Conroy and he lifted his glass with satisfaction, as the reluctant curate left the room.

He downed the drink recklessly. I'm going to find out, he told himself. Even if it comes to a court case, I'm going to find out. Be hanged to the village gossips, be hanged to the wits of the diocese! Watch the fellow closely from now on, he told himself. With the help of God, he'll let it slip.

The young man, however, let nothing slip as they waited for lunch. As the priests listened gloomily, he talked about other parish priests he had done business with, all in distant dioceses. From the next room, Father Conroy could hear the cutlery being slapped on the table. Father Tobin shifted apprehensively at every sound. Please God, thought Father Conroy, make that whiskey work! But the young man prattled on, only very occasionally pausing to take a cautious sip. All the time, Father Conroy felt the fumes within him rising higher and higher, until they mushroomed up through his brain. To keep a firm grip on his purpose, he lowered his head and fixed his eyes intently on those shining black shoes, which began to shift uneasily as if they were on hot coals.

A single knock at the door summoned them to lunch. As they entered the cold dining room, the door to the kitchen swung sullenly to. There was going to be trouble, he could see that. She might even give her notice. Well, if it was to be, let it be. Only he wished the final scene was over.

"Yes," the young man was saying, "it's so much more satisfactory with the seculars. Not like the nuns or the order men. No shilly-shallying. They know how to do business."

Without warning, Father Conroy swung into saying grace, and caught the young man off his guard. It was a shabby trick; he knew that even as he did it. The young man, however, recovered quickly and made a vague circular movement with his right hand. It could have been that of a slipshod Catholic crossing himself after a couple of large whiskies. Father Conroy grunted as they took their seats. Foiled again! Beyond the kitchen door, he could hear the kitchen range being raked out, the symbolic start of the cold war. He dipped the ladle in the stew and filled the young man's plate. Well, let it come, he told himself. Let them all come.

The young man had run out of clerical shoptalk. He looked from the heated face of the parish priest to the frowning forehead of Father Tobin, now centered on the dinner plate. He watched the curate's tireless fork pursuing a lump of meat, which finally yielded in the lee of banks of cabbage and mashed potatoes. "Well done, Father!" seemed the proper thing to say, but instead the young man blurted out, "I was surprised, Father, to hear that you weren't interested in the gun."

Father Conroy let his breath out slowly. He glanced carefully at Father Tobin, who had lowered the fork to his plate, releasing the lump of meat, as if he was restoring it to its natural habitat. Nobody spoke.

"I mean, with all those grouse," stammered the young man.

No, thought Father Conroy, no, it wouldn't be any use to tell him why Father Tobin was exiled here. You couldn't expect even a Catholic to believe it. That a priest would be diehard enough to appeal to his English congregation to help buy arms for the IRA in order to blow up more English barracks? No, it wouldn't do. Of course, it had been Easter week and Father Tobin was an excitable man. Still, the story was too out of the ordinary to use as a decent test of a man's faith.

The young man was picking nervously at his stew, his face scarlet. Poor fellow, thought Father Conroy, suddenly sympathetic. He was about to break the silence, when Father Tobin got there before him.

"What about this offertory table, Mr. Bourke?" The tone was magnanimous, almost jovial.

"What, Father?"

"The offertory table you're supposed to give us?"

"I'm afraid I don't understand, Father?"

"I thought you contractors always throw in a little something. You know! For goodwill and all that!"

"Not my firm, Father."

"Oh?"

"You see, as I explained to the parish priest, we prefer to cut our charges to the minimum than to offer inducements, which after all . . ."

"Besides, Father," said Father Conroy severely. "I wasn't aware that we needed an offertory table?"

"No, muttered Father Tobin, "maybe not." And he centered his forehead again on the plate and began the long methodical search for the lump of meat that was still at large.

Katie broke the silence, bursting in the door as if she'd been leaning against it. She dealt out the tapioca pudding (Father Conroy's least favorite) and a cup of coffee to each man. Then she gathered up the dinner plates and bore them away, as if they were not only soiled but unclean.

Father Conroy pushed back his plate ostentatiously and reached for his pipe. He was going to make things hot for someone, he promised himself that. When the others were ready, he stood up and took his coffee into the parlor. As he set it down carefully, he noticed that the fountain pen had reappeared in the young man's hand. Father Conroy cleared his throat, a rasping, brutal performance, which he sometimes found useful in getting a congregation into the right mood. The young man had drawn the briefcase toward him, snapped it open, and was stealthily reaching within. Father Conroy ignored the movement. He had thought of a final test. He was going to risk all, in a gambler's throw. He leant back in his chair, thumbs in his waistcoat pocket, a raconteur's pose. His voice, when it came, was merciless.

"Those old oak trees, Mr. Bourke, that you were admiring back in the churchyard?"

"Yes, Father?" The hand stayed its search.

"I had the divil's own trouble over one of those same trees." He paused to light the pipe, his eye on the hand, daring it to move. "This tree grew right up against the east window. It was that dark inside that I was hard put to it to read the missal at Mass. And, as we haven't got the electricity—"

"Yes, Father." The hand began to move again, then stopped, waiting indulgently.

"So what did I do but decide to cut it down. Well, I sent up Pat Lacey to do the job and, bedad, he was back to me within the half hour. 'I couldn't do it, Father,' says he. 'Why not?' says I. 'There's a crowd of the men gathered up there, Father, and they won't let me.' 'In the name of God, why not?' says I. ''Tis not my place to say, Father, but maybe ye'd best go up and talk to them yerself.' So up I went."

He paused to relight the pipe. The hand took advantage of the pause to draw forth the contract form, a single daring movement.

"There was a crowd there all right, idlers mostly and a few of the troublemakers. 'What's this all about?' says I. Well, ye know the way they are. They shuffled their feet and stood behind one another, until at last a voice spoke up somewhere. ''Tis Thady Moran, Father. 'Tis growing alongside his people's grave.' 'Where's Thady?' says I, 'let him come out and speak for himself.' Well, out he came at long last and he bent over his stick. 'Ye're not going to do it, Father!' says he. ''Tis my church,' says I, ''tis in my care and I'll see that it gets air and light.' ''Tis the grave of my people, Father.' 'The church must come first,' says I. 'Oh, no, Father. The church would never want us to disturb our dead.' 'Oh, what nonsense!' says I, losing my temper with him, 'and will ye tell me how'twould be disturbing yer dead?' 'How do I know,' says he, and he shaking his big blackthorn stick at me, 'or how do you know, Father, but that that tree isn't growing through the stomach of me poor dead mother?'"

Father Conroy looked up as the young man drew in his breath. "The stomach of his poor dead mother!" said Father Conroy with relish. "'Down with the tree,' says I. That started it. I thought some of them were going to come at me with their sticks, while others began groaning as if I'd beaten the heads of them. In the middle of the hullaballoo, I heard Pat Lacey's voice at my elbow. 'Maybe, Father,' says he, 'maybe if ye were to tell him I could use the timber for the new altar, maybe Thady would be willing . . . ' 'Get thee behind me,' says I, and I turned on my heel and left them there. Well, the tree came down. And the next day, I put the ads in the papers, asking for tenders." He rapped the pipe against the empty grate. "So that's what you're up against," he said, turning to the young man with a cruel smile.

Now! he was thinking, if the fellow's a Catholic, he'll split his sides. Why, the pubs were in a roar for weeks over the story of those devils using their holy dead to get Pat Lacy the contract. But the Protestants, now, wouldn't see it like that. They're so respectful toward death, it always has to wear a straight face for them. Father Conroy stared down at the black shining shoes and waited.

The young man gulped, then shut his mouth tight. He looked quickly toward Father Tobin, but the frowning forehead gave no help. Then suddenly, just in time, his hand made a vague circular gesture. "Lord save us, Father," he muttered.

Oh, God! thought Father Conroy. A city Catholic! Why didn't I think of that? The smile faded from his lips, as he watched the hands picking at the contract form. Was there any real difference between them? Catholic or Protestant, the city made them all the same. Add everything up and it comes to money! And even if the fellow was a masonic imposter, did it matter much? A devil to cast out devils! A step, a very small step toward the truth! Father Conroy snorted, stuffed the pipe in his pocket, and rose, reaching out his hand. "Give us the form," said he.

The young man clung to it a moment. Then, hesitantly, he handed it over. Father Conroy took it to the table and signed it with a flourish.

Outside, the young man shook hands with a sickly smile and got into the car. As it lurched forward, the St. Christopher badge slipped from the dashboard. His farewell wave broke off in midair as he hastily caught the badge and pushed it back with the palm of his hand. Father Conroy turned away, in his mind a vision of a group of parish priests, swinging their clubs and smiling on the first tee. He found himself facing the apprehensive but admiring gaze of Father Tobin.

"How did ye know, Father?" he asked his curate curtly.

"Haw?"

"How did ye know he was a Protestant?"

"Not Protestant, Father."

"No?" His heart rose, just for a moment.

"Some class of a Presbyterian, Father."

Father Conroy angrily waved aside the irrelevance.

"How did ye know?" he demanded.

"I asked him, Father, and he told me. I asked him right out as soon as he came."

"You did?"

"Yes, Father, John Mitchel was a Presbyterian, Father, the first republican!"

"Oh, confound John Mitchel!"

"Oh, no, Father!" The frowning forehead lowered on him reproachfully. "Oh, no!" And as he passed in, to carry on the unequal battle, the curate turned to follow, the squire, bearing the windmill-breaking lance. "They're a very honest people, Father, the Presbyterians. I mean—they must have been!"

The Pill

There was no doubt about it; several people had seen the young man tiptoe down the steps of number twenty-four. As the door eased shut behind him, he half-turned to whisper something back to whoever was within, almost kicking over the milk bottles, which had been left on the bottom step only a few minutes before. Then he straightened his tie, pushed at his tousled hair and, as he reached the street and turned toward the bus stop, ran his hand down—yes, this seemed the give-away—to check surreptitiously the buttons of his fly.

The elder Miss Byrne opposite, who had been dressing for eight o'clock Mass, was all for dialing 999 (she had wanted to for years), but Miss Eva was sure the man couldn't be a burglar. Why, she asked, would a burglar hurry out, as if he'd just been wakened by the milk-man? And besides, who let him out?

There was only one answer to that one, as Mr. Shannon told Mrs. Shannon with a tolerant chuckle. He stared over the curtain of the bay window and poured into his capacious trousers first one, then the other, vast wool-clad leg. "While the cat's away—" he rumbled, "By God, that's a good one!"

Mrs. Shannon was anything but tolerant.

"The idea of it!" she exclaimed, yet once more, though fortunately, she was incapable of really grasping the idea of it, "I can't believe it! Why, she's only—My God, I can't believe it!"

"Even the mousiest will play!" continued her lord and master, struck by an unusual flash of mental lightning. His delight showed that the phrase would last all day, if not longer.

Seriously, though, it was a problem. How were Mr. and Mrs. Casey to be told that, while they were up in Belfast at the dinner dance of the Institute of Cost and Works Accountants, a young man was spending the night with their Siobhán? Just to make sure that it was, indeed, Siobhán, those who had seen the man's early departure, together with several other hastily summoned witnesses, watched the front door of number twenty-four as school time drew near. Sure enough, at ten minutes to nine, Siobhán emerged, satchel under one arm, and came demurely down the steps. As she reached the street, she put a hand to the top button of her plum-colored blazer, as if suddenly conscious of prying eyes.

"Minx!" exclaimed the elder Miss Byrne.

"Little bitch!" Mrs. Shannon spat, from her corner of the dining-room window.

Whistling uneasily, Mr. Shannon swayed back and forth with his hands sunk in his pockets and noted with interest that that top button was under some stress. Miss Eva merely shook her head and said, under her breath, "No!" and again, more definitely, "No!"

Father Fitzpatrick was approached. He listened gravely to all they had to say, then shook his grizzled head. Sometime before, he had been prevailed upon by a deputation, which included some of those present, to inveigh against mixed bathing at the swimming pool. Against his better judgement, he duly inveighed. Later, when he went to see the effect, he was delayed at the ticket office to allow six sopping-wet Franciscans to scramble into their habits. He was going to make sure he was walked into nothing else.

Nan Casey was duly told, not in so many words, of course, though everyone did their little bit to help. She flushed at first, went very silent, then suddenly burst out laughing—she had rather a nice laugh—and said, "No, it was ridiculous!" The charge wasn't pressed; it was simply left lie there, just enough of it to keep her restless and to make her turn suddenly on Siobhán, several times during the day, and as suddenly turn away again.

It was left to her to tell Mr. Casey, which duty she had every intention of avoiding, if she could. Her trip to Belfast had been very pleasant; the hotel had been good and the entrance of their breakfast trays, borne by two smiling, clear-voiced northern maids, had established the honeymoon luxury she sought in all trips away from home. There was generally a reaction on their return—that was only to be expected—but she knew how to deal with Tom's grumpiness, too.

And, indeed, he was grumpy enough after tea, when he took some papers out of his briefcase and began to look at them, not even turning the pages, just looking at them as he sucked his empty pipe. When Siobhán came in, at nine, after putting away her schoolbooks, he grunted without looking around, "Geometry, I suppose?"

"No," she smiled, "QED's tonight. Some Falernian wine, though."

"Hah?" he roused himself, startled.

"Horace, that's all, but you wouldn't know anything about that."

I'd know about it, all right," he grumbled, as she kissed the top of his head. When she nuzzled her thick, chestnut hair against his ear, however, he smiled and held her against him for a moment.

"Goodnight, Mummy," she said and turned away smiling, but Nan left down her knitting, caught her hand and drew her down to kiss her with unusual warmth. It was a great relief to know that there would be nothing to tell him, after all, that things would not be spoiled.

He went to bed early with a copy of *Time* magazine and grumbled several times at her delay. She undressed, however, at her usual pace, brushed her hair and, just in case, took a pill from under the odds and ends of jewelry in the tortoiseshell box on the dressing table. There were only four left, but she had got more in Belfast. He switched off the light and turned away, as she got in, heaving the clothes about him. She waited a while, snuggled up close to him, then slipped a tentative hand inside his pajama top and after a while, he wasn't grumpy any more. In fact, it was even better than Belfast.

And yet, the question remained. Whenever she met Miss Byrne out for her two o'clock walk, pushing dead leaves off the pavement with the point of her umbrella, whenever Mr. Shannon lifted his hat to her, taking the lid off a gamey smile, she knew that it was there, waiting to be met and decisively rejected. Oh, yes, rejected, she was sure of that. Siobhán was a model child, in every evening soon after school, humming placidly as she helped with the washing-up, bed at nine after her homework. She didn't steal makeup or turn on Radio Luxembourg or do any of the things, which all the stodgier matrons of the neighborhood complained of. Nan did find that a black bra of her own was unaccountably missing, but the daily could had mislaid that. And anyway, any questions about it might have led to a discussion, which Nan had hitherto shirked. She had never had any trouble, herself, with the facts of life, which she had always rather enjoyed without knowing much about them. The thing was that she wasn't good on theory; Siobhán's existence was proof of that!

It was with a fairly easy mind, therefore, that she set off with Tom on Saturday to a rugby interprovincial in Limerick. As usual, Tom had wanted Siobhán to come—he'd wanted a son to play rugby, but would have settled for something like Nan's cursory interest; Siobhán, unfortunately, could not even manage that.

Before she left, Nan took a quick look around her room, noted her things on the dressing table, hesitated over the tortoiseshell box, but decided not to take it. Siobhán waved goodbye to them from the top step, her finger in one of the Doctor Doolittle books she had reread umpteen times since she was ten. She waved faithfully until she was out of sight.

They stayed for the dance after the match and spent the night, as arranged, with some rugby friends of Tom. When they returned, on Sunday afternoon, Siobhán was in the kitchen with sleeves rolled up, cutting out circles of dough on the pastry board—the job she had claimed for herself since she was four. Everything was normal, so much so that no shadow of the hovering question disturbed Nan—until next morning, when Miss Eva fell into step as she went shopping and remarked that her sister and herself had heard the door of number twenty-four close at about ten past four on Sunday morning and was everything all right. Well, of course everything was all right, she replied rather more peevishly than she intended; it could have been some other door. At which Miss Eva nodded and said, of course, but they just thought they recognized the sound of that particular door.

Pair of old snoopers, thought Nan, it must have been some other door, old Shannon possibly, slipping in less discreetly than he thought. She was in rather a bad humor that morning, in no mood to consider the question of Siobhán, until, making her bed, she discovered the black bra caught between the bed and the wall. That made her pause. There was an explanation, of course—the daily could have stuffed it down there, changing the sheets—she could even have put it there, herself, laying out her clothes on the bed. Still, it was strange.

She looked at the dressing table. Everything seemed untouched, the tortoiseshell box in its usual place—she even opened it and counted the pills—yes, all there. Then what was she worrying about?

What, indeed? Because she was worried, however ridiculous it all seemed. She should have told Tom at the very start; now, with each day that passed, it became more difficult to explain. She should, at least, have a talk with Siobhán, yet whenever a favorable moment came, she couldn't bring herself to face that clear, innocent gaze; she couldn't do it; she felt it would be like stirring up a spring well, that had been unmuddied since time began.

Tom asked her several times if she were all right and she told him rather impatiently that of course she was. They were healthy as trout, the pair of them, usually; in fact, she had come to share Tom's view that illness was a form of malingering. She had to admit to herself, however, that the worry was getting her down. Yet now, she had to admit to herself that the worry seemed to be getting her down. She even thought of going to their doctor, who was a big, strapping, rugby friend of Tom's, but decided that for once she could not take his peculiar brand of humor. Only as a last resort did she decide on Father Fitzpatrick—not in the presbytery, she felt, he might ask too much—it would have to be in the confessional.

He knew her, of course, as soon as she opened her mouth. A flighty one, he knew, never seen at sodality meetings or daily Mass or Communion, but then she wasn't the only one who barely made the Gospel at last Mass every Sunday.

"It's not about myself, Father, it's my daughter."

"Ah!" He stiffened. The Miss Byrnes at it again. He remembered the swimming pool, painfully. So determined was he to stay clear, that he hardly gave her a chance to make her case.

"But this fellow they saw, sure he could have been a milkman, a paperboy, anyone with a message for Mr. —." He copped himself on, just in time.

"Oh, no, Father!" Quite definitely! Not one of that class! From the several bits and pieces of description, she began to put him together—tall, tousled hair, not well-dressed, not badly dressed, more like a student or like—well like one of their sons, if any of them had had some.

"But sure, he could have called there by mistake, or be asking the way, or be a friend—or," he corrected hastily, "a cousin, perhaps?"

She shook her head, but allowed herself to be silenced.

"But what did she tell you, herself?"

She began to explain, or try to explain her difficulty, surprised how unconvincing it sounded.

"You haven't asked her? In the name of God, woman," righteous wrath here, "what d'you want me to do? What d'you think I am, a detective?"

She assured him that he was nothing of the kind, that all she wanted was—but what did she want? Hastily, she prepared to leave.

"You must have proof, you know, proof, not the gossip of old . . ." Hairpins he was about to say, but checked himself in time. "Now what about yourself?"

But she was outside the door by then, beating him to it. One thing at a time, she thought, confession could wait.

Proof, though, that was the thing! They were going to the races in Powerstown Park the week after next, staying over with Tom's sister in Clonmel. That would be her chance!

The fortnight dragged; she was moody and depressed. Siobhán was very attentive, even bringing her breakfast in bed before going off to school. Finding it hard to make conversation, she found herself noticing things, the clear cheeks, for instance, the shine of the eyes, noticing them with a surprising twinge of envy. The child was certainly growing out of the ugly duckling stage, she told herself chidingly; the poor thing badly needed a new blazer.

Tom was attentive, too, in a sulky kind of way. Partly worried, partly irritated, he wanted to cancel the trip, but she insisted on it, fiercely. Yet, she didn't enjoy the races, though it was a good day and Tom gave her two winners. Afterward, in his sister's home, she broke the news straightaway about going back; she said simply that she wasn't feeling well. He gave in, much more easily than she had hoped. Even his sister didn't seem put out; her face showed concern as she waved good-bye.

The streetlights were out when they reached home. While Tom brought the car around to the garage, she let herself in, banging the front door after her. As she waited in the darkness of the hall, she heard a door open upstairs, her own door—she knew it by its creak. Hearing no other sound, she switched on the light and began to climb the stairs. There was no one on the landing. She pushed in her door and switched on the light. Siobhán lay in the double bed, awakening reluctantly from sleep.

"What are you doing here?" Nan asked in a breathless voice.

Siobhán rubbed her eyes and half-rose on her arm, as if still unsure where she was. Before she could say anything, Nan heard the stairs creak. She rushed out and was just in time to see a tousled head disappear around the turn of the stairs. She reached the turn in time to see a figure in shirtsleeves and bare feet tugging at the front door. "Stop!" she called, "Stop!" but the door was open and the figure was through, slamming it behind him.

She climbed the stairs slowly to her room. Should she wait for Tom? But no, this was her problem, her responsibility as a mother. Tom's turn would come later. But what did one say?

Siobhán was on the floor, making up the bed, not hurriedly, but as if it had to be made properly. She was clad in a petticoat, which showed only too clearly that there was nothing beneath it. Nan put her hand to her mouth, feeling quite sick.

"We didn't know you were coming back," Siobhán said, looking up and making, as it were, polite conversation. The audacity of it was like a blow.

"Siobhán!" she heard herself shriek, as if in pain. She groped forward to the bed and as she reached out for the post, saw something on the floor, a tie carelessly tangled, yes, a school tie. Almost suffocating with the effort, she bent and picked it up. Siobhán gently reached out for it, but she snatched it away.

"What are you going to do?" she asked in a voice which sounded strange and high-pitched.

"Do, Mummy?" she was still making the bed.

"You can't—What's he going to—Who *is* he?"

"Jerry, Mummy. He goes to St. Paul's. He's doing leaving cert. this year. He's very clever. And he's on the first fifteen, too."

"Yes, but . . ." Was this proffered as an explanation? Surely to God, not! Was she dreaming all this? "You can't—What's he going to do?"

"You mean—us? You mean the two of us?"

"Yes, that's what I mean!" What did she mean?

"Get married, is that what you mean?" The idea seemed faintly amusing.

"But sure, Mummy," here control broke down and she giggled, "I had to give him his bus fare to get here!"

"Oh, my God! But what about—What if—"

"There's no fear of that, Mummy, a baby, you mean?"

"Yes," now that the word was out, it was easier. "Yes, that's what I mean."

Siobhán didn't seem to be listening. She had wandered over to the dressing table and picked up the tortoiseshell box. "Don't worry, Mummy. Honest! You needn't worry. You see," she lifted the jewelry box with her finger, "I used one of these."

Nan's legs gave due warning that they could take no more. She clung her way around the bedpost and seated herself on the bed. Her hands went to her face.

"My God!"

"Oh, but they're very good, Mummy. I've been using them for months."

"Months!" Nan leaped to her feet, strength suddenly renewed. "But how—I never noticed!"

"Ah, no." She was playing with the catch of the box, not even bothering to look up. "You see, I put some iron tablets back instead. You'd never notice the difference." She looked up suddenly at the slam of the back door. "Here's Daddy," she said, conversationally.

There was no response from Nan, not a word. Siobhán reached out her hand. "Jerry would like to have his tie, Mummy," she said, gently but firmly, "Would you like me to put back this box?"

Nan hardly heard; already she was listening for the secret movement within her. Slowly, absentmindedly, she yielded to the ultimatum, handing up the tie just before Tom's footsteps sounded on the landing.

Night Thoughts

The gates were gone, but from the pillars on either side the animals still stared down out of empty stone sockets. He stopped the car and turned to ask: "What are they, Johnny-bon?"

Johnny screwed up his eyes against the sun to study the two crouched animals. He took his time: as the family zoologist, the others had to respect him in his field, even as they scoffed at his efforts in their fields.

"Wildcats," he said at last.

"They look like wildcats now," Goggo broke in from the back seat, "but people don't put cats on their gateposts. Those are lions that the rain wore down, lions from the time of the knights."

"Lions are cats," said Johnny. Even at six years old he had learned how to keep an escape route open, that was one thing one learned as the third from the top.

"But they're not quite the same species," Goggo was beginning to get out of his depth. He had been hoping to lure Johnny on to the fields of history, there to demolish him.

"Yes, they are. And anyway, they're Irish wildcats. Knights in Ireland never had lions."

"Ha! That's what you think! Didn't they go on the crusades? Didn't they have lions prowling around the tents every night? Why, the knight who lived here was probably eaten by two lions, which is why her ladyship put those up on the gateposts, to remind her of him."

"Why didn't she put him up?" Johnny asked with interest, as usual not realizing how deadly he could be.

Goggo looked to Peter, the oldest, for help, but Peter was looking ahead where the dusty road led into the shadow of the trees. "Oh, don't be stupid," was all Goggo could think of to say.

"We can't go in there, Daddy," Peter said to his father.

"Why not?"

"There's men working."

"Oh, they won't mind," he said, driving on in.

"But, Daddy—"

"They won't mind," he said, irritated by Peter's ten-year-old respect for the conventions.

"I suppose," ruminated Johnny, "that it would have been too sad to put a statue of him up, by the time the lions were finished with him."

But Goggo had decided to let the subject drop.

A truck was backing in toward a pile of logs under the trees. Men were standing around. One of them left the group and came limping toward them, making for them with a sort of uncanny directness over the humped and hollowed ground.

"He's a dwarf," Johnny whispered, as the car drew to a stop.

"No, an elf," said Goggo, "they live in trees."

"He's a dwarf-elf."

"Shh," ordered Peter.

The little man's eyes raked into the car, over the three boys, and the man at the wheel.

"Where d'ye think ye're going?" he demanded. His eyes were very black, with no shine in them.

"We thought we'd camp here for the night."

"You can't come in here."

"But I know people who've been here. I've been here myself . . ."

"Camping?"

"No, not camping, but I was in here."

"Well, you can't camp here now."

"We're not going to light fires."

"Fire or no fire, you can't come in."

The father eased his hands on the wheel. His sons were watching, frightened. They weren't used to violence.

"All right," he said and began to reverse the car. He did it slowly, to infuriate the little man waiting so impatiently. He stopped for a moment and asked, innocently, "I suppose we can camp in the Forestry Commission's place further on?"

"No, they won't want you either." The little man moved quickly along beside the car, with that limping, pushful, frenzied gait. "Ye think ye can drive in anywhere ye like. Drive down out of Dublin and trample over everyone. Why don't ye camp in yer Phoenix Park or in yer Stephen's Green?"

The father said nothing, just spun the wheel and spurted away. He was slow to anger, too slow always. In the mirror now he saw the men standing by the truck, watching and the blood began to rise to his head, flushing his face and neck. His hands tightened on the wheel and for a moment he slackened speed. Then he thought, Oh, hell! And drove defeatedly out the gate on to the road.

"I don't think I like dwarves," Johnny-bon murmured.

"Elves," said Goggo.

"Oh, shut up," Johnny shouted.

"That's enough," called the father.

They drove fast up the narrow road. Peter was looking at him with that cool, critical look which so infuriated him.

"I told you, Daddy, not to go in there."

He said nothing, but held himself in.

"How d'you know, Daddy, we can camp further up?"

"Look, shut up," he said.

There was a small whisper of "that's enough" from the back seat. He forced himself to ignore it.

The estate wall was on one side, open farmland on the other. The high wall ended and another estate began, this one lined with beech hedges. A massive gateway ahead was guarding, rather than being guarded by, a small Gothic gate lodge.

"Boys, let's ask in here," he said, placatingly.

The two smaller boys in the back leaned forward, breathing over his shoulder. Peter was still in a huff, looking out the side window.

"It's Hansel and Gretel's house," said Goggo.

They watched him get out and walk up the flagged path between heaps of fine chopped logs.

"Mind yourself, Daddy," Johnny called after him in a peaked voice.

A man was watching him from the dark above the half door, with face oddly suspended in midair. As he approached the door, he saw that the man was so big that his head was bent forward as if to fit under the rafters. A big hand descended on the half door and pushed it open, then the man came out, straightening up as if in relief at being uncramped. The big, ruddy face smiled at the sight of the boys.

"Camping, is it?" the deep voice said, "Ah, sure we can fix you up someway. Go down that lane over there and into the field and if anyone stops you, tell them I sent you. D'you want anything before you go? Any milk?"

"Thanks. We could do with some milk."

"Well now, ye could do with some milk. Let me see."

And they could hear, at the back of the little house, the clanking of a bucket and the pouring of milk, all the time the deep voice humming a tuneless song.

"Good luck to ye now and a pleasant stay," he said as he handed back the billycan. The boys looked through the rear window, as they drove away, to watch him stoop at his doorway and fit himself into his house.

They found a good camping place in the corner of the field, not too close to the hedge. Before they set up the tent, Johnny picked all the buttercups and dandelions to prevent them from being crushed. Then while the others worked, he sat down with the flowers and held forth on his surroundings. He was a great one for choosing a job to suit his talents.

The sun was still high and there was no wind here in the corner of the field. It was stifling in the tent, where Peter was smoothing out the ground sheet. He emerged wiping the sweat from his face and looked around to see if there was some job that could be foisted on Johnny.

Johnny, oblivious, sighed reminiscently and said, "I think I like giants."

"You get good giants and bad giants," snapped Peter.

"He was a good giant," said Johnny.

"The thing about giants," said Goggo, "is that they have the same amount of bad in them as everyone else, but it's spread out more."

They worked on, at least the others did, while Johnny sat holding the flowers. "I hope I don't stay a dwarf," he said.

"You will," said Peter, sweating as he tugged on the rope, "if you never do any work. Your muscles won't grow if you don't get exercise, that's what Brother says."

"You're always saying what Brother says," said Johnny, who was still at school with the nuns. "I don't think I'm going to like Brother."

"He won't like you," said Peter, drawing the rope tight with satisfaction, "That's one sure thing."

"Of course he'll like him," said the father, "everybody likes my Johnny-bon." A remark that was greeted by jealous silence.

Flies gathered, buzzing around their hair, their sweaty faces. Johnny slapped at a horsefly on his leg and gave a cry at the sight of the blood. Before there were tears, the father decided to go across the fields and down through the woods to the river. A swim first, then they would come back and eat, when the flies were gone to rest.

The boys climbed excitedly into the next field and ran down the line of haystacks. The earth showed red beneath the cut grass and the air was loud with twittering of crickets. Ahead of them loomed the wood and the boys fell silent as they passed under its shade—but only for a moment. They plunged down the path toward the sound of the river and the father, following, could see a fair head now and then flitting between the bushes of laurel and rhododendron.

He crossed the path he had taken the last time. It led along above the river then swung gradually upward until it brought them out into the sunlight again. They had found a spot there in the ferns. It must have been a familiar honeymoon spot of his father and mother, too high to be overlooked from the far side of the glen. They lay there all day, his father and mother, while the boys played wild in the woods.

It was a day he had remembered, which was why he always wanted to go back and camp there. Recently, moving house yet again, he had come upon the photo of it—a shaky, rather underexposed snapshot taken by Nellie, their maid of all work. It was the last photo taken of his father and mother, the last of the whole family. Soon after, perhaps that very year, his own childhood had ended suddenly and he had entered into a long period now lost to his memory, remembered only because of the light at either end of it, a long, dark tunnel, which lay behind him ever after, blocking the view back to childhood.

He wanted to find the exact spot where his father and mother had lain, but his children were gone on ahead toward the sound of the river, and he hurried after them.

The river tumbled from pool to pool under the green brambles. Already, the boys had pulled off their clothes and were stepping into a level stretch of shallow water on which the sun played through the leaves. He sat down to watch, leaning back against the roots of a tree.

Peter moved away by himself, looking down, occasionally stooping to wrest a stone out of the riverbed and examine it. He moved deftly. Yes, the man thought, a beautiful mover, like his mother. He could still see the boy's white figure between the branches of a sally tree that leaned over the stream. The light of the leaves gave the skin a faintly green, luminous quality against the dark water. He's mine, he thought, I made him. Christ, amn't I the lucky man to be lying here, watching my son.

The boy came back toward him slowly, turning over something in this hands, looked up suddenly and held it out. "D'you think it's gold, Daddy?"

He glanced at the veins of feldspar, glittering in the quartz, then smiled at the intensity of the boy's gaze. "It could be," he said, that being the easiest, the least upsetting thing to say.

The boy gave him one of his straight glances. "D'you really think so?" He looked at the stone more closely and shook his head. "Brother says there's no gold left in Wicklow."

"Oh, well." He decided to take it lightly, "Brother's always right, isn't he?"

"Yes, nearly always," the boy said seriously, then bending slightly, he skimmed the stone away over the surface of the water. As he turned away, he caught his father's eyes upon him and offered, with an easy smile, "You taught me that."

"Did I?" the man said, and felt compensated, returned to ownership.

When they had dressed, they moved downstream through thickets of birch, past fallen trees overgrown with moss, with the noises of the stream always close by. When they emerged at last into the open the sun was low and the light lay on the piles of logs which the dwarf and his men had been loading.

"We shouldn't be in this part of the woods," said Goggo. He drew back, plunging again into the dimness under the trees. "Things will happen now," he said, and though the others mocked at him, they followed quickly. They ran back down to the stream and found it here flowing deep and quiet below steep banks. High up on the far side, on the edge of a cliff, the ruins of a big house stood outlined against the reddening sky.

"A castle!" Goggo cried, "Golly!"

They looked up at its massive butt, at the gaping window, the broken chimneys like bunched fingers. The man didn't remember the castle, yet it must have been there, hidden deep in the woods while he and his brothers played.

"Let's go up," said Goggo, but without great enthusiasm. Peter slithered down the steep bank and stopped beside the stream to assess the jump. The far side gave no foothold. Higher up were rocks and deep clefts of gorse and briars.

"I think," said the father, "it might take us all night to scale those ramparts."

"Yes," said Goggo, "and I'm hungry."

"My legs are empty," complained Johnny.

"All right, troops, back to the cookhouse and fill up the tummies."

Peter hadn't heard. He was poised on a rock in the stream, staring up at the empty windows from which rooks circled clamorously. Like Cúchulainn, his father thought, the boy here, facing the dark things of the air.

"Peter," he called sharply, perhaps a little anxiously, "Come on."

"I didn't much like that place," Goggo said, as he pushed rather quickly through the thickets, "It might be where the dwarf lives."

"It's only a ruin," said Peter, "With crows in it."

"And owls," said Johnny, "and bats."

"And Dracula," Goggo whispered and made a vampire scream.

"Oh shut up," said Johnny and pushed up close to his father.

The sun went down as they ate. It settled into the cleft of the glen, reddening all around it.

"It's an eye," said Goggo.

"The eye of Mordor," said Peter, who spent his nights secretly reading Tolkien and drawing maps of the hobbits' journeyings. Their father broke the uneasy silence with the scrape of a match. "To keep off the flies," he explained, defensively, as he lit a cigarette.

"Oh Daddy," said Johnny, "not again!"

"First one today."

"Peter's brother says you'll never make a miler if you smoke."

"It's all right, Daddy," Peter said, "It's more important that we don't get germs on the ham."

"I'd like Daddy to be a good miler," said Johnny, who wasn't quite sure what a miler was.

"One cigarette won't destroy his wind."

"Did Brother say that?"

"No, but I don't think Brother would mind one cigarette, for the sake of the ham."

It was getting dark. They were waiting, not quite sure what to do, when the first shots went off, a quick, sharp fusillade.

Johnny's eyes opened wide. "Injuns," he whispered and bundled himself in panic against his father.

They looked at the hills around which the sound was still rolling. The father laughed and held Johnny close. "Not at all. They're only scare guns. They keep off the rabbits and the foxes." And he told them how they worked.

"But how d'you know, Daddy?"

"Of course he knows," said Peter, "He was a soldier once. Among other things."

"An actor, too," Goggo moved a little closer in the twilight.

"And a cowboy and a fisherman."

They looked at him. Some day he would have to qualify all these callings, but not now, not when their faces showed such a need of him.

The guns fired again as they lay in their blankets.

"There now," said Peter, "Daddy was right."

Johnny nestled up to one side of his father. "I only hope that none of the small animals get in the way." And he sighed contentedly when his father explained once more about the blanks.

There was a long silence and it seemed that the boys were all asleep. Then Peter's sleepy voice said, "Daddy?"

"Yes?"

"This is the first time we've all slept together, all the men of the family," and then had no more to say after his father replied, "Yes, so it is."

But of course, he had slept before with each of them, brought into bed at some time or other, crying, night tormented, as now when Johnny, reawakened, felt for his hand and said, "Daddy?"

"Yes, Johnny-bon?"

"Are you sure the bullets don't kill the little animals?"

"Yes. Now go to sleep, little man."

And the man reached an arm over Johnny-bon and felt the two other boys beyond heavy with sleep. All mine, he thought, given to me to make men of. He was aware of them together and yet distinct, each of them clearly marked by the night on which they had been given to him. Peter's night was the restless chuffing of a goods engine in the railway yard across the city. Robert's was coming out into the warm, damp air to wait for the doctor and finding red lamps on the roadside, and a glowing brazier beyond which a night watchman sat in shadow. Johnny's night went past unnoticed, as he sat outside the delivery room in the small American hospital, reading "The Country of the Tall Pointed Firs." When he went outside at last, the sun was coming up, overflowing the little prairies town and all the hills and rolling valleys. Yes, all born at night, summoned for him out of the darkness.

He did not remember withdrawing his arm, when he awoke, it was still night but lighter as if the moon was hidden somewhere, not too far away. The echoes of the shots were still cannonading around the hills. A dog howled in the distance and near at hand was immediately answered by the deep bay of hounds.

Goggo crept suddenly into his arms.

"I don't like this place, Daddy. I think . . . I think the devil's here."

"Oh, nonsense," he said, impatiently. He had always been careful not to frighten his children. The devil had never been mentioned, except lightly as one would mention Rumpelstiltskin or Dracula. He was determined that their childhood should be different from his own.

"But I heard him, Daddy."

"Go to sleep, little man."

"He walked past outside. I heard him in his rubber boots."

The father laughed. Goggo hated wearing his rubber boots because of some fad or fashion in his class. "Nonsense, why would he wear rubber boots when it isn't raining?"

"Yes, Daddy." Goggo relaxed, lay back with a sigh. "I didn't think of that." He was softly curled for sleep, when he said suddenly, "That dwarf was wearing boots, Daddy."

"Yes, but it's not raining," the man said in exasperation.

The boy made no reply, and after a while the man could feel him slumping reluctantly into sleep.

He himself lay trying to sleep. He turned on his back and began to relax himself muscle by muscle, composing himself for sleep, which he never had to do at home. Damn it, he thought, I never had any difficulty before in sleeping alone, in tents or haystacks or Salvation Army hostels. I'm too used now to carpets and central heating, too bloody well used to the double bed, to her shape, her warmth enclosing me. I'm too used to love, mine, hers, my children's, theirs for me, for each other, all plaited together, secure and snug, a proper nest of love. And God there too, in whose love they (or at least the children) had never come to doubt, buoying them up, so that even he who had doubted, no longer did so but like them, took love for granted, rested in it.

He thought of his father and mother asleep that day in the heather. They were happy together, too happy, his aunt the nun used to say, as if happiness tempted Providence. Maybe it did, maybe happiness had to be expiated. Had his parents ever known that, ever guessed at it?

It was their last year, the year they lay there—had they known what was to come into their own lives, out of the blue, blasting them apart?

Oh Christ, he turned over quickly. I never gave them five minutes thought in all these years. What's this in aid of?

He slipped a hand along the canvas and found his cigarettes. He lit up, quickly striking the match.

The moon was coming out, or maybe it was the dawn. The air was very still. He could see the hedge, the dark blur of trees, quite motionless. He lay waiting for the shots to ring out, for the whole infernal mechanism to be set off once more—the howl of the distant dog, the bay of the nearby hounds—but no sound came. That was the way, of course, when you were prepared for something, it never came. Christ, what a night! He flung the cigarette out on to the grass and watched its glow being doused slowly by the dew. He knew that cigarette; his eyes seemed to have sharpened so that it glowed before him as if in another dimension. How long more, he wondered, hours it must be!

A cry came from the edge of the field, a very small, very thin cry. He heard it distinctly, not too far away. It faded slowly and then was gone. A rabbit, that was all, trapped, perhaps in pain. He felt Johnny stir beside him and put his hand on the small, hot, uneasy body. Just as well Johnny-bon hadn't woken up; he would think those bullets did kill after all. That cry might be hard to explain away.

The gray world under the trees was no longer empty. The animal, whatever it was, was out there, eyes open, panting with fright as heavy boots moved nearer over the wet grass. Around were the waiting dogs, ears pricked, muzzles raised. He tensed himself, waiting for the shots, all the noises to be triggered off, exploding the silence in terror and pain. Nothing came, but still he lay waiting, unable to relax.

His children slept on, breathing quietly. How sure of him they were, how confident of his protection! And how little protection, really, he was able to give, as little as his father had given him, nearly thirty years ago, his father who had lain here, thought perhaps about him.

He saw his father again, suddenly, after thirty years, turning to wave back from the station entrance. There were people around, crowds waiting at the entrance, women seeing their men off to the war and the munitions factories. People seemed to move together more, in crowds; there seemed to be more of them.

He felt his father's lips brush his cheek and then he turned away, coldly it seemed, but really because he did not know what to say. The streetlights were still on and Westland Row looked black and not quite real in the dawn. In a moment his mother joined him and they moved out along the pavement together, she so vaguely that he had to put a hand on her arm to guide her. They stopped once more to look back, but his father had already passed on through the crowd and was gone. A train passed over the bridge above and its smoke rolled against the fronts of the houses and filled the dark hole of the station entrance.

Years later, after the war, he visited Cardiff and found his way out to the street where his father had died. The house, the whole street, was gone, nothing lcft only a heap of rubble and pools of stagnant water. Was that all, he wondered, was that what lay beyond the tunnel in which his childhood was passed, through whose smoke-blackened entrance his father had gone?

He lay on his side; he could feel the pulse in his temples, its throbbing amplified through the pillow. Surely it beat too fast, too unevenly? He felt for his heart and passed his hand stealthily over it. Suppose his heart, too, was to stop, suddenly, for no reason, as his father's had done? What would happen to him? What would he find beyond, where his father had gone?

He pushed the sleeping bag down from his chest but the air still held him, wrapped close and warm about him. The silence seemed waiting to be broken by threatening sounds and while it waited, all he could hear was the laborious thump of his own heart. How small a thing it was, how faint a sound, and how great the gray, clammy light all about, in which it found not even an echo.

He drew himself up in a panic, reaching out to feel for his children. His movement upset Johnny. At the child's whimper, a chocking noise, he sprang up but he was too late. The smell of vomit rose up at him even as he half-pushed, half-carried the child out through the opening of the tent. He felt the warmth flow over his hands; then they were outside and the child was choking again as another tide forced its way up through him.

The other boys were awake, blundering about in the tent. The man looked at the bushes, black in the cold light. The stench was over everything, but as he held the whimpering child, he began to laugh, quietly, with relief. "Come on, boys," he called out, "We'll take the Johnny-bon home."

Goggo came stumbling out of the tent, eyes half-closed. "I told you, Daddy, we shouldn't have stayed here. The devil's here."

"Oh, shut up, don't be silly."

"But he is." He pointed at Johnny. "There, the devil was inside him."

And just then, the first cock crew.

They drove home in the early morning sunlight. The sea glinted between trees. Birds skimmed the roadway. There was no one in their street, not even a milkman.

"We're the only people up," he told them, "the world's not aired yet."

And even Johnny-bon, pale, still remembering to give an occasional sob, permitted himself a smile.

Their garden was deep in green; there were drops of dew on the roses and small apples on the boughs that they hadn't noticed before.

They threw pebbles up at her bedroom window and called in softened shouts of "Mummy! Mummy, look who's here!"

After a long time, she came to the window, flushed, pulling her dressing gown together over her breasts. As they waited for her to open the door, Goggo said, "It's nice to be in a place where God is."

"God's everywhere, of course," said Peter.

"Yes, but he's in some places more than others."

"That must be it," said the father, as they waited, happily, on the sunlit step for the door to be unlocked so that they could enter in.

The Mohair Boys

Part II

Andy turned over in bed in his basement apartment in the town of Aurora, not a stone's throw from the Mississippi River. Beside him, Kit had drifted off to sleep; he moved away from her, seeking some fresh area of coolness under the single sheet, but the whole bed stretched about him, a steaming bog of heat. Moonlight shone through the small slit of window under the ceiling. Even though it was jammed with polythene to keep out the humidity and the mosquitoes, he could hear faintly outside the tireless scraping of the cicadas, the most alien sound he knew.

He twitched the sheet aside, a moment's cooling gesture, and lay naked facing the ceiling. He thought of his thesis that had to be urgently retyped—he had forgotten to check about the margins with the Graduate College and now, it seemed, the inner margin being a quarter of an inch too small ruled out his effort, according to the sour old harpy of the Graduate College. The use of capitals was also inconsistent, she said. When he had asked Professor Shellerbacker if these conditions couldn't be waived, the professor had been noticeably cool. "I'm surprised you should ask me that, Mr. Gandon; you should have known it's a regulation of the Graduate College, which has nothing to do with me."

"But I thought you said my thesis was a major contribution to the history of—"

"It may well be, Mr. Gandon, I don't recall I ever went further than to say it may well be. As you know, only the committee is competent to tell you what sort of contribution."

Nor had his application for a renewal of the assistantship for next year been approved. How quickly one's foreignness wore off, even here in Aurora. Last year, his application had gone through in a matter of hours, but that was before the professor had said to him "By the way, Mr. Gandon, if you do have to buy American clothes, may I recommend some place other than Kresge's Supermarket." And had later, rather ostentatiously, let his coat fall open to show the Tyson label from Grafton Street, Dublin.

Where had he begun to go wrong? Looking back over the year, he remembered a few needling remarks that Shellerbacker had passed during the one-thousand-strong Core Classes—like an actor up there on the podium, skimming the surface of European history, while Andy and the other assistants stood at the back like wardens to take attendances and prevent anyone from slipping out—a few references to Ireland's social history, narrowmindedness of the Irish Church ("Oh yes," he said, staring up at Andy, as he did when he answered any question of Irish interest, "Parnell, of course was excommunicated by the Roman Catholic Church. He was an adulterer and they don't allow those in Ireland"), and the venality of Irish political parties, with thin references as exemplified in Joyce's "Dead Souls," to stagnation and decay. "'Great hatred, little room,' as the famous Irish writer Joyce once said." Granted, there was a look of complicity as if to say, naturally the better Irish got out and made their names abroad, and a smile up to the gallery, as between two who knew the problems of the Irish only too well, but Andy had glared back. He had tried to get to the professor afterward, but Shellerbacker had gone. "I'm going to ring the bugger up—"

"Wait till you get the thesis done."

"Bugger the thesis," he retorted, but perhaps Kit was right, and he should play it cool until the thesis was through. Damn it, he thought now, maybe there is stagnation and decay at home, but that bollocks is not going to pronounce on it after his three-day visit to Dublin's Intercontinental, while on his grand tour. But if he brings it up at one of his bloody soirees, I'll let him have it. But there were no were soirees, not for the Gandons, not after Andy had at last gone American in a red and yellow check shirt and pair of loose blue denims he later found to be identical with those worn by the college janitors. How different everything had been when he first came and still had the bloom of Europe upon him—or that attractive musty bloom which got them in Aurora. All his friends of the first year, that had come on the late-night skating parties, the St. Patrick's Day skits through the Mississippi River towns, had somehow vanished away to other courses on other universities, or else picked up with the newest campus arrivals, a grim Icelandic couple, a Korean, and a Saudi Arabian with a tiny child-wife, before whose ritual face scars the Mothers' Clubs used to just sit and stare and say "Oh, my!"

Another year to go, so he had been promised; if he was a good boy and did all his courses, they would let him go away and finish the PhD at home. Lately, however, there had been no word about the renewal of his assistantship. He dreaded having to go to see the professor. He would have to set right the misquotations and also, for good measure, point out that Parnell was a Protestant and so could not have been excommunicated by the Roman Catholic Church. National pride demanded that these errors be rectified before he could discuss the subject of the assistantship. And yet, if he rectified them, he mightn't get his assistantship and what would he do then for his PhD. There was barely enough in the bank to carry them over till the start of next term. That was assuming that she would let the rent stand over for another month.

He stared up into the darkness where the flue was which carried heat in winter to the floors above—he couldn't see it in the shadows, but now, listening intently, he could hear her singing again, drunkenly. In an automatic gesture he pulled the sheet back over his lower half; it struck him suddenly, that if he could hear her, perhaps she could hear what went on in the basement; he flushed even hotter at the thought. Maybe that was why she had come down again that afternoon.

Kit and the two boys were gone to the supermarket—the only place they could enjoy really good air-conditioning, apart from the church. After a particularly long bout of typing—getting the margins right this time—he had been taking a rest, lying on the bed in his shorts and playing with the baby. He liked playing with babies, and this one was smart the way it stood up in the cot, pleading to be taken out. It was crawling over his chest when she appeared at the foot of the stairs, the usual clothes basket in her arms. "Hi," she said and smiled. "No, no, don't let me disturb you. I'm just on my way to see to that little old machine of mine."

But she stood a moment smiling; she was wearing only her two-piece bathing suit and her dark hair was damp and coiled up as if she'd just washed it. She was small with breasts that lifted gently toward him as she walked. "No, no," she said, as he tried politely to struggle up. She went past, then stopped beyond the foot of the bed to look again and say: "My, he's got real big, hasn't he?" And she laughed and added: "The baby!" and then passed on.

"Yes." He got up at last, lifting the baby to one side and sat on the edge of the bed. He could hear her in the boiler room, running the water into the washing machine. Should he dress? That would be the gentlemanly thing to do. But what was the point, now that she had seen him there in his big hairy chest? He could go back to his typing, but that would seem unfriendly and damn it, he owed her the month's rent. I'd better just sit here, he thought, not lie down, just sit and see what happens. His throat suddenly went dry on him—no, not that, he thought, God no; anyway, Kit might be back any minute.

She flicked the switch inside and the machine began to throb gently, then seemed to gather momentum. Next moment, she appeared at the door, unencumbered by the basket, but for that very reason seeming a little unsure of herself, hands at her sides as she moved toward him smiling. Oh Christ, he thought, what's going to happen? I'm not going to be able to let her pass. Then, too late, he saw the baby topple over the edge of the bed—its bottom hung a moment there while he tried to grasp it. There was a sickening thud, and then silence.

He rushed around the side of the bed to pick up the child, panic in his heart, thinking: it's the price of me—what could I expect. Naturally God would send some punishment like this. The baby lay inert in his arms, then it swallowed hard and suddenly a yell burst on his ears. He lay back, weak with relief, rubbing its back and saying: "Poor little fellow. All right, poor little fellow." He had forgotten her until she stooped over his shoulder and said, a little dully, "He's all right. Yes let me see. There's not even a mark. You're lucky I put a mat there."

The baby continued to yell, staring at her with an expression that said, "All your bloody fault." "There now, there, little fellow," he soothed. "He's all right," he turned to her, "when they can yell you can be sure they're all right."

"Guess you'd know," she said. "Why not put him back in his crib? Give the poor little fellow a rest from his mean old dad."

He tried to put the baby back but it turned appalled eyes on him now. "Leave me there!" it said, its eyes filling. "Why, you low-down son of a bitch." And its mouth opening wide. "Wah," it yelled, "I'm not going back there, Wah! Wah!"

She waited a little longer while he patted it and persuaded it. Then, when it gave way to a paroxysm of yells, she moved to the stairs. "Ah well," she said, "I'll leave you to it."

Hardly had the door closed upstairs, when the baby stopped crying. He eyed it enquiringly and it squealed gleefully in his face. "Blast you!" he said. Gently he put it back in its cot. He sat on the edge of his bed and found he was shaking. So well he might. He was hardly there five minutes when the car door slammed outside and he heard the piping voice of Tom, the oldest, pass the window. "No, Tom, no," called Kit, "Don't go down. Daddy's busy."

He looked across at the typewriter. There was just time to dash for it, start pounding away—but no, why should he? He had always been honest with Kit, as honest as man was expected to be. He let himself sink back on to the bed and lay there, trying to look stricken with heat and in dire need of a glass of salt and water. At least, it was the more honest pose of the two.

She restored him with salt and water, then sat awhile and touched his fevered brow with the back of her hand. That, of course, started something, as it always did in this barbarous climate; only in Ireland did people seem able to confine sex to its proper time and place.

And now, she lay beside him under the single sheet, the long slim body whose every nook and cranny he knew so well, warm and relaxed and so confident of him that he had but to put out his hand to draw it toward him. Every sweet nook of her he knew so well and yet would never know enough. But he could not put out his hand. He was listening to the tuneless singing that came through the pipe overhead, a distant sound, then what seemed like a heavy weight being dragged across a floor—was it herself—perhaps, because the singing was never more raucous. Poor thing, he thought, deserted, widowed, childless—

He turned over again restlessly then at last sat up: the baby was in the cot at the foot of the bed, arms splayed out. Thank God, no worse for its fall. In the bunks around the corner were the two boys; soon in an hour or so now, at break of day, they would be piping for their "*podgie, podgie*," the bowls of porridge which he insisted Kit made for them with proper salt, as a protest against the world of cornflakes and sugar.

He sat there, in the hot, bright night, the sweat on his forehead and small of his back, his family breathing trustfully in their sleep, and he felt suddenly afraid of that wild force that was singing outside, wild and conscienceless under the moon. Christ, he thought, this is not really the place for me and for mine.

Andy watched the old dame in the Graduate College thumb her way slowly through his thesis, ruler at the ready. Here and there she checked on a page to make sure both margins were within the limit. "Of course, we'll be taking a double check on this later," she said and smiled, "and on these capitals you slipped up on." And she gave him an admonishing wag of the ruler.

He smiled back. He had Phil's letter in his pocket. Wait till I tell Phil and the boys about you, he chortled. I'll drown you in a bloody big pint of stout.

Back in the apartment, he pulled off his shirt and took the phone to the far end of the room, away from the kids, who were shouting for *podgie*. He dialed the professor's number and while he waited for an answer, cupped his hand over the phone and yelled, "Do those kids never stop looking for *podgie*?"

"There's damn little else," Kit shouted back.

"All right!" he motioned up to the heating shaft, "Needn't shout." And then the Professor came on the line.

"Ah, Mr. Gandon," said the professor, "I didn't know you were still around."

Damn well, you knew it this time last year, thought Andy, bathing parties by the lake, tea on the lawn. That was before the Icelanders and the Korean and the Saudi Arabian with the scar-faced child-wife came along.

"Yes, I'm still here," he said. "I just rang to say that Parnell was a Protestant."

"I beg your pardon."

"He couldn't have been excommunicated as you said, since he wasn't a member of the Roman Catholic Church."

"Is this some joke, Mr. Gandon, because if so, I don't quite see—"

"And that reminds me: you misquoted Joyce on one occasion and the title of his famous story is 'The Dead.' It was Gogol who wrote 'Dead Souls'—remember?"

"I fear you must be drunk, Mr. Gandon."

"No. I just want to put you right, professor. And while I'm on the subject, you remember the six sports coats you asked me to get?"

"Yes, yes, but please, now—"

"You can stuff them, all six of them, leather patches and all!"

He put down the phone, smiling with satisfaction. Kit had come halfway down the room and was staring at him.

"Why, professor!" he said, and he did a few steps of a hornpipe toward her, whirling his shirt. "I wanted to put him right for a long time." He caught her and twirled her with him while the children in the kitchen looked up from their bowls of porridge to stare.

"Pack up, girl," he said, "We're going home."

"Home where?"

"Home to Ireland," he said. "Where else?"

"Oh God!" And she flung herself against him. "Oh Andy! I thought we were here for all eternity."

Glossary

Works by Richard Power/Risteárd de Paor

Selected Materials about Richard Power

Glossary

anamundeel. Irish: *Th'anam don diabhal—T'ainm do'n diabhal*: "Your soul to the devil"; equivalent to "damn you." References to the devil were thought impolite in Power's youth and would not be uttered in the presence of women.

Anam 'un Diabhal. Aran Islands variant of the above entry.

Baggot Street. East of Trinity College, an area of pubs thought to be frequented by artists and literati.

Ballinasloe. Town with a current population of 6,722, located in eastern County Galway, a long distance from the Aran Islands.

banbh. Irish word for a piglet.

bawneen. Anglicized spelling of *báinín*, diminutive of *bán* (white). The white Aran sweater, especially as a workaday garment, before its international chic.

bedad. A mild oath; euphemism for "by God."

bob. A shilling; British colloquialism common in Ireland. 1/20 of a pound in Power's youth; did the service of a quarter in North America.

boreen. A country lane; small, seldom used, possibly unpaved. In Irish, *bóithrín*; diminutive of *bóthar* (road).

bowsie. Malicious, evil, bad.

brigade, brigade ambulance. Dublin Fire Brigade: the fire department.

Bundoran. Seaside resort in County Donegal. Renowned in the 1950s for dance halls.

Carrick Fair. A farmers' market.

cess; bad cess. Luck; bad luck. Possibly from assessment (i.e., levy, or success).

chancer. One too confident in his own abilities; implications of lying.

cipin. Twig, little stick; the Irish employs diacritics: *cipín*.

cleamhnas. Authentic Irish spelling for word denoting items or events pertaining to marriage.

Clonmel. The largest town (now with a population of 17,140) in County Tipperary; far to the south, the opposite direction from Dublin from what Belfast would be.

coddin, codding. To joke, to hoax; to lie. English dialect term of obscure origin but common in Ireland.

conacre. Sublet land by a tenant farmer, usually of small portion, prepared for crops or grazing.

Cúchulainn. Hero of the medieval epic *Táin Bó Cuailnge* in the Ulster Cycle.

currach. Anglicized Irish word, *curach*, for the coracle: a small, rounded boat made of waterproof material stretched over a wooden or wicker frame.

Dáil. The Irish parliament, the term by which it is usually known in Ireland.

divil/devil a bit. Not a bit; in no way.

Drumcannon. Former parish in County Waterford.

Emmet's day. Robert Emmet (1778–1803), a leader of the United Irishmen, who was hanged.

Falerian. A sweet, white Italian wine from a region near Naples.

feochan. An unspecific term for undesirable seafood. Related to *feochadán* (thistle).

gach acis a chomhluadar féin. Every age its own company, in Power's translation.

Glenbride. An exurb south of Dublin in County Wicklow.

Guard, Guards. Police. In Irish, *Garda Síochána*.

hooker. Single- or two-masted ship of Dutch origin with a Dutch name, a fishing smack. Thought to be clumsy in use. Once commonly used in Aran Islands transport.

Kresge's Supermarket. S. S. Kresge's "dime stores" flourished in the United States in the early twentieth century but had disappeared by the time Power lived in Iowa. Kresge is nonetheless alluded to in the naming of Kmart discount stores.

leaving cert. Certification, requiring two years preparation, that a student has completed secondary school and is prepared for university. In Irish, *ardteist*.

Lough Derg. Lake in County Donegal, northwestern Ireland, known for St. Patrick's Purgatory, site of a religious pilgrimage, often of three days duration, at Station Island in the lake.

MacDonagh. Thomas MacDonagh (1878–1916): participant in the Easter Rising, who was executed for participating in the rising.

Midleton. A town (pop. 12,000) in southeast County Cork employs this nonstandard spelling. Known for its distillery.

mitch. To play truant; from the Old English word *mycan* (to steal).

Mitchel, John (1815–75). Irish patriot, son of a Presbyterian minister, sentenced to penal servitude in Van Diemen's Land (Tasmania) for leading passive resistance by small farmers against landlord oppression.

morra. Variation of *moryah*, an expression of strong dissent or disbelief. From the Irish phrase *mar dhea* (as it were).

Múchadh is báthadh ort. May you suffer and drown.

Muise, a Phadraig, nach tú an trua Mhuire. Indeed, Patrick, Mary's pity on you.

oinseach. In Irish, *óinseach*. A stupid or foolish person, usually a woman, sometimes a man.

Pearse. Patrick Pearse (1879–1916): leader of the 1916 Easter Rising; he was executed for participating in the rising.

RUC. Royal Ulster Constabulary, Northern Ireland's police force (1922–2001). Resented and feared by the nationalist minority, it was renamed the Police Service of Northern Ireland in 2001, with greater participation from the minority population.

Radio Luxembourg. Luxembourg's national radio station broadcast rock 'n' roll when other European national radio stations would not.

raimais. Nonsensical talk; borrowed from the Irish word *raimeis*.

Rose of Mooncoin. Nineteenth-century romantic ballad of thwarted love. Ascribed to poet-schoolteacher Watt Murphy, but often thought to be a folk song.

scut. A contemptible person. Possibly an Irish borrowing of the English dialect word denoting a hare's tail; or the Irish word *sciota* (snippet).

spillet. An Irish variant of spiller, a long fishing line provided with a number of hooks; a trawl line.

sprong. An Irish variant of *prong* (a thrusting, piercing instrument with sharp tine).

streel, streeled. As a verb this means to saunter aimlessly, after the Irish word *straioll*. As a noun this is a pejorative, describing anything slovenly or untidy, usually female.

Synnott's. A pub in south central Dublin.

tack. Food. Dublin slang of English origin.

tinker. Opprobrious and no longer current term for the native, migrant population living in camps along country roads. The polite term is Itinerant, but the preferred term within the group is *traveling people* or *travelers.* Although not ethnically separate from the majority population, they are immediately identifiable by speech and dress.

'25 drive, also 25s. An ad-hoc charity competition, often a card game, usually among young people, popular in the 1950s and 1960s. The sum of the admission fee, paid up front, was delivered to the charity. Any contest was often undemanding.

Vincent's Men. Workers from the St. Vincent de Paul charity.

wisha. An assertive exclamation, often at the beginning if sentences. In Irish, *más ea* (if so, even so).

yerra. An expression of disbelief; from the Irish phrase *Dhera, A Dhia ara* (O God, well).

Works by Richard Power/Risteárd de Paor

Published Books

The Hungry Grass. London: The Bodley Head/New York: Dial Press, 1969. Dramatized on RTÉ radio by Owen Ashe, December 1978. Reprint: London: Catholic Book Club, 1970; London: Pan Books, 1973; Swords, Ireland: Poolbeg Press, 1988; London: Head of Zeus, 2016.

The Land of Youth. New York: Dial Press, 1964. London: Secker & Warburg, 1966.

Úll i mBárr an Ghéagáin. Dublin: Sáirséal agus Dill, 1958. Dramatized on RTÉ radio by Liam mac Uistín, April, May, June 1978. Translated as *Apple on the Treetop* by Victor Power. Swords, Ireland: Poolbeg Press, 1980.

The Mohair Boys. 1971. A fragment of the uncompleted novel appears in *Irish Press*, February 27, 1971, 9. A fuller manuscript is in the archives of the National Library of Ireland, Dublin. The story "Pike," found only in manuscript form, appears to be a chapter from it.

Publications in Serials and Collections

Stories in English

"Alone." *Icarus* 2, no. 5 (October 1951): 18–23.

"An Outpost of Rome." *Dubliner* 3, no. 1 (Spring 1964): 14–26.

"Peasants." *Bell* 8, no. 7 (December 1952): 424–30.

"The Rebels." *Dial* 1, no. 1 (Fall 1959), 132–52. Reprinted in *Midland: Twenty-Five Years of Fiction and Poetry Selected from the Writing Workshops of the State University of Iowa*, ed. Paul Engle, 233–49. New York: Random House, 1961.

"Republicans." *Icarus* 2, no. 6 (February 1952): 52–58.
"Saving the Bacon." *Pioneer* 3, no. 1 (January 1950): 2–4, 6.
"The Threshold." *Icarus* 1, no. 3 (January 1951): 79–84. Reprinted in *The Saturday Book*, no. 13, ed. John Hadfield, 18–23. London: Hutchinson, 1953.

Stories in Irish

"Breithiúnas Dé." *Comhar* 12, no. 5 (Bealtaine 1953): 15–18.
"Deor na hAithrí." *Comhar* 9, no. 10 (Deireadh Fómhair 1950): 9–11.
"In am an Dóchais." *Comhar* 12, no. 3 (Márta 1953): 9–11.
"Sleá na Fírinne." *Comhar* 11, no. 9 (Meán Fómhair 1952): 13–19, 22.
"An tAonarán." *Feasta* 8, no. 7 (Deireadh Fómhair n.y.): 9–10, 22.
"An Táirseach." *Comhar* 12, no. 2 (Feabhra 1953): 12–13, 24–25.
"Na Treabhadóiri." *Comhar* 11, no. 2 (Feabhra 1952): 9–10, 18, 24.

Poetry

"Geneva." *Icarus* 2, no. 6 (February 1952): 69.
"Grá sa Chathair." *Comhar* 13, no. 9 (Meán Fómhair 1954): 5.
"Poem, (Translated from the Irish)." *Poetry Ireland* 19 (October 1952): 7–8.

Miscellaneous Prose

English

"A Literary Letter from Ireland." *New York Times Book Review*, July 11, 1965, 44–45.
Review of Seán Ó Riordáin, *Earball Spideóige* (Dublin: Sairséil agus Dill, 1953), *Bell* 18, no. 2 (Autumn 1953): 129–30.
Review of Liam Ó Flaithearta (O'Flaherty), *Dúil* (Dublin: Sairséil agus Dill, 1953) and Maírtín Ó Cadhain, *Cois Caolaire* (Dublin: Sairséil agus Dill, 1953), *Bell* 19, no, 2 (January 1954): 60–61.
Review of Benedict Kiely, *Honey Seems Bitter* (London: Methuen, 1953) and John Brophy, *The Prime of Life* (London: Collins, 1953), *Bell* 19, no. 5 (April 1954): 56–58.
Under the pseudonym Nomad, "The Aran Islands." *Ireland of the Welcomes* 11, no. 2 (July–August 1962): 10–14.

Irish

"Cladóir: Scéalta le Criostóir Mac Aonghusa." *Combar* 11, no. 12 (Deireadh Fómhair 1952), 2.
"Gaeligeóir sa tSeapáin." *Combar* 8, no, 11 (Samhain 1949), 16–18, 22.
"Dún Deireannach na Drámaiochta?" *Combar* 13, no. 9 (Meán Fómhair 1954), 19–24.

Dramas, Unpublished

"The Blind Mouth." By Desmond Walsh (pseudonym). A Play in Three Acts. Written c. 1960. Manuscript on file at the University of Iowa, Iowa City.
"Charon iBponnc." Manuscript in the archives of the National Library of Ireland, Dublin; also exists in short-story form.
"Cluiche Solo." 1964. Manuscript in the archives of the National Library of Ireland, Dublin.
"The Faithful and the Few." Manuscript in the archives of the National Library of Ireland, Dublin.
"A Green Grave—Aran." Manuscript in the archives of the National Library of Ireland, Dublin.
"A Home for Heroes." By Michael Roberts (pseudonym). Manuscript in the archives of the National Library of Ireland, Dublin.
"Kevin Barry." Manuscript in the archives of the National Library of Ireland, Dublin.
"Oidhreacht." Winner of the Oireachtas Literary Competition, 1957.
"An Oighreacht Drama Einghnimh." Manuscript in the archives of the National Library of Ireland, Dublin.
"Mo Mhile Slán Le Éirinn." Manuscript in the archives of the National Library of Ireland, Dublin.
"Saoirse." Co-winner of the Oireachtas Literary Competition, along with "Úllghlas Oiche Shamhna," by Mairead Ní Gráda, n.d. (possibly 1958).
"Screen Frame." (1956–57). Manuscript in the archives of the National Library of Ireland, Dublin.
"Songs by Cóilín." Manuscript in the archives of the National Library of Ireland, Dublin.

Film Scripts, Produced and Unproduced

As the Ball Bounces. Directed by Colm Ó Laoghaire, 1964.

"A Boy in Ireland." Manuscript in the archives of the National Library of Ireland, Dublin.

Game of Chance. Directed by Jim Mulkerns. Released by the Department of Local Government (c. 1967). Shown at the Berlin Film Festival.

A Tale of Two Cycles. Directed by Billy Bowles. Released by the Department of Local Government (c. 1961).

To Save a Life. Directed by George Morrison. No date.

Water Wisdom. Directed by Colm Ó Laoghaire. Released by the Department of Local Government (c. 1967).

Miscellaneous

Three Stories. Master's thesis, University of Iowa, 1960. "The Rebels," "The Land of Youth," "A Province of Rome."

"The Irish in the Middle West." Radio recording made by WSUI in Iowa City, spring of 1959, and broadcast by RTÉ in 1959. Richard Power leads a discussion with William Cotter Murray and Patrick Morrissey.

Unpublished Stories

English

"The Alchemy"
"The Anointed"
"Brothers"
"The Critic," under the pseudonym Michael Roberts
"Cuckoo Call"
"A Damp Soul"
"End of a Criminal"
"Extrajero"
"First Class Compartment to Dublin"
"Highway to the Sun"

"In Sincerest Sympathy"
"The Intruder"
"Ivory Tower," "Ivory Towers"; different titles in different drafts
"The Land of Youth"; appeared in in MFA thesis, 1960
"The Love Potion"
"The Man of Kerioth"
"Mr. Cox's Crowded Hour"
"Neighbors"
"Pike," possibly a chapter in the uncompleted novel *The Mohair Boys*
"A Pilgrim"
"The Pill"
"The Strange Game"
"A Stranger Came"
"Summer Evening"
"Thumbscrews"
"The Trespassers"
"The Voice"
Untitled #1 begins: "Tony snuggled deeper . . ."
Untitled #2 begins: "He knew she would open her powder compact . . ."
Untitled #3 begins: "A gray October day . . ."
Untitled #4 begins: "Mrs. O'Reilly nervously fingered . . ."
Untitled #5, no first page, second begins: "happened. He had managed to kill time . . ."

Irish

"Cé hÉ sin Amuigh"
"Charon in bPonnc"; also written as a one-act play
"Cúl taca na Cúise"
"Na Pictíuri Ailne"
"Níl Miss Culshaw sa Bhaile"
"Oh, My America, My Newfoundland"
"Oileán agus Oileán Eile"
"Poblachtánaigh"; a version of "Republicans" (1952)
"Sclábhaithe"; a version of "Peasants" (1952)
"An Túr Éibhir"

Selected Materials about Richard Power

Battersby, Eileen. "Last Days of a Doomed Everyman." *Irish Times*, September 17, 2016.

Brown, Terence. 1976. "Family Lives: The Fiction of Richard Power." *Cahiers irlandais* 4; rpt. 1975. *The Irish Novel in Our Time*, ed. Patrick Rafroidi and Maurice Harmon, 245–53. Lille, France: Publications de l'Université de Lille.

Foster, John Wilson. *Colonial Consequences: Essays in Irish Literature and Culture*. Dublin and New York: Lilliput, 1991.

Kiely, Benedict. "In Memory of Richard Power." *Hibernia*, February 20, 1970, 20.

MacAmhLigh, Dónall. "Údar Gaeilge a d'imigh le Béarla." *Irish Press*, November 16, 1976, 9.

MacKillop, James. "*The Hungry Grass*: Richard Power's Pastoral Elegy." *Éire-Ireland* 18, no. 3 (Fall 1983): 86–99.

Mulkerns, Val. Untitled appreciation. *Irish Press*, February 27, 1971, 9.

Ó Direáin, Máirtín. "Do Risteárd de Paor." *Comhar* 29, no. 2 (Feabhra 1970): 4.

Poss, Stanley. "Richard Power, 1928–1970." *American Committee for Irish Studies Newsletter* 1, no. 1 (February 1971): 11–13.

Thompson, Douglas. "The Novels of Richard Power." Master's thesis, University College Dublin, 1979.

Richard Power was born in Ireland. He worked as a civil servant in Dublin and earned an MFA from the Iowa Writers' Workshop. He is the author of *The Hungry Grass* as well as numerous short stories and plays.

James MacKillop is the author of *Fionn mac Cumhaill: Celtic Myth in English Literature* and the *Dictionary of Celtic Mythology*, and is coeditor of *An Irish Literature Reader: Poetry, Prose, Drama.*